"Over here!"
"What ya got?"
"Looks like a baseball cap. Yeal
"Jim! What color was the cap
like a woman's voice.

Last week there were more women than men out here. I was surprised how stoic they were. The men swore under their breaths, damned the heat, cursed a rock or broken piece of glass. The sun was too bright, too many bugs. They grumbled and searched. But the women just walked and swung their rakes—whatever they'd brought from home. With heads down, eyes focused, they held all the fear back along with their frustration and discomfort. The louder the men got, the quieter the women became. But every so often there'd be a whimper and I'd realize it came from the females.

I straighten up, waiting to hear if it's Steven Kracher's Cardinal's baseball cap that's been found.

"No! No! God, no!" a man wails. "Stevie!"

Gordian Knot Books is an imprint of Crossroad Press Publishing

Copyright © 2015 by Christine Matthews
Cover illustration by Dave Dodd
Design by Aaron Rosenberg
ISBN 978-1-941408-31-5 — ISBN 978-1-941408-32-2 (pbk.)
For information address Crossroad Press at 141 Brayden Dr., Hertford, NC 27944
www.crossroadpress.com
First edition

BEATING THE BUSHES

CHRISTINE MATTHEWS

To Bob, because of Bob, only for Bob. I love you.

PART ONE

VINCENT

CHAPTER ONE

"If you find anything don't touch it! Stand back and wave for help."

After the first six days some sort of half-assed order settles in. The agitation seems to calm somewhat too, but it's always ready to boil up again. And that pain punching away at my heart now rips through every inch of me like a dirty piece of barbed wire.

My left arm, plagued with bursitis years before all this began, throbs on a good day. But the last few mornings it's been hell getting dressed as I wrestle into a clean shirt. In the evening it's worse. Both arms burn as I struggle to get undressed. My feet look like wads of dough. The skin cracks open in a crease across each ankle when I have to stuff them back into those damn boots the next day.

Rain, heat and claustrophobic humidity. While my feet swell, my boots shrink, and as much as I want to put on the dark glasses in my pocket when the migraines come, I don't for fear of missing something. Something important.

The megaphone clicks on again. It's only a matter of moments before another warning blares.

"If you think you've spotted anything, shout!"

I can't stop—even if my brain serves up excuse after excuse why I should. I'm being fueled by the fear. All of us are.

"Over here! I think I found something!"

Every single goddamn time I hear those words I freeze. And wait. My heart vibrates, aching, sometimes even stopping a second. I inhale small breaths so shallow my chest doesn't move. And I stand there. And I wait.

"You're crazy. Ain't nothin' but a garbage bag. See?"

I don't bother looking. It's so hot. I'm hungry; my back aches and my knees bulge beneath stiff jeans. After a few minutes I shuffle along, focusing on what I'm here to do while that horrible sadness rips at my soul.

"It's been twelve days since anyone's seen or heard from Steven Kracher, the fifteen year old from Kimmswick, Missouri. Behind me are several volunteers who have worked so hard helping the family look for Stevie. If you would have passed by this stretch of rural highway yesterday you would have seen at least fifty men and women out here. But today's Monday, the weekend's over and everyone's either at work or in school. Except these dedicated men who still search."

I've been inches from that bitch for days now and every single time our eyes lock, she smiles. That fuckin', plastic I'm-someone-important smile she has plastered across her face whenever she's on camera. Her hair looks like it's painted on. Fake, tomato-red—a color unnatural to anything in nature. God help me, I hate her guts.

"Sir? Can I talk to you for a moment?"

Why? I wonder. We've been through all this before. Have you gotten any smarter since our last interview? Somehow become more sensitive? Will anything, any damn fuckin' thing get resolved because I stop to talk to some woman jamming a microphone in my face?

But hope makes you do things. Even if those things feel wrong.

"Sure."

"How long have you been out here?"

"Five days."

"Are you a friend of the family?"

"No."

"A relative?"

"No. I heard about Steven on the news and just came to help."

It's his father that really got me there, but I don't tell her that. Mr. Kracher had been composed the first time I saw his face on my TV screen. But with each update the torment started to show. In his eyes especially. When he spoke, his words got tangled as he fought to get them out. And the last time I saw him, he was crying, pleading for the return of his son…his only child.

She stares at me for a moment. There's no way in hell she can understand. "Well, I'm sure the Kracher family appreciates you being here."

I shrug, stand there with my hands shoved into my pockets.

"It's getting windy out here, feels like it might even rain. How long do you intend to stay?"

How long can a parent wait, I want to ask her. "I don't know."

She turns back toward her cameraman. "Police will continue canvassing Stevie's neighborhood. So far no clues have been found to indicate he was taken by force. If you have any information that could aid police in this investigation, please call the eight-hundred number at the bottom of your screen." She flashes her whitened smile. "And I'm Laura Ann Bonetti for Channel Four news."

That's it. Another news item thrown out on the air waves to report the absence of anything new.

She suddenly remembers I'm standing next to her. "So what next?"

I want to knock some sense into her with the stick I hold in my hand. "Nothing to do but wait, I guess. Nothing any of us can do except keep looking. Keep beating the bushes."

CHAPTER TWO

A leaf swirls past my face. It's the color of her hair—warm amber—a rich brown and gold that only comes from deep down on the family tree, passed from mother to son to father to daughter...

When she was so very little I'd rock her. She was this smiling, bright, baby person who made my heart feel as though it had been shot through with joy. I'd study her face as I gave her a bottle. Never had I known a face so well that I could have sketched it from memory. Still can. Such love, such deep, glorious, unconditional love. I could feel it radiating from her. It was almost too much at times. I'd kiss her soft, baby-powdered belly. Give her a bath. She'd giggle and I'd laugh. Everyone who saw us together grinned.

As she got bigger, she'd push away from my hugs. My kisses were suddenly "gross." My wife, Kathy, would give me that look and roll her eyes as if I was supposed to know. But I never saw it coming. One morning she called me "Daddy" and the very next, as I walked into her room, bent down to pick her up, she scolded me. "I'm too big for that, Dad."

Overnight. No time to prepare or get ready for so many changes. They just had to be accepted without questions. Onward and upward–forever different.

I tried explaining to Kathy that for me, the feelings we'd shared the day Gabby was born, that heart-straining, euphoric, sublime happiness never changed. It didn't matter how old she was or what she was doing. When she was in her crib, or crawling across the kitchen floor, running out to play or reading a book, I was enchanted with my baby girl. And every time I saw her face, every single time, I swear, I felt overwhelmed.

When Gabby started school, I asked Kathy as we watched our daughter walk away from us, if she still felt amazement knowing we had created this perfect human being. She studied me, trying I suppose, to see the crazy person peering out though my eyes. "Try spending every moment of the day with our perfect human and see if your amazement is still intact."

"I plan to do just that."

"What do you mean?" she asked, facing me, blocking the sidewalk.

"I quit yesterday."

"And just when were you planning to tell me this?"

"Today, just the way I did."

"And I'm supposed to be happy?"

"Look, Kath, Gabby's going to be in school all day now. They want you back at the magazine. And you know you miss it. Go. I'll stay home and do all the demeaning, tedious jobs you hate so much. Hey, I thought you'd be happy."

A frown took hold of her face. Her gorgeous face. Then she brightened up. "Can we afford this? I've never made as much as you."

"We have savings. And I can do some work from home—keep a few of the private clients I have."

She started walking quickly. Her long hair pulled back in a ponytail, bounced as she went. "This is exciting. I have to get some new clothes. I need a haircut..."

I practically had to run to keep up with her.

"Over here!"

"What ya got?"

"Looks like a baseball cap. Yeah, that's what it is!"

"Jim! What color was the cap Stevie was wearing?" It sounds like a woman's voice.

Last week there were more women than men out here. I was surprised how stoic they were. The men swore under their breaths, damned the heat, cursed a rock or broken piece of glass. The sun was too bright, too many bugs. They grumbled and searched. But the women just walked and swung their rakes—whatever they'd brought from home. With heads down, eyes focused, they held all the fear back along with their frustration and discomfort. The louder the men got, the quieter the women became. But every so often there'd be a whimper and I'd realize it came from the females.

I straighten up, waiting to hear if it's Steven Kracher's Cardinal's baseball cap that's been found.

"No! No! God, no!" a man wails. "Stevie!"

The cap could have been in that spot for months, I tell myself. Stevie could have lost it and just been afraid to tell his old man. There could be a dozen reasons it's out here, mashed down in over-grown weeds along Highway 61.

A man comes walking up behind me. "You hear?"

I nod. "How can they be positive it belonged to the boy?"

"His name's inside. It's his alright."

"Ahhh, geez."

"You friend or family?" he asks.

"Neither."

"Yeah, me either. Got laid off a few months ago, figured what the hell, I got some free time. But, Jesus, this is tough. Hey, I'm takin' a break. Wanna get some lunch? There's a place…"

"That's okay, I'm not hungry."

"Suit yourself," he says and walks over to a blue pickup.

I look at the long stick I hold. For a moment it seems such a foreign thing. I can't remember exactly how it came to be in our basement. Somebody's cane. But whose? The handle is smooth, the length just right for poking in hidden places where something might be…

Kathy was wrong about the love changing. Gabby and I grew closer with me at home more. And I swear, every time…every damn time she walked through the door…I felt the wonder.

CHAPTER THREE

Kimmswick, Missouri. St. Louis, just twenty miles north, breathes down the neck of the quaint town. But no one here seems to notice. I can feel it though.

Rape—murder. Rape—murder. Rape—murder.

My arms once again fall into a rhythm as I swing that stick, looking for Stevie.

Rape—murder. Rape—murder. Rape—murder.

Then I become aware of the words swinging back and forth in my head. Still there. Always and forever living back behind good times and memories I've managed to salvage.

After what happened to Gabby, Kathy and I tried but it was like picking through wreckage from a flood. Everything ends up in two piles: salvageable and garbage. The salvageable falls into two categories: needs cleaning up and almost good as new. No matter what pile things end up in though, everything stinks. Nothing's the same; your home is contaminated. But you work, pick up, put away, disinfect. And just when things are almost back to a new kind of normal, you find mold growing under the couch that seemed barely touched by the disaster. That's when you realize it was garbage like the other stuff you threw away, it just took longer to get that way.

Rape—murder. Rape—murder. Rape—murder.

I want to take this stick and beat everyone in this town with it.

Coming down here from Chicago I got caught driving through St. Louis during rush hour. Orange cones everywhere. Someplace there has to be a goddamn highway that's not under construction. Trying to find some music on the radio while I pretended to be patient, all I could get at that time of day was local news. Police chasing a drunk driver had crashed into a car, killing three people. Drive-by shooting left two elderly people dead. The parents of three small children perished in a fire last night. One robbery, a kidnapping...

Rape—murder. Rape...

And when I arrived, they seemed surprised, the citizens of Kimmswick. They looked stunned. Shrugging, telling me they didn't know how such a thing could happen in their town. Smugly, as if I, being from a different universe, couldn't understand their way of life, they proclaimed loudly, proudly, that they didn't even lock their doors at night. How could this happen, they asked each other.

Ask Steven Kracher.

I want to knock his teeth down his throat when some idiot says the same old, tired words. Words Hollywood screenwriters pound out on neon colored computers. Words pampered stars recite again and again, in movie after movie: "Gee, we never thought this could happen to us. Not in this town—it's so quiet here."

Surprise!

Who was it supposed to happen to, then?

Don't they take one minute to skim through a newspaper? Cause there it is—in black and white. Try turning on some real, reality television. What about all those statistics popping up on the Internet? And if for once someone would kindly turn down the volume, they'd hear stories.

I want to line every one of them up. Woman, man—it doesn't matter. Smash every citizen in the face. And when I've finally managed to wipe the complacency and ignorance away, I'd shake them and shout, "What the hell did you expect? This isn't fun and game time. It's twenty-first century duck-for-cover-run-for-your-life time. So why are you still standing there smiling? Acting as though bad is never supposed to happen to you?"

St. Louis, famous for being the host city of a World's Fair, the arch—Gateway to the West—and...the city with one of the highest crime rates in the nation. Twenty miles north. But here the Mississippi lazily winds by gift shops where wooden geese wearing calico bonnets stand guard. And I have to admit, it feels more than twenty miles from danger, it feels light years away from any city I've ever lived in. Appearances can be so very deceiving.

Rape—murder. Rape—mur…

"Sir? Ahh, mister?"

"Yeah?" I don't make eye contact. My rage would frighten her.

"There's gonna be a pot luck supper over at the VFW tonight. Mr. Kracher's invitin' everyone to come."

"Thanks."

"See ya there, then?"

"I'll try."

"Okay." She just stands there. Maybe I should say more? But when I don't, she walks away. "Bye."

CHAPTER FOUR

When the unthinkable happens, it frees you up from all the bullshit. What else is there to fear? What more can anyone do to you? Kill you? If only. Death would be the easy way out …

Kathy had been calmer than I'd ever seen her. She lay there, covered in white. Surrounded by white. Something so dirty looking so pure.

"Why the hell would you do this to yourself? And me? You're nothing more than a weak, cowardly bitch."

"This is the first time I've ever done anything without thinking about who I was pleasing. Or who might get hurt. I didn't think about anyone except myself. And it felt great, Vince. I did it for me. Get it? Me…just me."

"What if I hadn't found you? Do you realize what I'd have to go through? Jesus Christ, it would be Gabby all over again."

"Come here." She held her arms open to me.

The valium they'd given me hadn't kicked in yet. It probably wouldn't. Spasms chilled me and I zippered my jacket up as I walked toward her bed.

"Sit."

I sat.

"They say my sight in one eye will be a little weaker but…"

"You shot yourself in the head, Kath." I lost it and hugged her, hiding my face in her chest. "Do you understand what you've done?"

She laughed. I couldn't believe it but she laughed. "Yeah, I screwed up my own suicide."

I jerked away from her. "Stop it! Don't you dare laugh, you heartless…"

"Vince, I'm tired. Go home."

"And do what? Change into a shirt that isn't covered with your blood? Go sit in Gabby's room until I ache so bad from missing her that I can't stand it anymore? What, Kathy? Please tell me what I'm supposed to do?"

"Stop it. Just stop all of it, Vince. I can't help you. I don't want to suffer with you any more. Something happened to me last night…"

"Oh no. No, no, no. Don't you dare tell me some fuckin' story about seeing God. Or going through a tunnel…" How could I ridicule her like that? We had gone to hell together and all the time I wondered if we'd ever find our way out. Finally, we were seeing just a glint of light and now this.

She turned her head away from me. "I won't tell you any of that because it didn't happen. I'm different that's all. Like I'm seeing things for what they are. Seeing without looking. Or analyzing. Not wondering why but just accepting."

I couldn't take anymore. "I gotta get out of here."

"We both need some rest. I'll see you…" She stopped. Maybe that was when she realized she might never see me, or anything, again. Maybe for that one second she got it.

"Yeah, I'll see you." I rubbed it in.

Before I left, I turned back to look at her and damn it, she was smiling…

I was alone. In the dark. Afraid. Lonely. Madder than I'd ever been. I paced through the halls of the only house I'd ever owned. The Real Estate Agent had called it a "starter home." She'd gone on to explain that someday we'd want to move up. Everyone did.

But Kathy and I weren't everyone. The modest house was perfect for the three of us; we never wanted to move. And now I have a difficult time believing that I hadn't even wanted to buy a house in the first place. Kathy agreed when I explained that our apartment was affordable, near shopping, restaurants and friends. We had more than enough room. But when Gabby was born, things changed. Kathy started looking for a home near a good school, for months she kept pointing out how our little girl needed a yard to play in, a real neighborhood. Next thing I knew, we were moving into the three-bedroom ranch. We used to kid it was Gabby's house. Because of her—for her.

And when Gabby stopped coming back to that home, Kathy and

I managed somehow. We held on to each other. We took care...I thought we'd healed until she betrayed me by trying to kill herself. Leaving me alone in Gabby's house.

CHAPTER FIVE

The light's going; I figure unless dumb luck or fate leads me right into something, I'm not going to be any more help today. Man, how I need to lie down. My arms are dead weight, hanging painfully from sore shoulders. I can feel my eyes starting to rattle with exhaustion.

Daddy?

I drag my feet up to the road, not knowing how I'll make it back to the car.

Daddy, I'm so hungry.

"You'll be fine until tomorrow," I whisper.

But I know you're hungry, too. Remember what you'd say whenever I'd ask if you were hungry? You'd always say the same thing. It didn't matter if you'd just eaten a whole pizza or one cookie. Member? You'd say...

"Guess I could eat something," I finish her sentence.

She giggles. *Even at Thanksgiving or Christmas, Mommy would ask if you had enough to eat. All of us were stuffed. But you'd just smile and say the same thing. You were funny, Daddy.*

"I remember."

I saw a place down there. It looks like a log cabin. Come on, slow poke.

By the time I reach town it takes everything left in me to keep my eyes open. "Maybe I should just go back to the motel."

You need food.

"I don't have enough energy to chew."

The restaurant is closed. The whole area seems deserted and I wonder where the hell everyone is.

Over at that VF place the lady told you about.

"There'll probably be a crowd."

Just go eat and then you can leave.

I don't have a clue where the place is but just as I turn out of the restaurant parking lot, I see a sign and follow the arrow. It isn't far. Nothing's far in a town the size of Kimmswick.

It sounds like a party inside. When so many people congregate there's bound to be commotion. Even at a funeral there's that human rustling. Feet moving across a floor, words mumbled or jokes told to lighten the mood.

A woman, cradling a baby in her arms, walks ahead of me toward the building. She moves steady, deliberately. When she gets to the door she stops, holding it for me. Her unnecessary kindness prompts my feet to move quicker.

"Thanks."

We exchange positions and I hold the door as she and her child enter.

It's your typical VFW hall. The first thing that hits me when I walk inside is the smell of warm beer and stale smoke. An old juke box hunkers in the corner, dark and silent. The walls are covered in cheap wood paneling, the floor looks chewed up. The ceiling, made of those big white acoustic tiles, is stained. There's a dart board against the far wall and a bar all the way in the left corner, behind it hangs neon ads for Budweiser. The atmosphere is subdued. Strange how it had sounded so lively outside but now that I stand in the midst of the crowd it feels more like a church before the sermon.

"Help yourself," a man says and points toward a long table set up with plates of food. "There's more than enough. Drinks are over there." He waves me toward the bar.

"Thanks."

So much food—too much. I pick up a paper plate and stand in line behind a man who looks like he has eaten his way through one too many buffets. Licking his lips, he shouts to the person behind me, "Try some of that chicken. It'll make ya swear off the Colonel— go cold turkey."

"Turkey! That's a good one," his buddy laughs and shouts to someone behind him, repeating the joke.

When I finally get my plate full, the sight of the food makes me nauseous. I walk back to a table in the corner and after arranging my silverware, go up to the bar to get a soda, hoping the carbonation will help.

It doesn't

"Are you okay, mister?" a kid squeals as I head for the floor.

Daddy! Daddy!

"Gabby?"

The last thing I remember is blessed, cool, nothingness.

CHAPTER SIX

"And you're a relative of Mr. Lloyd's?"

They know my name.

"Nope. He's in town helpin' me…"

"So you're a friend, then?" A woman interrogates the man. I'd speak up if I knew where the hell I was. And if I had the strength or will to open my eyes, I'd look over to see who's talking.

"Nope, not that neither. To be honest, I didn't even know his name, until just now."

"So, you were passing by and Mr. Lloyd happened to keel over right in front of you? How lucky for him."

"Ain't exactly how it happened, neither."

"Well, Mr…?"

"Kracher."

"Huh, Kracher? Have we met?" The woman hesitates a moment; the man offers no help. Then she has it. "Oh. Kracher. Are you," in a lower, softer voice, she asks, "are you Stevie's father?"

He must nod because I don't hear a reply. Without looking, I know too well the pity that now creases every line in her face. I'm trying to get enough strength to say something, help the poor guy out, but before I can, the door opens.

Another man's voice. Things get fuzzy and I go with it again.

This time when I come to, I realize I'm lying in a bed. Slowly I open my eyes. Alone, I try moving my left arm but can feel it's hooked up to something. Light comes in under the door and I hear activity on the other side. A woman moans from someplace, scuffing of shoes, rolling of wheels. A laugh. Carefree laughter. It sounds good.

I'm starving.

I sit up and when I do, must have set off some sort of intercom. A voice comes out of the wall. "Mr. Lloyd?"

"Yes."

"I'll be right in." The same woman's voice as earlier.

Before I can locate the control panel, she's here. "Well, how are you feeling?"

"Hungry."

"Now that's a good sign." She switches on the light and I nearly go blind.

"What happened to me?"

"You passed out. Doctor said it was from exhaustion. You're dehydrated. That can put a person right into a coma, you know."

"How long ago was that?"

"About fourteen hours. You scared poor Mr. Kracher half to death. And with what he's going through right now, we were afraid he'd end up in the bed next to you."

Am I supposed to feel guilty? Because I don't.

She presses her cool fingers against my wrist and stares at her watch. "I'll have one of the orderlies bring you something to eat. The doctor left a list of what you're allowed but I'm afraid it's a very short list. For the next few days we're going to have to watch you closely. Is there anything else I can do for you?"

I think about trying to get up, telling her I don't need to be in a hospital...for a minute...until everything starts to hurt. Even the sheets feel like sandpaper grinding away at skin on my legs. Besides, it feels good to rest. Having an anonymous, pretty woman take care of me feels good, too. "No, I'm okay."

"Sure?"

"Well, you could tell me where my clothes are; I need my phone."

"Hanging in the closet. But there's one next to you." She nods toward the nightstand. "It'll be a lot easier. Just dial nine first to get an outside line."

"Thanks, I'll do that."

"Alright then." She finishes changing the bag suspended on a metal stand next to the bed. The liquid drips slowly down the tube into the needle taped to my left arm. "I'll have something sent in. It shouldn't be too long."

"I'm in no hurry here." I smile, trying to be pleasant. She's trying—everyone's trying—why shouldn't I?

After she finally leaves, I struggle out of bed. The phone next to me might be easier to use but I need my cell number to register on Kathy's caller ID. Thankfully the IV stand is on wheels and I'm able to drag it behind me over to the closet. It takes all my energy to find the phone, bring it back to the bed, crawl under the stiff sheet and dial. Obviously I'm a lot weaker than I imagined.

Kathy answers on the third ring.

"Hey, it's me."

"Hi sweetie, how's it going?"

"Slow."

"They haven't found anything? Not one thing?"

"A cap, I think. That's about it."

She groans. "Are you okay?"

"Fine. Just a little tired."

"Really, Vince? You don't sound good. Maybe you should come home now."

"Stop it, Kath, you know I gotta do this."

"No, I don't know. Tell me again why you had to run down there. Why the hell you think you can help that family when you couldn't..."

"Help my own? Go ahead, say it."

"Vince, I'm worried, that's all. This has got to be so hard on you. Why would you want to put yourself through all of it again? And you've been getting those terrible headaches."

"Look, you work through things in your way—I work through them in mine."

She exhales a long, suffering sigh. "So, a week? A month? Can you give me something here cause I'm trying to be patient."

"When they find his...when that poor kid is safe in his own bed."

"Yeah, well, that could be awhile."

"I know. Look, I don't want to fight," I tell her.

"Me neither."

"So how're things at home?"

"Quiet."

We both breathe across the miles into each other's ears for a long moment. I finally break the silence. "Kathy, I'm a selfish, stubborn bastard, I know that. And I can't come home and play at being the good husband right now. Please...I just can't."

"I miss you."

The door swings open. A tall man stands holding a tray.

"I miss you, too."

He unloads dishes onto a table next to my bed.

"What's that? Where are you, Vince?"

"I'm picking up a pizza before I head back," I lie.

"Good, go eat and get some rest. Call me tomorrow."

"Promise."

PART TWO

BAYLOR

CHAPTER SEVEN

Hospitals. I hate them damn places. But after all the hours that guy put in lookin' for my Stevie, it's the least I can do—give him a few hours. So I plant my butt on one of them hard, plastic chairs in the waitin' room of Jefferson Memorial and wait.

I drink two cups of coffee and still have trouble keepin' my eyes open. The TV is on but the volume ain't—no matter—I can't concentrate on much. I try movin' over to the couch in the corner and think maybe I can stretch out for a while when I hear the two of 'em laughin'.

"If I buy one more pair of shoes, Joe'll kill me. I mean it."

The other voice laughs in this high squealy kinda way, reminds me of that old commercial when Ella hits a high note an' glass shatters all over the place.

They come round the corner an' I spot 'em before they see me. Aides, not real nurses, dressed in pink uniforms, both look so happy 'til they see who I am.

An' then it comes—the pity face. Just like before. People conversatin', all happy 'til they see me, same like when Jean was around. 'Cept this time it ain't just my pride an' manhood that get snatched away but my boy. Come on God, help me out here, cause I can't make it without my boy.

When Jean left I can't honestly say I was anythin' but mighty glad. Glad for me an' Stevie both.

"I didn't want that damn kid but you forced me into havin' him. What did ya think, fool? While you was changin' shit pants an' prayin' did ya think some miracle would turn me into a saint or somethin'? You knew damn well what I was—I told you the kinda person

I was—when I moved my stuff into this dump, I warned you. But here you stand, lookin' all disappointed an' hurt. Come on, Baylor, give us a tear. I swear you cry more than that kid does."

Poor Stevie, he was just a baby but he knew. Kids are tuned into their folks even before they get born, especially their mothers. But Jean never felt nothin' back. Stevie would hold out his arms, beggin' to be picked up or just hugged a little, but Jean, she'd keep on walkin' right past him. Cigarettes an' beer was always more important than either of us was. The baby, he'd start to cry an' she'd laugh. If only we knew then how much better off we'd be without her... both of us.

Stevie don't talk much about her anymore but I know somewhere inside him, he blames me, even after all the years of not hearin' one damn word from that whore.

"Oh...Mr. Kracher." Them two little aides have come over to comfort me...I guess. The tall one smiles when I open my eyes. "How are you doing?" She leans forward an' I think she's gonna pat my poor pitiful head.

"How do you think he's doing?" Giggler looks over at her friend and rolls her eyes.

"It's okay, I'm fine."

"My brother and his friend were over at the VFW tonight. I heard that poor Mr. Lloyd just fell right off his chair. Good thing Frank Watson was there to catch him or he could have banged up his head really bad."

"Yeah, Frank's a good guy alright."

"There's a phone over there if you need to talk to the police or something."

"Got my cell." I pat my shirt pocket.

"So," Giggly asks, "are you stayin' the night?"

"I'm hopin' he'll wake up soon 'cause I have to get back an' try to grab some shut-eye before the sun comes up."

Both girls nod sadly.

"Well, I'm prayin' for you, Mr. Kracher, sir. You an' Stevie." The tall girl speaks with so much sincerity that I have to look away.

"I appreciate it."

After a few sorrowful blinks, they finally leave me alone.

The couch smells like sweat an' Fritos but somehow I guess I fall asleep. A sliver of sunlight burns through my eyelids as I wake up. Damn, why didn't no one wake me up? Jesus, what time is it?

I jerk the cell phone outta my pocket, there are two messages. How the hell did I miss 'em? What if? Panic is all I can feel. Calm down, I tell myself . You're not doin' no one a bit of good if you lose it. Calm down!

Message one is from my neighbor, Bill Nelson: "Heard you were in Crystal City at the hospital, waiting to hear about that guy who passed out last night. Hope he's okay. Try to get some sleep, will ya? And don't worry, I got things covered here."

As soon as Bill hung up, his wife Dottie musta grabbed the phone an' called me back. "Don't you worry, Baylor, everything's gonna be fine. Eat something!"

Since Jean run off, the Nelsons have been a godsend. Their kids are like brothers an' sisters to Stevie. I still remember that afternoon, more than ten years ago when Dottie couldn't hold it back no more an' told me how much she'd always hated Jean. The stories that came pourin' outta her. Most of 'em I knew by heart already, though. The cheatin', drinkin', lies, to cover up more lies, but I could see she needed to talk. Then she told me 'bout the time she'd heard Stevie cryin' from a beatin' an' I broke down. Said she'd gone to Jean, threatenin' to call the police if she didn't stop.

As I sit here, not wantin' to start one more day without my son, I wonder if all this is payback. Maybe God's tellin' me I don't deserve such a great kid.

Sweet Jesus keep him safe. I'll do anything, anything in the world, just as long as you carry him back home to me.

A woman walks into the waitin' room with two toddlers. They spot a box of toys against the wall an' squeal. I stand, try brushin' some of the wrinkles off my shirt before headin' for the nurses's desk.

"Can I help you?" Morning shift nurse is older.

"I was wonderin' 'bout Mr. Lloyd? He was brought in last night. Is he conscious? How's he doin'?"

After some typin', she reads the computer screen. She stares for a while an' finally frowns. "Sorry."

"He's not…? He's alive, right?"

"Oh, yes. He's just not allowed visitors now."

"Does that mean he's in a coma or somethin'?"

"I'm not a doctor, Mr. ahh...?"

"Kracher."

"Mr. Kracher. Oh...Kracher...I saw you on the news."

Before I get the pity face I ask, "Can you at least tell me Mr. Lloyd's first name?"

"Sure, of course, I can do that." Now she's fallin' all over herself to be helpful. "It's Vincent. If you'll wait here I'll go get Doctor Wallace. He can explain everything..."

"Sorry, that's real nice of ya, but I can't wait. If Mr. Lloyd wakes up, tell him I'll be back to see him later. Will ya do that?"

She nods, then reaches up and pats my hand. "I know they'll find your boy, I just feel it in my bones."

CHAPTER EIGHT

The police said we should have a headquarters. I ignored 'em. Stevie would be home; he just got carried away an' lost track of time, is all. An' I stuck to that idea for as long as I could. But then night came, an' by mornin' I knew somethin' was mighty wrong. My basement got turned into volunteer headquarters on the third day.

Then the questions started comin' fast 'n' furious, the police grilled me for hours. Had we been havin' trouble, my son an' me? They tell me how teenagers are all the time causin' trouble an' Stevie bein' fifteen, chompin' at the bit to get his driver's license—they seen it all the time. Treatin' me like a complete idiot, they explained how boys his age get all charged up with hormones an' maybe he had a girl? I know for a fact that he ain't goin' with no one special.

Oh sure, Stevie's your typical kinda boy in the hormone department. He chases or been chased by females. But he's a good kid, never gives me one bit of trouble...'cept for that time when he was twelve an' run away to see his mother. But I swear on my old man's grave, Stevie's one of a kind, everyone says so. It's probably because there's just the two of us. He's responsible, looks out for me. Many's the time I come draggin' my butt in the door after a long day an' there he is, settin' the table, servin' up his famous mac 'n' cheese.

We take care of each other. He loved...loves me.

Puttin' together a headquarters makes everything seem so official like. Now instead of a lost kid, we got a missin' person, posters, news crews. I lose my son right along with my privacy—any life I have—not to mention a few friends. Oh yeah, they ran away real quick. Not all of'em, mind you, but some. Like I'm contagious now an' if they get too close their kid'll go missin'. Well, fuck 'em.

The green top of the pool table is covered over with stacks of envelopes, newspapers an' pizza boxes. The picnic table I forgot we even had, got hauled outta the garage an' is now the phone center. Stevie's eyes stare at me, beggin' for help, from dozens of posters taped to the cement walls.

"Yo, Baylor." Bill, from across the street looks up as I walk over to the coffee pot. "How's that guy doin'? I heard that you spent the night at the hospital?"

"He's still out of it."

The ceiling above me creaks, a sure sign that someone's runnin' cross the living room floor. Then I hear 'em comin' down the steps.

"Oh, thank God, Bill, there you are! Have you heard?" Dottie asks.

"Heard what?"

"They found something!"

"Jesus. What do you mean, 'somethin'?'"

"The police are putting up that yellow tape, just like they do on TV."

I can't move.

"Calm down," Bill tells her, "remember your blood pressure." He's stallin', I can tell.

Dottie takes a deep breath.

"Now, tell me what exactly it is that they found?" he asks.

I don't want to hear this. No...I do. I have to.

"Bones. That's all I know. Nothin' else except it was Larry Olson who found 'em; he called for help and now the place is swarming with..."

Then she comes off the bottom step, walks into the room, and sees me.

"Baylor. Oh, I didn't know you were..."

"Where?"

"Back of Max's place."

And then I can't do nuthin' 'cept run.

Bill comes chargin' after me. "You're not going over there by yourself."

"I'm comin', too." Dottie shouts. "Bill, watch him!"

No need to turn round, I know she's pointin' at me.

CHAPTER NINE

Can't be. No way in hell. Awww, not Stevie. Not my sweet boy. No. No. It just can't...

I run. Can't remember much but I'm all of a sudden movin' fast with Bill 'n' Dottie right behind. None of us say a word; all I can hear is breathin'. An' there's this metal taste in my mouth, coatin' the back of my throat. It tastes like blood an' for a minute I think maybe I bit my tongue without even knowin' it. But there ain't no blood. It has to be the fear risin' up that I been tryin' to swallow back down for days.

"This is Laura Ann Bonetti reporting to you from Kimmswick where a grizzly discovery has been made."

I push my way up to one of the cops.

"Sorry sir, you can't—"

"Look, just tell me if it's true. Were some bones found?"

"Sir...Mr. Kracher, right?"

I wonder if he recognizes me from all the stuff on TV or if he can tell who I am just by the look in my eyes. Anyway, I nod that he's right.

"Stay here; I'll get the Chief."

I stand, stiff as a statue, not wantin' to see what everyone else can't get enough of seein'. Some guy crawls along the ground takin' pictures. That damn Bonetti woman rattles on an' on, bullshittin' herself into more time in front of the camera. I've heard all her theories—I've heard everyone's. Experts from New York, cops, reporters—all talkin' their heads off but comin' to the same conclusion. None of 'em knows nothin'.

I've known Chief Stoffel since we was boys. But as he comes up on me, he looks like he wishes we'd never been acquainted. "Baylor, you shouldn't be here. It's no good you getting worked up about..."

"Just tell me what ya found. For the love of God, I have the right to know!"

"Please don't—"

"I can handle the truth, Dwayne, just spit it out, will ya?"

He puts a heavy arm around my shoulder an' leads me to his car. "Look, two large bones which appear to be femurs—thigh bones— were found along with several smaller ones."

I can't say nothin'. Maybe I can't take it after all.

"Now, please, Baylor, we can't know if they're human remains until the Coroner arrives and then he has to send them to a lab. But believe me, it's probably nothing to get upset about. Those bones are more likely what's left of a deer or big dog. It happens all the time."

He keeps on talkin', tryin' to reassure me, sayin' things every-body's been sayin' for days. I watch his mouth but am listenin' to my own thoughts.

It don't matter where them bones came from, they can't be Stevie. No way. A body can't rot away that fast. Summer started up just a week ago. No...it ain't Stevie.

I realize he's pattin' my back like I was some over-sized baby an' it makes me mad.

"Don't you think you'd be more help at home? Man the phones, in case your boy calls? It's about all you can do now, besides, we have plenty of volunteers and you look exhausted. Go home, try to get some sleep."

"Yeah, thanks." Bullshit—that's all any of 'em keep handin' out.

A song starts up, sounds like an ice cream truck, but I can't see nothin' on the road.

"I think that's yours." Dwayne points to the cell phone in my pocket.

I'm still not used to the thing. Bill bought it an' passed the num-ber out to all the volunteers. But Stevie don't know I even got it, so whenever it rings the only thing I know for sure is that I won't be hearin' his voice on the other end.

I guess I don't move fast enough to satisfy Stoffel because before I can do it myself, he flips open the phone an' holds it up to my ear. But I don't talk til he struts away.

"Yeah?"

I recognize her voice, it's that reporter lady, Laura Bonetti. "Mr. Kracher, I need to talk to you."

Lookin' out over the crowd of bobbin' heads, I finally spot her red hair. She's in the driver's seat of a white news truck. The door's open an' she sits sideways, danglin' her feet like she's spendin' a nice day at the beach. A camera guy is standin' on the roof, aimin' one of them big lenses at the area the cops roped off.

"Did the police tell you somethin'?" I ask before she can say another word. "Cause if they did, I got every right to know."

"Sorry. If they had, I'd tell you."

"Yeah, sure."

There's been phone calls, visits from neighbors, all my friends warnin' me that this particular female is ruthless, a real cut throat among blood-letters. She does anything to get a story, and I do mean anything. But even if no one told me nothin' I sized her up after the first interview when she asked me to turn my head so that the light reflected off my tears better. She said it would "inspire" people to help find Stevie if they could see my pain real good. What kinda world is this anyway, when they measure a person's sufferin' by TV ratin's? Here I was, wounded like a dumb animal caught in a trap, sufferin' more than ever before in my life and all she cared about was turnin' me an' Stevie into some kinda sideshow.

"Look, Mr. Kracher, we're here because of Stevie. That's all any of us care about."

"An' I suppose it's your love an' concern that makes you go pokin' round my neighborhood, lookin' in garbage cans? Spyin' on people I knowed my whole life, good people who love my son an' would help me look for him without any of your fancy reports. Because, Miss Bonetti, as far as I can see, you've managed to stir up more trouble durin' your stay here, an' I for one wish you'd get the hell out. Let the big guys from CNN or some real news station help us instead of a sorry flunkie like you."

"Mr. Kracher..."

"What?" I surprise myself at how loud I shout.

"I know you're upset but I'm only trying to..."

"If you don't know where my son is, then leave me alone."

"I called with information about Vincent Lloyd."

"I don't know no one named Lloyd."

"Sure you do. He's the man who passed out last night? You visited him in the hospital."

Come on, I think, I can't take no more guilt. That guy has to be okay. Don't make him be dead an' especially don't make me have to hear any bad news from this woman. "What about him?"

"Two years ago he raped and murdered his own daughter. I just thought you should know what kind of person's in town helping you. Maybe the police should be notified?"

I slap the phone shut.

Bill comes huffin' 'n' puffin with Dottie tryin' to catch up. "Ya okay, buddy? I saw you talkin' on your cell. Any news?"

Before I can answer, Dottie starts cryin'. "First Stevie's cap and now this. Oh, God, Baylor." She throws her weight on me, grabbin' round the waist, huggin', screamin' into my shirt.

Bill pulls her off. "Calm down, woman."

"I'm sorry. I'm so sorry." She looks at me like a scared little girl, maybe she thinks I'm gonna yell; maybe she needs me to…I don't know.

"It's okay," is all I can get out.

"I gotta go back to the house. I can't take this." She turns an' runs away.

"It's gettin' to all of us," Bill says. "This not knowin'. Beats the hell outta me how you're holdin' up." He's gonna pat my shoulder but stops, instead shoves his hands down into the pockets of those old jeans of his. There's paint spots all over the knees an' his stomach hangs over the silver belt buckle Dottie had his initials engraved on. My friend has endured high blood pressure, diabetes, an' sixteen year's worth of AA meetin's during the years I've known him. Hell, we've all gone through a lot. But this ain't like them other times. This time I'm scared outta my mind. Cause if Stevie was to all of a sudden show up, he wouldn't find none of us the same people we was two weeks ago. Not Bill or Dottie, not me or Stevie himself, not even our town. I guess that's how POWs must feel.

A big cop holds up his hands 'n' shouts for everyone to get back but waves at me to come over. I don't wanna go.

Bill knows what I'm thinkin'. "You want me to go with ya?" he asks.

"No, thanks, I'm fine. You go take care of Dottie."

My feet feel like they're covered with glue, but I push them over to the cop. It's like I'm in the nightmare I had all the time when I was a kid. It started off where I was walkin' down a dark street, in a big city somewhere but there weren't no lights on in none of the houses. I feel the cement under my feet cause I'm always barefooted. Then someone's chasin' me an' I try to run cause I know if I don't, I'll end up dead. When I fall down, I start crawlin', pullin myself along by my fingernails, grindin' my knees into the sidewalk until the skin rips open an' I'm all bloody.

"Mr. Kracher, I need the name of your family doctor." He holds a pad 'n' pen, waitin' for me to answer.

"Edward Jamison. He's been our doctor for years. Delivered Stevie."

"He's here, in town?"

I nod.

"Okay, then, we'll get ahold of him."

"That's it?"

"For now, yes. Thanks."

I stand there feelin' like I'm bein' sent to the Principal's office… dismissed on account of I done somethin' wrong.

"Baylor! Hey, where ya goin'?" Bill shouts, but I keep on goin'.

My stomach growls an' I wonder if Stevie's hungry. I'm dead tired an' feel guilty for even thinkin' of sleepin' cause I might miss a clue or a call.

Then I remember Vincent Lloyd.

CHAPTER TEN

I stop by the house to check in with whoever's there. Sid an' Andy from work, their wives an' a baby crawlin' round fills up my livin' room.

"Hey, Baylor, you're on TV," Andy says all amazed like I'm a movie star,

Sure enough, there I am standin' in the field, talkin' to Stoffel. No need to bother listenin', just more reports of nothin' to report. I thank everyone in the room then head downstairs to check out the basement crew.

There's food laid out all along the counter in the kitchen 'n' I grab a slice of cold pizza, stand over the sink to eat it. The way I figure it, if I don't sit down at a real table, with a proper knife 'n' fork or even a napkin, I'm not really eatin'. It's hard to take any pleasure outta tryin' to swallow down hard, dry pepperoni. It would be wrong to enjoy anything 'til Stevie gets home.

The basement's fuller than the upstairs. There must be ten people down here; every last one of 'em busy doin' important lookin' business. When I walk in, a boy—I think he went to school with Stevie—holds out the phone to me. "Mr. Kracher, they want you to go to New York and be on The Today Show."

"I got People Magazine on the line," a woman calls out like she's just hit Bingo.

When did I become a celebrity? I hold up my hand an' shake my head. "I need a shower, an' there'll be no interviews or trips to New York City. None! You tell everyone that I ain't leavin' here. Not for nothin'. Got it?"

I hope they don't get all mad or think I'm bein' unreasonable. I'd hate for them to leave. But the room stays quiet. By the time I make it to the bathroom and into the shower the commotion starts up again.

When I leave the house I notice someone has tied a yellow ribbon to a tree in the front yard. How long has it been there, I wonder. Didn't see it when I came in. Whoever done it was only tryin' to show their concern, I know, but to me it might as well be that yellow police tape. It's like my house has been marked…same as they done when the plague hit.

The hospital's buzzin' now that it's later in the afternoon. Nurses push beds, rushin' back an' forth. The visitor's room full of kids 'n' bored grown-ups. I take the elevator up to the third floor where I know Lloyd was last night 'n' stop to ask about him.

"He's doing much better," a pretty young thing with bottle-cap glasses tells me.

"So, he's awake?"

"Yes." The nurse doesn't have time for me; it's plain she wants me gone.

"Can I see him, then?"

"Are you a relative?"

This time I know what to answer. "Yes, I'm his cousin."

"All right then. Right down the hall," she points, "room three-oh-four. But just for a few minutes; he needs his rest. The doctor should be stopping by soon to check up on him."

"Got it."

As I walk toward his room, I feel calm. If what Miss Bonetti says is true, I can just pick up the phone an' have Mr. Lloyd carried off by the police if he gives me any trouble. I'm in charge now; it's my call. I'm gonna look Lloyd straight in the eyes an' ask him 'bout his daughter. I'll be able to know if he's tellin' the truth. An' if I think he had anything to do with Stevie bein' gone, I can kill him right here. Course I've never killed anyone before, well 'cept for some deer an' quail, but I can kill him with my bare hands an' gladly go to jail for the privilege.

I just have to ask the right questions in just the right way…

PART THREE

VINCENT AND BAYLOR

CHAPTER ELEVEN

*D*addy?

"I'm fine, honey. Don't worry."

You don't look fine.

The man rocked himself from side to side as he lay stretched out in the hospital bed, banging the IV bag against the metal hanger with each jerk.

"Mr. Lloyd?"

Swiping at the moisture on his cheek, he straightened up. "Yes?"

"Mr. Lloyd, I'm Stevie's dad. I was here last night to see ya but you was out like a light." He smiled, tried a slight laugh but received only a blank stare for his effort.

Walking around the bed he faced the man full on, studying the sad brown eyes. Crazy is always in the eyes, he thought. Extending his hand he tried again. "I want to thank you for eveythin' ya done. I've been hearin' how you drove all the way from Chicago."

"No big deal." Vince tried to avoid making eye contact, the pain he was all too familiar with, was sure to be staring back at him.

"Well, maybe not for you, but it's a hell of a big deal for me. I mean, ya don't even know me an' you—"

"Thank me after we find Stevie."

"So ya ain't headin' home, then? From what I been hearin', ya ain't doin' too good, Mr. Lloyd."

"Why don't you call me Vince, okay? And from where I'm sitting, you don't look like you're' doing too good, either."

"Okay, Vince, an' I'm Baylor. We'll agree, neither of us is doin' too good, today. But right now I think we need to get ya home. I'm sure someone will be glad to—"

"I'm not leaving until I know something…one way or the other."

Baylor tried figuring out an argument that would persuade Vince to leave. All he needed now was one more person to worry about. But if this guy was willing…well, God only knew he needed all the help he could get. "Mind if I sit?"

"Be my guest." Vince watched as the tall man dragged a chair next to the bed. He looked worn out all over, from his blue flannel shirt, frayed along one sleeve, to his jeans, faded, pock-marked with small holes around each knee. His eyes were dull; gray strands glistened, mixed in with his thinning brown hair.

After Baylor settled himself into the chair he started. "I…I… wanted to say somethin' but it seems to have slipped my mind right now. Give me a minute."

"Confusion is part of it. Bet you can't sleep, eat or even decide what to wear. But who really gives a shit in hell if your pants match your socks when my little girl…I mean your boy… is missing."

Baylor stared at the sunburnt man. He reminded him of an animal that had been caught, runnin' round 'n' round tryin' to find a way out. Desperate, wiry, angry as hell. "Yeah, I heard you been through all this yourself."

Vince nodded. "Have they stripped you yet?"

"What?" Baylor wasn't sure he'd heard right.

"Have the police stripped away your dignity? Your pride? Have they accused you and your wife of harming Stevie? Made you doubt yourself and every friend you've ever had?"

"I ain't been through near as much as you, Vince, at least not yet, but I do know what you're talkin' 'bout, that's for sure. It gets harder an' harder every day. I don't know how much of this I can take. I never hurt no one. Why is this happenin' to me an' my boy? I don't understand what's happenin'?"

"I'll tell you exactly what's happening, Baylor. Some motherfucker didn't think about me and you. He did what made him happy. That's all. He just did whatever the hell he wanted and screw the rest of us. Plain and simple. Now we gotta live with it."

As Baylor listened to Vince he knew this man was the only person in the world who wouldn't lie to him. He knew it straight down to his core. "Man," Baylor said, "that first week I thought I was dyin'. All them questions, everyone tellin' me to calm down. Calm down, shit, my son, my only child is gone. My wife—ex-wife—has been in prison for years. Stevie never really knew her. All that crap come back to me, all the bullshit I gotta sift through an' look at over an' over again. Got me to thinkin' maybe I been a lousy father."

Vince felt so sorry for Baylor.... and guilty. Here he had come to help and look what he'd done—beat the poor guy up even more. Damn this anger. When was it going to let up? With as much compassion as he could muster he said, "It's not you. You can't think that way."

"Jean had an alibi, given to her by the state of Missouri, thank you very much. So while she's sittin' in her cell, I have to waste precious time defendin' myself. I begged 'em to start lookin' right away, Stevie needed every minute of us lookin' for him. But he'd run away from home once before. An' he ain't no baby, he's fifteen—a teenager—a headstrong, average, good kid."

"Gabriella—Gabby—was only six."

"Only six? Aww, geez. Did they ever catch the guy?"

"No."

The room seemed to swallow up their breathing. Sterile, void of any character of its own, at that moment it contained only the two men and their pain.

"Did you take a polygraph?"

Baylor nodded. "First thing I done. An' I passed it—no problem. But they want more—"

"They always do."

"Well, I finally convinced 'em, I think," Baylor said, "The police, reporters, radio people, all of 'em. I think they believe me when I tell 'em I was buyin' groceries, just doin' somethin' simple like that, while my boy was taken. I have the receipt an' everythin'."

"Listen, Baylor, they'll act like they believe you but you're always a suspect. Always. No matter what happens or how much time passes, you're going to be remembered with suspicion."

"That what happened to you?"

Vince nodded.

"Well, for what it's worth," Baylor leaned forward and patted the foot of the bed, "I'm real sorry. An' Stevie an' I appreciate that you're here."

Vince was touched by the man's sincerity.

"I guess I better be goin'. Nurse Friendly out there told me the doctor was on his way."

"Nurse Friendly." Vince laughed. "I know exactly who you're talking about."

The chair skidded loudly as Baylor stood up. "You know where to find me, Vince." He extended his hand to say good-bye.

"Could you stay a while longer? If you've got your cell with you…"

"Never leave home without it," Baylor said as he pulled the small phone out of his pocket.

"I'd be glad for the company," Vince said.

"Sure. But if ya start feelin' bad, let me know an' I'll skidaddle."

Vince smiled weakly. "If you don't mind…I mean if it's too hard you don't have to but…I'd sure like to hear about Stevie."

CHAPTER TWELVE

Baylor's face lit up, a wide smile gave away the absence of a tooth in the back of his mouth, on the top right side. "Now that's a subject I could go on about for hours."

"I got plenty of time." Vince settled back in the bed, getting comfortable.

"He's the kinda kid that always makes ya proud, ya know? Oh sure, he ain't at the top of his class when grade time comes 'round, but he's a decent human. Better than me, that's for sure. I don't know how it happened, but that kid has the morals of a saint. An' I ain't exaggeratin', ask anyone 'round here."

"I can't wait to meet him," Vince said. "Does he have a girlfriend?"

"He says he don't. I suspect he tells me that 'cause I'm alone an' he feels bad that I get lonely at times. That's the kinda heart he's got. Compassionate. He thinks I don't see but sometimes when the news comes on an' there's one of them drive-bys in the city an' a little kid gets killed, I see him cry. An' those dog commercials—the ones where they show a little pup shakin' or missin' an eye... he wants to save everyone. Ever since he's been four, whenever anyone asks what he wants to be when he grows up, he says 'A cop!' He's all the time talkin' 'bout how he wants to be a cop. Help people. Ya know?"

"Sounds like a great boy; you should be proud."

"I am. He'll always be the best of me."

A nurse hurried into the room. When she saw Baylor Kracher, she hesitated, obviously recognizing the man. To Vince she said, "Oh, I didn't know you had a visitor."

"Am I in the way?" Baylor asked.

"No...no...stay where you are." She didn't make eye contact, covering up her uneasiness with busy work. She scurried around like a little bird.

"Will I live?" Vince managed a weak smile.

" 'Fraid so."

A joke. It hung in the air, producing a relaxed moment.

"I came in to check the IV." Back to business. "The doctor's running late. Is there anything I can get you while I'm here?"

"No. But I would like to know when I can leave." "That's for the doctor to say."

"Ahh, come on, I bet you got some idea when my friend here can get his walkin' papers," Baylor said playfully.

"No idea." The woman obviously wasn't in a playful mood.

Both men watched her walk out of the room. Baylor looked back at Vince and rolled his eyes. "So where have ya been stayin'? There ain't exactly a lotta choices 'round here."

"Over at the Drury Inn on fifty-five."

"That can add up after all these days."

"I don't mind..."

"How 'bout you come stay with me? I got plenty of room. But if you have to get home, I understand. 'specially after bein' in the hospital. You must wanna get back—"

Vince's cell phone rang. He knew it was Kathy. If he didn't answer, she'd get upset. Baylor stopped talking as soon as Vince picked up.

"Hey."

"Vince: two things."

When Kathy was angry she got cold and detached.

"Okay, what are they?"

"The bones. You never mentioned anything about them finding bones. Is a forensic team there? Because there should be."

It was the first time Vince had heard about any bones. He couldn't let her know he'd been in the hospital. So he bluffed. "I'm out in the boonies here, Kath. I haven't heard any news today."

She was quiet. He could hear the clicking of her keyboard. Since Gabby was gone, Kathy spent most of her day sitting in front of the flat screen, constantly checking websites listing missing children, answering emails sent to her organization, WE'LLFINDYOU, networking with the police. She was obsessed.

"And what is two?" Vince asked.

"When were you going to tell me you're in the hospital?"

"How'd you find out?"

"Come on, Vince. This is the twenty-first century, for God's sake! I've gotten seven emails just in the last hour. People know you're there, they recognize your name. There are eyes and cameras everywhere. And that reporter, Bonetti? She did a story on you while she was standing in front of the hospital. Congratulations, dear, you're famous!"

"I didn't want to get you upset," Vince said weakly. "So are you mad that I'm in here or that I'm trying to do something—"

"What the hell do you think I'm doing all day—and night? Huh, Vince?"

"I didn't mean—"

"Just because I'm not out there with a stick, traipsing around doesn't mean I'm not working on Stevie's case. I'm doing more good than you are right now."

Baylor stood to leave, it was obvious there was trouble at home for this poor guy. Vince motioned for him to sit back down.

"Kathy, I don't want to fight."

After a heavy sigh she said, "Neither do I."

"I'm fine, it was just the heat and I didn't get enough rest. I hadn't eaten anything…"

"Are you coming home?"

"Not yet. I can't until I'm sure there's nothing more I can do."

"We each have to deal with this new life in our own way, I guess."

"We do. But I love you, that hasn't changed."

"I know." Her anger was gone. "They're going to suspect you, now that everyone knows who you are. It could get rough there, Vince."

"I'll be fine."

"Okay then, do what you've got to ya do, but come back in one piece. And if I find out anything I'll let you know."

"We'll talk tomorrow."

"Okay. Love you." She hung up abruptly.

"Sorry," Baylor said. "I didn't mean to listen but this is a small room an'—"

"Don't worry about it; my wife gets very excitable whenever she hears about another missing child."

"I can imagine."

Vince pushed himself back into the pillows. "Baylor, can I ask you something?"

"Shoot."

"Had you read stories about me when my daughter went missing?"

"Some."

"And now, do you think I'd hurt your son and then stay here pretending to look for him? Be honest. Because if you're uncomfortable being near me...I'll go home right now."

"Life's educated me, Vince. I ain't got no degrees, an' live in this little bump of a town, but I've learned from other things. Like my gut." He pounded his chest. "If it feels good in my gut, I go with it. Ya know, people are all the time fillin' their heads with TV, an' them little earplugs that blast music. Then there's them guys that want to preach all day 'bout how smart they are. I learned a long time ago that alls I need to do is be quiet and let the answers come to me.

"So, to answer yer question, no, I don't believe you'd hurt Stevie. I can see it in yer eyes. The hurt, the fear. You're not a killer, Vince, an' I'm not afraid of you."

Vince blinked back a few tears. Christ, he thought, am I getting soft or old? I was never like this before... His life had been split in two. Before Gabby was killed and after. There was no middle place to rest and think. Just the two halves that he teetered between, trying to keep his balance.

"Thanks, Baylor."

"Before yer wife called, I asked you somethin'. Remember?"

"Yes. And with that reporter stirring things up now, I think I should stay with you. But that's for my safety...what about yours?"

"Hey, things can't get any worse for me. I'll chance it."

CHAPTER THIRTEEN

"Why don't you leave the poor guy alone? His kid is missing, for christsake. Can you imagine how that must feel? How crazy with worry he must be?"

Laura looked up at her cameraman. "It's my job. Like your job is to get the footage. That's it. I'm the face and voice out here; it's my ass on the line. No one ever complains about crappy camerawork. Ever notice that, Ken? No, they just say, 'technical difficulty.' You always have an excuse. But if I screw up? It's my reputation."

"I hope you can live with yourself."

She pretended to be checking her make-up, but it was just a ploy to avoid his blistering glare. When he realized he wouldn't be getting any more from Laura, he spun around on his heels and stormed off.

What were the odds, she wondered, as she walked to the set then around the long desk to take her seat. Her first job had been at WGN in Chicago just around the time Gabriella Lloyd had gone missing. And now here she was in St. Louis and here was Vincent Lloyd—again. Of course there were coincidences. Life, she believed was timing and coincidence...and maybe just a pinch of planning. But this was something more. Fate maybe?

Strange how they had both pretended not to recognize each other yesterday. She knew what her reason had been: surprise. And she never came unprepared. At least she always gave her viewers the impression she was the driver, never the passenger in any situation. Holding the bull by the horns, that was her role, not running away from the beast. Okay, and maybe there had been some guilt. She had put the Lloyds through another level of hell, hounding them, accusing them. But at the beginning, all signs pointed to their role in the disappearance and then death of their daughter.

She'd been visiting her father when the news came in that Kathy Lloyd had tried to kill herself. "That poor woman," Dad had said over and over. "If I ever lost you... especially with your mother gone...I'd want to die. That poor woman." But Laura had felt nothing. Some people are weak; some can't take the pressure. Kathy Lloyd just caved.

But why hadn't she eased up a little after that? There was a heart beneath her Anne Klein blouse. She didn't have to have children of her own to feel the pain of losing one. What had she hoped to accomplish that the police hadn't?

National recognition, that's what. CNN recognition. Or maybe a show of her own.

But it hadn't worked.

Thousands of reports and two years' worth of updates. The police had found nothing and the couple had survived...somehow. Vincent Lloyd must surely hate her. But if he did, why hadn't he said something? Laura would have, if the tables were turned. No one could ever accuse her of possessing one tiny shade of shyness.

She adjusted the microphone and waited for her cue.

"Good afternoon, I'm Laura Ann Bonetti and this is Live at Noon. Our top story: Fifteen year old Steven Kracher from Kimmswick, Missouri has still not been found. Stevie was last seen two weeks ago, walking home from his part time job at the Bargain House on Elm Street. His Cardinals' baseball cap has been found in the woods about three miles from town. He was wearing jeans, black tennis shoes, a purple t-shirt and black hoodie. Hundreds of volunteers have been searching the area. Yesterday several bones were found and sent to a forensics lab in St. Louis. It should take a week to ten days for the results to come in. I interviewed Police Chief Stoffel about the discovery."

Her producer signaled that a video would play next. Laura ran her fingers through her bangs while the interview wound down.

The camera was on her again. "Another ten thousand dollars has been added to the reward from WE'LLFINDYOU, a group based in Chicago that helps locate missing children. This brings the reward total to twenty-five thousand dollars. If you have any information, please contact your local police or call the eight-hundred number below. The family is asking for your help in finding their boy.

"There was a five car pile-up on Interstate two-seventy East at the Earth City exit during the morning rush. Two people were injured. The driver of a semi fell asleep and veered out of his lane causing the accident. Traffic was held up for three hours until the area could be cleared."

Two people hurt. Accidents happen. She felt nothing.

Several more stories and then the weather was reported by the new guy, what's-his-name, and she pretended to care if it was going to be "mostly cloudy" or "partially cloudy." Did anyone really believe what those guys said, anyway?

By the time the sports came on, all she could think about was how big the ex-jock's neck was who spouted baseball scores she was sure a lot of people cared about. She just didn't happen to be one of them.

"Time for our traveling critic, Barbara Wellington."

A pretty brunette, fresh out of college, smiled her petite little smile on her petite little face and gushed about the new Disney movie. "It's a winner for the whole family, Laura. I highly recommend it."

She liked everything she saw or did, or ate, Laura thought.

"Thanks for that report, Barb, I'll be sure to check it out."

Big smile. Wait for her cue. "And that's it for now. Be sure to tune in for News at Five, this is Laura Ann Bonetti wishing you a happy day."

Hold that smile, wait for the cue, don't move and…

"That's it!" her producer shouted.

She took off the tiny microphone and laid it in front of her. On the way back to her office she stopped at her assistant's desk. "Tracy, can you get me the number of the forensics lab where those bones were sent? The ones they found in Kimmswick."

"I'm one step ahead of you."

Laura took the slip of paper from the woman. "Love you— mean it!"

"No need for sarcasm," Tracy shouted over her shoulder.

Laura shut the door and took off her blazer, carefully draping it over a padded, scented hanger. "Does everyone here think I'm a cold-blooded bitch? Well, I'm sorry if I don't cry over every sad story that comes into this office," she grumbled. "I'm sorry that I don't fall down and die when I hear about abused cats or homeless people. I could make a list a mile long of things to cry about. Or die for." She swiveled her chair toward her computer screen and frantically began typing. "Over-population, cancer, AIDS, world hunger, war orphans, oil spills, torture, droughts, floods. And missing children. Air pollution, endangered species, the IRS (that one made her laugh) unemployment, retirement benefits, rape, identity theft."

She stopped and read what she had just typed. "I can't possibly care about all these things. How would I function? I know what we should do." Her face lit up when the idea dawned. "Every person should be assigned a cause to cry for. What will mine be?"

CHAPTER FOURTEEN

"Are you sure you're okay?" Baylor asked as Vince got out of the car.

"I'm fine. If you keep treating me like an invalid, I'll go back to the hotel."

"Sorry."

The yellow ribbon had multiplied since Baylor was last home. A warm breeze waved them like so many cheerful hellos. He hated every one. Why yellow? he wondered. Yellow was cheery, sunshiny an' happy. Or yellow was cowardly, meek an' frightened. He sure as hell wasn't none of them things. If he had his way, they'd be gone. Or black. Black was how his heart felt. Black was the color of everythin' 'til Stevie got home.

Vince hesitated to look at the ribbons. They covered trees and bushes on Baylor's property then continued down the length of the street on both sides.

I think they're pretty, Daddy.

He smiled as Baylor led the way into his small house. Or maybe it just felt small because there were so many people inside. He didn't have to be told why they were there. This same scene had played out in his own home when Gabby first went missing. Volunteers, neighbors bringing hope and casseroles. And reporters, of course. The phone constantly ringing with tips leading nowhere. Psychics who "felt" Gabby was nearby. Legitimate news shows: *Good Morning America, The Today Show,* all wanting interviews. And those not so legit. Everyone calling or visiting, trying to get inside his life. Until the confusion settled into accusations. Then his house got even fuller.

"This here's Mr. Lloyd, the fella from Chicago."

"Aren't you the guy who ended up in the hospital?"

"Yes, that would be me." Vince attempted a smile.

"Well I'm Bill Nelson, from 'cross the street. That's my wife Dottie over there."

He pointed to a short woman wearing a white t-shirt with Stevie's picture across her large chest.

"Hi Bill," Vince said as he shook the man's hand, then waved at Dottie.

Baylor leaned in. "I'm not real familiar with everyone here so we'll skip the names. Let's get ya settled an' you can rest up a little."

"I'm going out with you," Vince said. "And don't argue."

"Ya know," Baylor said as the two made their way down a short hall, "you're just about the rudest house guest I ever had."

"I know."

"There's the bathroom on the right, we only got the one... sorry." He pointed to a small bedroom, also on the right. "This here's my room." The door was open and Vince could see the mess. An unmade bed, clothes scattered across the floor, a closet doors ajar. It was obvious there had been a large dresser against the far wall. Indentations in the carpet marked where it had stood. Vince assumed Baylor had removed it when his wife left. The room needed fresh air and sunshine.

On the left was a closed door with a large black skull and cross bones poster taped to the cheap wood. The word RESTRICTED was printed across the bottom in red. "Stevie's room. His poster," Baylor said.

Vince knew what was on the other side. Not much left of Stevie. The police and FBI would have taken any computers, cell phones, personal belongings. They probably stripped the bed, maybe took the mattress. There would be spots of carpet ripped up, spaces where books, CDs and magazines had been. It would feel like a ghost had once-upon-a-time inhabited that small part of the house, but had suddenly vanished. It would feel sad and empty.

"I hope this is good enough," Baylor said as he stopped in front of the room at the end of the hall. "Course it ain't no Drury Inn."

"Are you sure you're okay with this?" Vince asked, touching the man's shoulder. "With all you're going through...I know how difficult and overwhelming—"

"Yes you do, Vince. You know exactly what I'm goin' through. That's why I need ya here. We'll look out for each other."

"I have to admit, it would make me feel a whole lot better knowing I helped you in some way."

A woman's scream suddenly shattered the moment. And then it seemed as if everyone was running. Without thinking...Vince and Baylor ran, too.

"What the hell's happenin'?" Baylor shouted.

When no one answered, the men followed the others downstairs.

Dottie was spread across the floor, Bill knelt down beside her, holding her head. "She passed out when she heard."

"Heard what?" Vince asked.

"Shhhh." An older man held up his hands. "We're trying to listen to this."

Vince recognized the spot where the reporter stood.

"It was here that a black tennis shoe spotted with blood was found. Police confirm it belongs to Steven Kracher the fifteen year old who went missing in Kimmswick more than two weeks ago. This is the second article of clothing that has been retrieved. Bones were also uncovered but we are still waiting for the lab report on those to come in so a positive identification can be made. No comment from the boy's family yet. We'll keep you updated. This has been a special report. Be sure to tune into your local news for more details."

"How do they know it's Stevie's shoe? No one called here. Have you talked to anyone, Baylor?"

Baylor stood, staring at the big screen TV.

"It doesn't mean anything," Vince said. "Come on, I'll go with you, we'll talk to the police. They have no right putting these kinds of things on the air without consulting you first. You have rights, you know." He wasn't going to let this happen again.

Baylor allowed Vince to pull him back upstairs and outside to the car. "You can't believe anything anyone says. You'll go crazy if you do," Vince said.

They drove the short distance to River Park, right on the Mississippi. News vans with huge satellite dishes mounted on top were parked in a half circle. Police and reporters holding microphones with their call letters affixed to the front, huddled in a tight knot.

Vince shot out of the car, not waiting for Baylor to follow or take the lead. When he spotted the policeman holding the sneaker that had been bagged in plastic, he demanded to know, "Who verified that's Stevie's shoe? I've been with Mr. Kracher all day and no one from your department has called. How can you just put a report out like that without checking first? What if you've made a mistake? Have you stopped to think how devastating this is for Mr. Kracher? How excruciating it is to hear all these reports? Have you?"

By the time Baylor reached the men, he had worked himself up into an angry panic. "Let me see that shoe!" he demanded. "Mr. Lloyd's right—"

"Mr. Lloyd?" Chief Stoffel asked as he approached. "You two are friends now? I thought you said you didn't know Vincent Lloyd, Baylor."

"Oh no you don't. I know what yer doin' an' it ain't gonna work," Baylor said as he glared up at the Chief of police. "I have a right to see that shoe!"

"Come on, Baylor, you were the one who gave us a detailed list of everything Stevie was wearing when he went missing. An' we all know, especially those of us who've been around Stevie since he was born," sarcasm was spicing up the Chief's tone, "that Stevie an' a bunch of his friends always hung out down here, that they liked to shoot hoops right where we're all standing."

"Why can't I see that shoe?" Baylor asked.

"It's evidence now. We'll run it up to the lab so they can test the blood."

Baylor had been holding it together pretty well until he thought of Stevie's blood being spilled. As he started to slump over, the Chief grabbed him and led him to a picnic table a few feet away. When Vince tried to follow, Stoffel signaled for one of his deputies to stop him.

Gently, the Chief lowered his friend onto the bench. "We're all upset about Stevie bein' missin', Baylor. Look around at all the good folks here to help find him. But some people come to gawk, our misery makes 'em feel superior. We gotta watch out who we trust at a time like this. There could be a killer watchin', takin' pleasure in our fear. We can't trust no one, Baylor."

"An' that includes Mr. Lloyd?"

"There are lots of folks, my friend, up in Chicago, for instance, who believe he killed his own little girl an' got away with it. Maybe the urge overcame him again an' he grabbed Stevie. Ever think about that?"

"Sorry, there ain't nothin' you can say that'll make me believe a decent guy would just up an' kill his own little girl. An' even if he did, why on earth would he all of a sudden—years later—drive down to this nowhere place an' grab my boy? Out of the blue? It don't make no sense."

"Well, it really don't matter what you think. I'm leading this investigation an' I have to suspect everyone, Baylor—"

"Even me?" It was the first time he had honestly considered that people might be thinking the worst of him.

"Even you."

CHAPTER FIFTEEN

The house seemed to deflate late at night. Like a balloon with a slow leak, it would lose its energy. All day long it churned with anxiety, fear polluting the atmosphere, always too warm, even though the air conditioner was hiked up. Nothing fresh and clean circulated within its walls. Baylor found it hard to breathe since Stevie had disappeared.

But when everyone settled back into their own homes, the anxious father could relax—just a little. The phone stopped ringing. No news is good news, right? No one was giving up—there just wasn't anything to be done in the dark. And while he settled down, hoping for a few hours of sleep, he'd imagine his son sleeping also—safe 'n' sound. Because even the bad guys had to sleep—sometime—and while they slept, everyone was safe.

Baylor Kracher stood outside, letting the muggy air hold him in a comfortable hug. Summer—his least favorite time of the year. And from now until he died, he would remember this particular stint in hell and hate July even more.

The stars were bright, one blinked. Or was it a plane? People goin' somewhere, havin' a life. Movin' on. Would he forever be stuck here? Is this how his life would end? What if they never found Stevie? Could he stand the not knowin'?

Baylor turned his face up to heaven. "Lord, please keep my boy safe. Help him to be brave an' let him know we're lookin'. Let him know we're never gonna give up. Never."

Vince lay on the lumpy twin bed, under a fleece blanket. Baylor kept his house so damn cold that the tips of his nose and fingers were on the verge of freezing. But he'd never complain. A streetlight, planted between the house and its neighbor, made total darkness in the small room impossible. His neck hurt; pain traveled up to the top of his head then spread back down, settling in each temple.

He sat up to look for something to read. A stack of magazines in a corner, piled at least three feet high, intrigued him. Wrapping the blanket around him, Vince turned on the small light above the bed. Then like a mummy, he shuffled across the room, pushing his feet, covered in white cotton socks, ahead of him.

"*Field & Stream, Fisherman Magazine,* 'Fishing for Trout,' 'Fishing for Bass,' 'Lures,' 'The Best Fishing Spots in the Country,'" Vince read off the names of magazines and articles. "Guess Mr. Kracher likes to fish—or at least read about it." Did Stevie fish with his father? he wondered.

Vince's stomach growled. If he were home, Kathy would heat up some leftovers, all the time complaining that he should have something lighter so late at night. No, if he were home, he'd be up watching an old movie—probably a western. He used to love true crime programs but after Gabby...

Cautiously, Vince opened his door and crept down the hall toward the kitchen. Baylor had been so kind, said to help himself to anything he wanted.

You used to be that way, Daddy. Member? You were the nicest Daddy in the whole world...

"Yeah, I was a big ole teddy bear. Nice and stupid."

Baylor stepped into the kitchen, closing the back door behind him. Flipping the light on, he was surprised, yet happy to see Vince standing there.

"You okay, buddy?"

"Sure. I didn't mean to...I was cold...and I thought maybe if I had something to eat...but if I'm bothering you..."

"Hey, you're fine. I was just outside gettin' some air. My chest feels like a two ton gorilla's sittin' on it. You're cold? It's hot as hell, even now; Missouri summers are like sweatin' in a sauna."

"Yeah, it's unbearable outside—"

"Sorry. It's just that I'm so hot all the time now. Must be what hot flashes feel like, huh?" They both managed a grin. "But it's all the time. The doctor down at the clinic says I'm fine 'n' I should try to relax but I tell him he's crazy if he expects me to just... Sorry."

"Don't apologize," Vince said. "Don't let any of us make you apologize."

Baylor cinched the belt around his plaid robe even tighter. It had been a present from Stevie but he'd never worn it until this past week. When he found it in his closet, he remembered how the boy had been so proud givin' it to him last Christmas. But Baylor had told him that it just wasn't his style. Why had he done that? Would it have killed him to wear it sometimes, just for Stevie? Now look at him, he was wearin' it because of a stranger.

"You mentioned wantin' somethin' to eat? Good, cause there's so much food in that frigidator that it'll surely spoil if we don't clean it out some."

Baylor walked over to the thermostat and set the room temperature higher. Then he turned to Vince. "Let's have a look now an' see what we got. Think I'll join ya, if that's okay?"

"Sounds good."

Baylor opened the refrigerator while Vince folded up the blanket he had been clutching. He felt foolish now, like a crotchety old man. Then quickly he looked down to make sure his t-shirt wasn't dirty. His flannel pajama bottoms had a small rip across the right knee.

"We got part of a ham, some Velveeta, turkey, and all sorts of casseroles." Then as if to prove what he said was true, he started pulling foil covered platters and clear plastic containers out, setting them on the counter behind him. "There's some bread over there," he pointed, "if a sandwich sounds good. If not I can nuke ya a plate."

"Sandwich is fine." Vince grabbed a loaf of white bread off the small table against the wall. "Got any mustard or mayo?"

"You like yellow or spicy?"

"Whatever you're having."

"I like spicy. Stevie used to laugh when I'd get ahold of somethin' so hot it would make my face turn all red."

"Hot's good."

The two men stood quietly layering meat and cheese on top of Wonder bread, comfortable in each other's presence. The stillness hanging in the air calmed them.

"Milk, soda or beer? Maybe a cold one will help ya to sleep," Baylor said.

"I don't drink alcohol…anymore." Did he sound pathetic or like a snob, Vince wondered. Not wanting to come off unfriendly he decided to explain. "I had—have—a drinking problem."

"Two milks, then," Baylor said.

They each pulled a stool up to the counter.

"Oh, we got chips or maybe a pickle?"

"Baylor, sit—eat."

"Sorry, I just don't know how to act no more. I don't even know who I am…"

"I know," Vince said as he took a bite of his sandwich.

"I like that ya know what I'm goin' through, Vince. It's comfortin'."

"Good."

Baylor picked up his sandwich, unsure if he even wanted to eat it. The first bite was more of a nibble but then he realized how hungry he really was.

"So," Vince said, "I see you like to fish?"

"Used to. But the past few years it seems I'm always too busy. So I read about it. Livin' here on the river you'd think I'd get the chance every day. But there's always so many other damn things needin' attention. My dream though, is to go fishn' in the ocean."

"Which one?"

"Don't matter. Ya know, they say that all of us have this urge to return to the sea—cause we come from there."

"I've heard that, too. Guess it has to do with the tides."

"Do you live near any water in Chicago?"

"Not far. We do have some great beaches there. My folks used to take us to the beach every Sunday afternoon. I loved it."

"Seems like we got more than a tragedy in common," Baylor said.

Vince just nodded.

CHAPTER SIXTEEN

"We're outside the home of Baylor Kracher, father of missing teen, Steven Kracher. It has now been twenty days—almost three weeks—since Stevie was last seen walking home on Elm Street, near his home in the small town of Kimmswick, Missouri. Volunteers have been working diligently every day in hot temperatures and high humidity. So far Stevie's baseball cap has been found, then several bones and most recently, his tennis shoe. Today we have word that the results from the forensic lab in St. Louis has identified those bones as human, not animal as first suspected. We are now awaiting positive identification and reaction from Stevie's family."

Dottie walked across the street, agitated as she hurried toward Baylor's house. "Git away from here! You ain't nothin' more than vultures! All of you!"

Laura turned, holding the microphone out to the angry woman. "And you are a friend of the family?"

"I am none of your fuckin' business!" Dottie shouted over her shoulder, never breaking her stride as she made it up the stairs to Baylor's front door. "Let 'em bleep that one out," she laughed to herself.

That handsome reporter from NBN Cable News was standing by the bushes and she almost went over just to see him up close but didn't give in to the temptation.

Dozens of cameras flashed when she turned around, just for a second, and held up her middle fingers.

"Can you believe that woman?" she asked as she walked over to the sink to make a pot of coffee like she had done every morning for too many days now. She stopped when she saw the pot was full. Touching the side she could also tell from the heat, that it was fresh.

"Vince made it," Baylor said.

Dottie pulled her Stevie t-shirt down over her extra thirty pounds. "Well, that was nice of him. But I guess since he's living here now...I guess he should pitch in..."

"Are you kiddin' me?" her husband asked. "That man come down here just to help find a boy he never met. He don't know none of us. An' from what I hear, he's got a fancy place up in Chicago. I'm sure bein' here is not his idea of the ideal vacation. Where is your Christian heart, woman? Have you forgotten that Vince lost his own child?"

"How could I forget?" She grabbed a sponge and wiped crumbs into the sink. "Excuse me if I wonder about Mr. Lloyd's part in his daughter's disappearance. Maybe I'm just not as trustin' as you. Life ain't all gumdrops an' puppies, ya know?"

"I would ask you to please refrain from talkin' 'bout Mr. Lloyd that way," Baylor said. "I have found him to be a decent man an' after many conversations, I don't believe for one moment that he had anythin' to do with what happened to his precious little girl."

Dottie kept her back to the men while she busied herself tidying up. "Where is he...if I may ask."

"Where he's been every day since he got here—out lookin' for Stevie," Bill told her.

"An' why are you just sittin' here on your fat ass?" She spun around to glare at her husband.

"Come on, Dottie," Baylor said as he walked over to calm her. "Bill's been here since six. You both have been great; I don't know what I'd do without all yer help. I'm the one you should be hollerin' at. I'm dreadin' goin' out there to deal with them reporters. I feel guilty when I'm out lookin'; I feel even worse when I stay here. If only I had picked Stevie up that day..."

"Stop it!" Bill shouted. "Beatin' yourself up over an' over ain't helpin' no one. That boy is fifteen for christsake. He ain't no baby an' he sure as hell ain't no little wimp. Most kid's 'round here are afraid of him, Baylor. He's taller than all the rest; he's got a good ten pounds on most kids his age. An' let's not forget that Stevie weren't no angel. He could be real intimidatin', scary sometimes."

"Bill, Stop!"

The frustrated man watched his friend drop to the floor. It

seemed to be happening in slow motion. It never occurred to him that Baylor might hurt himself when he hit linoleum. Nothing occurred to him as he watched the scene like it was all playin' out on TV. He wasn't even hearing the soft sobbing escalating into a guttural howl.

At first Baylor beat his fists against the wall and then his head. His feet kicked wildly at the floorboard. The howling lasted a good minute before it turned into a piercing scream.

Dottie looked helplessly at her husband, all the while stroking Baylor's head. "We're here, sweetie. We're all gonna have a good laugh when Stevie's home safe 'n' sound."

Bill knelt down, and when he realized the crying wasn't going to end soon, he sat on the floor, making sure his knees touched Baylor's back, hoping the closeness would comfort the traumatized man.

CHAPTER SEVENTEEN

Was too much information a good thing? Kathy Lloyd struggled with that question daily. Did she really want to know every little detail about every sordid situation? Or was Vince right when he reminded her that ignorance was bliss? He also said that she hid in her office and didn't want to face the reality of a life with just the two of them in it. Maybe there was more than a small bit of truth in both statements.

When Gabby had been gone for more than two years, Kathy thought she was pregnant. She wasn't surprised…or happy. She was overwhelmed with questions, fears and doubts. Hour after hour a new one would work its way from some dark hole in her brain and end up either smacking her full on, or lurking, wriggling out unexpectedly into her consciousness. All the sleeping and work she did never smothered any of those dark thoughts entirely.

Was she trying to replace Gabby? Was it too soon? Or was it too late to have another child? Were she and Vince in the same place—ready to start making a new family? And did she even want to be bound tighter to a man she wasn't sure she liked anymore?

Vince was drinking heavily by the time the search finally ended. She took the easy way out and ignored him. The very sight of him, the smell of him, sounds he made when he ate or sucked down his booze, space he occupied—he was having a life when their child had none. And she hated him, all the while hating herself more. When she couldn't stand those feelings, she decided to check out. Better dead than in such pain.

The gun was old. Her father had given it to her after she signed the lease on her first apartment. He was worried about the neighborhood, her being alone and just twenty years old. He'd taken her to the shooting range a few times to get used to holding the .25 and they'd found something they could do together. It was a nice time.

The hardest part had been deciding where to do it. Always wanting everything clean and in its place, Kathy couldn't leave a mess behind for Vince to deal with. At first she thought she should wrap herself in a shower curtain and lay down in the tub. It got to be a game she played with herself. Not the woods—animals get to a body before the mortician. And she was a private person, the thought of strangers looking at her that way...no. Finally she decided to use her own car. Death in a can. She liked it. Vince would just have the car towed away—no muss, no fuss.

But all she managed to do was sever some nerves. When she woke up she was partially blind in her right eye. But her clarity was brilliant. Suddenly everything was in focus. Priorities shifted so totally she was surprised the room didn't shake. Her suicide attempt had left her changed and Vince...just angrier. It was his turn to hate her. But, she reminded herself daily, she had to be more understanding than he ever had. She wasn't the one who had been accused of murder and rape.

At first they were both suspects. Standard procedure. But when the police and FBI eased up on her, treated her more like the grieving mother she was, they came down harder on him. It hadn't been fair; she'd had the advantage of working downtown, being out of the house. And that day there'd been an added bonus—her dentist appointment.

"We can fit you in this morning. If you get here at eight Dr. Goodwin will see you—first thing."

No problem. Vince was home all the time, the perfect house-husband/stay-at- home-dad. He was reliable, dependable, in love with his family and everyone was happy.

And so their day had begun the same as always with her rushing, only everything had been amped up because of her temporary crown. Vince stayed out of her way, being considerate, making Gabby's lunch. He held out a cup of coffee to her as she rushed through the kitchen, kissed him and her daughter good-bye and hurried out the back door.

She had witnesses from the dentist office, her own office and even a neighbor who saw her leaving the house that morning. Dr. Goodwin, his assistant, the receptionist, strangers in the waiting room, and a cop who'd given her a warning to buckle up (she always hated that damn seat belt). All had been questioned. Thirty-two witnesses could vouch for Kathy Lloyd that day. They would give statements and swear to authorities that her hours during the daytime at least, were all accounted for.

But the FBI speculated that maybe she was trying to draw attention to herself by establishing an over-inflated alibi. Maybe she was protecting Vince. Gabby could have already been dead when Kathy left the house.

No one wanted to hear the truth. It was boring and uncomplicated—black and white instead of the Technicolor version they made up. She had simply left Gabby with Vince, safe and sound at home, and gone to the dentist and then to work.

Could she have withstood what Vince had? Not only the accusations but the self-loathing? Be gentle with him, she told herself all the time. But the more understanding she gave him, the more he seemed to expect, taking her love and concern for granted. Nothing ever came back to her. She was soon so empty inside that she ached.

The only comfort she found then and now was the certainty. One hundred and fifty percent on a bad day—two hundred on a good one. The certainty that her husband had never hurt their little girl kept Kathy warm at night. Even when evidence was twisted and analyzed, rearranged to make Vince look guilty, she never believed any of it.

After six weeks of holding the secret in, she told Vince there would be another baby coming.

He just nodded.

But when she went to her gynecologist, he told her she had been mistaken. There was no baby.

And when she told Vince...he just nodded.

Then had come his insomnia. While he paced and drank, she slept. Not wanting to disturb her with his constant uneasiness, Vince started living in front of the TV, on the couch. She hibernated in the bedroom, feeling safe under the covers. And then she realized how the sex had changed. When one of them broke down, the other would comfort. The level of despair dictated their level of passion. And when the despair eased up, they didn't really need anything from each other anymore. Statistically, most couples who lost a child got divorced, so it followed that they were doing better than most. "Just hang in there," a therapist had told them. And so they did.

Then Vince saw the story about Steven Kracher on the news and got off the couch. Thank you, God. But when he left, he took his anger with him. He packed up his resentment and fury along with his clean underwear. And the house sighed with relief when he drove off.

She sat down at the computer, her cell phone on the right corner of the desk, a "real" phone on the left. Her office was crammed with donations: FAX machine, another computer set up on another desk, a laptop, digital cameras, a TV and radio. Posters of missing children covered the walls. The desk lamp had been in Gabby's room, Kathy loved it; it made her happy. Tinkerbell sculpted from a colored resin. The shade had stars cut out of it and when the light was turned on, they reflected across the wall. It was silly, out of place and...perfect.

Her hair was still wet from the shower. She set the half-filled glass of orange juice on the side table and turned on her lamp. "Okay, let's get started." While she waited for the computer screen to light up, she rocked in her squeaky office chair.

"Only fifty-three emails today? Huh." She started by deleting the familiar crack-pots, messages she recognized as coming from people who confessed to every crime imaginable. Next she got rid of ads, jokes (a total waste of time) and then she was left with fifteen worth reading.

She started at the top and about a third of the way down, froze when she recognized Laura Bonetti's address.

PLEASE CALL ME. YU HAVE MY # AT THE STATION. TODAY!

"What the hell?"

Kathy picked up her cell, thinking she'd call Vince before doing anything. That bitch had to be stopped from hurting the Kracher family. Maybe Vince could confront her...no...calling him would only make things worse. Vince was finally feeling useful.

She put the phone down.

Then she picked it up again. Should she just call that Bonetti woman to see what she wanted? She'd worked a long, hard campaign to run that witch out of town. And now, here she was again, dammit, messing with their lives.

She put the phone down. Wait a minute, she thought, things are a lot different than they were a few years ago. I have supporters now, the police listen to what I have to say; I can take any story to any channel. WE'LLFINDYOU is respected nationwide. I'm one of the good guys.

She reached for her desk phone, didn't want to chance getting cut off, and quickly leafed through the phone book a local office supply store had donated. When she found the number, she dialed.

"Laura's not at her desk now, can I switch you to voice mail?"

"No." She took it as a sign. "Just tell her Kathy Lloyd called." And I won't be calling back, she thought.

"Hold on, she just walked in."

I bet she did.

"This is Laura."

"I got your email, Ms. Bonetti and I want to make myself clear before you say another word."

"I'm listening."

"I don't like you. In fact I hate you. You are a cold-hearted, calculating, bitch. You have no integrity, no class, and certainly no compassion. If you are attempting to start more trouble for me or my husband I will make sure you —"

"I know—never work in this town again. We've been through all this before, haven't we, Mrs. Lloyd?"

"Just so we're both straight here."

"Oh, I hear you, loud and clear."

"Then tell me what's so urgent and I can hang up on you."

"Look, I respect what you and your organization do for missing children. I know you won't believe me but, I admire you."

"And? You're running out of time, Ms. Bonetti."

"There was a shoe found—"

"I know all about it, a black sneaker—"

"With blood on it," Laura said.

"You still haven't told me anything I don't already know. I have sources now, Ms. Bonetti. And they reach around the world."

"Really? Do you know whose blood is on that shoe?"

"No, and I'll bet you don't either. Come on, those kinds of tests take weeks."

"Sometimes."

"Okay, so you got the results. Whose blood is it?"

"Baylor Kracher's. Stevie's own father."

Kathy sat stunned. "I don't believe you. Who's your source?"

"Oh come on, Kathy; you know I can't reveal that."

"Why would you call me with this news flash? Why aren't you out shouting it to everyone watching your show?"

"I feel as if I owe you something..."

"And just what am I supposed to do with this information?"

"Tell your husband to get his ass out of the Kracher house. Make him go back to a hotel. He has to distance himself from Mr. Kracher—at least until that kid's found. Better yet, make him come home. Do you want him suspected, accused and maligned...again?"

"I'm touched that you care so much about me and my husband," Kathy said sarcastically. "Suddenly you have a heart. Too little, way too late, Ms. Bonetti."

CHAPTER EIGHTEEN

"Course my blood's on Stevie's high-tops," Baylor told Stoffel. "And why is that?"

"Come on, Chief, how many pairs of shoes you think my boy got? Well I'll tell ya—two. One for church an' one for the rest of the time. He wore them things to school, he wore 'em when he went fishin' with me—or by hisself. He wore 'em to work—"

"I get it, Baylor."

"I bet you found animal blood from when his dog, Buster, caught a hook in his paw. That dumb animal got into everythin'. Stevie held him down while I worked it out. Cut myself...so did my son. Between me an' Buster an' my boy, there was blood everywhere."

"Well you'll have to come with us." The Chief felt badly, it was obvious in his tone. "We just need you to answer a few questions."

"Why can't you question him here, in his own home?" Bill asked.

"The man has rights. You're treatin' him like a common criminal," Dottie shouted.

Vince pushed his way through the crowd of reporters and rubbernecks camped out on Baylor's front lawn. After Kathy's call he felt an urgency to be with his friend.

A single squad car was parked in the driveway. The front door of the small house stood open. Through the screen Vince could make out a dozen people and hear Dottie's high pitched irritation.

"I just heard," he said to Baylor. Then realizing he was clutching the pole he'd used looking for Stevie, he propped it in the corner and wiped his hands on his dirty jeans. "I'm Vincent Lloyd; I'm a friend." He extended his hand to the Chief. "We haven't been formally introduced."

Stoffel had a strong grip but he was shorter than Vince and didn't like having to look up at the man. Puffing out his chest he tried to re-establish his authority in the middle of the angry crowd surrounding him. "It's good of you to come help find Stevie. We all appreciate it."

Turning to Baylor, Vincent asked, "Do you have a lawyer?"

"No."

"Well you're going to need one."

"Now look here, Mr. Lloyd. I've known Baylor before Stevie was even born. We trust each other, ain't that right?" The Chief smiled weakly at his friend.

"Thanks for the advice, Vince, but Stoffel's right. This ain't Chicago. There's only a hundred of us livin' here. We all know each other—"

"Can we have a minute, Chief?" Vince asked.

"Just one."

Vince eased Baylor into the hallway, away from the front door and police. "This is how it starts, Baylor. The questions, the doubts. You have to stop making statements to the press. You have to just concentrate on finding Stevie now."

"I appreciate your concern, Vince, but if I don't talk or go on them TV shows, beg for my boy's life, then I look guilty."

"And if you talk too much, they'll say you're covering up something. You're in a horrible position. That blood just pushed you into enemy territory as far as the authorities are concerned. You have to defend yourself, my friend. And I'll help you get someone who will do that."

"But I wouldn't even know how to get a lawyer; I ain't never been involved with the law."

"What did you do when your wife was sent to prison?"

"A court appointed someone; can't even remember his name. Besides, I was out of it by then. I didn't care what they done with her. I didn't even go to her trial an' I sure as hell didn't bring my boy anywhere near that place. I shielded him from all her shit."

"So let me help you. I have a friend who's a lawyer. I'll call her right away. But until I do, don't talk to Stoffel. Tell him you're invoking your right to have a lawyer present. Don't sign anything and don't say anything referring to Stevie."

Baylor stood defeated. "Okay, Vince. You been through all this... you're the only person I know who has. But it didn't end so good for you, did it?"

"Hey, I'm not in jail, am I?" Vince offered a weak smile.

"No."

"This is just bullshit to get through. Please, believe me."

Baylor nodded.

As Vince watched his friend walk back into the living room, he tried not to give in to the panic that was escalating in his chest. Oh my God, he thought, it's happening again.

"Can Mr. Lloyd come with me?"

Stoffel looked at Vince with suspicion, then at his deputy. "No need. I think he can be of more help here. Right, Mr. Lloyd?"

Vince recognized those eyes. They betrayed every kind gesture Stoffel's body tried to convey. They stood out, set in a face creased with accusations. But there was also something Vince hadn't seen in the eyes of the Chicago police when they brought him in for questioning—fear. This small time cop was in way over his head and he knew it.

"Right."

"How long will this take, Dwayne?" Baylor asked the Chief.

"No tellin'."

Vince followed the men out the door and down the front steps. When they got to the car, he stopped and called Kathy.

"You'll never believe what's happening here," he told her.

"Come home, Vince. You've done so much and I'm worried about your health. Please—"

"I can't just leave this poor guy. They're taking him in for questioning...again."

"What did you expect?"

"Right. And that's exactly why I'm going to help Baylor. He's all alone—no wife no child—"

"All right, all right. What can I do?"

"He needs a lawyer, Kath."

"You mean all this time he hasn't had one?" She couldn't believe it.

"Things move a little...differently here. Slower. Call Medora."

The deputy was helping Baylor into the back of the police car.

"I'll do it right now," Kathy said.

Vince held the phone to his chest and yelled, "Baylor, I'm getting a lawyer now!"

Baylor nodded toward Vince and gave a slight wave.

PART FOUR

THREE YEARS LATER

BAYLOR

CHAPTER NINETEEN

"What a surprise." Why can't they take a hint an' leave me the hell alone?

Dottie pushes through the front door, lookin' like another ten pounds has settled round her hips. "Well it's your birthday, for goodness sake. Did you think we'd forget?" She holds a white box out in front of her. "Your favorite."

"Now what ya got there?" It's a game we play every year an' I'm ready to call it quits. She makes a red velvet, two-layer cake, covers it with blobs of cream cheese icing, an' I act surprised. "Ya didn't have to do that."

Bill has gone completely bald since I last seen him, before he moved to South County, an' I swear he polished his head this mornin'. "Happy birthday, ya ole' son-of-a-bitch." He follows his wife inside, holdin' a stack of presents. "Damn, you're old!"

"Now, Bill," Dottie scolds, "be nice."

After pattin' my shoulder she walks straight through to the kitchen. The back of her sweatshirt has sparkly butterflies all over it—same as the front.

Bill sits the gifts in the middle of the coffee table. "Fifty! Where does the time go?"

"I sure as hell don't know."

An' that's all we have to say for a minute or two.

He makes a big production of strugglin' out of his jacket, finally tosses it over the back of a chair by the window. "Strange weather we've been havin'."

"Sure is." When in doubt, talk about the weather.

"They're predicting tornadoes," he says.

It's one of them October days that can't make its mind up.

Left-over summer or almost winter? The sky's been gray all day while the wind shuffles leaves down the street and in-between houses. How many more seasons will I watch pass outside my windows...without Stevie here?

"Good thing ya got that nice big basement at your new place." An' I smile...like I care.

"So? When are ya comin' to see it? We've been in South County for over a year now."

"Oh...I don't know."

"When was the last time you been out of this house, Baylor?"

"I get out—"

"That's not what I hear. The Witts say they ain't seen you in months—not unless they come to you. What's that about? Ya can't just stay in this house forever—all by yourself. An' I know it ain't any of my damn business, but what the hell are you doin' for money? UPS said they'd hold your job, but that was years ago."

"Sorry, Bill, I know ya mean well, but my finances ain't none of your concern. I got a life, thanks. I don't need no help—or well-meanin' people tellin' me what to do."

I hear Dottie openin' an' closin' drawers. Clankin' an' searchin'. I can't imagine why she has to work so hard out there; nothin' has changed places in years. Everything's the same as when Stevie was here.

"Look, Bill, let's have a nice visit. Take a load off—just not in my chair."

"You still so particular about that beat-up old thing?"

"Yep." Stevie used to sit on my lap in that "old thing" when we watched TV.

I see he's beefed up a little, like his wife. Them two never miss a meal.

"Here we are." Dottie has everything laid out on a tray. "Bill, go get the cake."

As she sets out the forks an' napkins, she never looks up at me. Then she puts three small plates out like she's dealin' cards. We don't exchange one word but all the while she's hummin'. Next comes the creamer an' sugar bowl, three spoons, coffee mugs an' finally a knife to cut the cake. I don't know where to look when she's finished, afraid if we make eye contact, I'll have to think of somethin' to say.

When Bill comes back, he's singin', "Happy birthday, old fart, happy birthday old fart…"

"Stop that!" Dottie yells. "Now Baylor, make a wish and blow out the candles."

We all know what my wish will be.

"This looks real good, Dottie."

She's already settled in on the sofa and starting on her slice, bobbing her head in thanks as she happily chews.

"Did you make coffee?" Bill asks, but it's more like a command. Dottie nods.

I push the cake around on my plate.

"Come on, Baylor, you know how ya love Dottie's cake. If you lose any more weight we won't be able to find ya."

They laugh. I smile.

"I'm fine."

Dottie finally comes up for air. "He can eat it later…there's plenty. Presents now." She puts her plate down and claps like a hyper kid. "Open the little one first."

Everything's wrapped in that black paper that says OVER THE HILL all over it. There are three presents stacked in a tower, the smallest on top. I pick it up, shake it and then tear the paper off.

"I seen these in my 'Game and Fish' magazine. How'd ya know I was wantin' 'em?" I hold up the small, clear plastic box filled with hard lures.

"They light up, did ya know that?" Bill asks. "I got me a set, too."

"You boys'll have to go fishing some weekend."

I nod, knowing the gift will never get wet. "We'll do that; thanks."

The largest box ends up havin' a fleece jacket inside an' the middle one is a heavy pair of cotton socks. All dressed up an' nowhere to go. They insist I try on the jacket. Have to admit it's a whole lot nicer than my old one.

I can feel Bill watchin' me undo every button, rip off some tags, maybe he's tryin' to figure out if I'm crazy or not. I stand up an' slip it on. It's too big an' I wonder if I shrunk.

"You can roll them sleeves up," Dottie says then hustles off to get the coffee.

Bill sits, all tight an' uncomfortable.

"I hope I didn't hurt yer feelin's," I say, tryin' to apologize but resentin' that I have to try.

"We're just concerned, is all. This has been hard on all of us. We loved Stevie, too, ya know."

Yeah, I know. But neither of them has been humiliated or terrorized by angry cops tryin' to wear 'em down.

After Stevie never showed up, all the volunteers went back to where they come from. The TV people lost interest in me an' my boy. Bigger stories, more important people, interestin' places to report on. Them bones turned out to belong to someone long dead, they figured more than twenty years. And that opened up a whole new can of worms. Cold cases got hauled out, so did some cops long ago retired. DNA tests, experts and everyone got all wrapped up in that mystery.

At first the suspicion didn't matter. I knew I didn't do no harm to no one. But it's always the bad stuff people remember ya for. Neighbors moved away, either to get far from this town where they didn't feel safe no more...or me. Them that stayed changed. Do they really think I can't see 'em shut their doors when I ride by? Or hear 'em tell their kids to stay outta my front yard?

I'm the Boogie Man now..

Even after the police said I weren't a "person of interest" no more, nothin' changed right away. But maybe each year that passes kinda dilutes their fear some. An' with no wife, no children, not even a damn dog, I can understand why I'm not considered the friendliest guy around. So after a few months I just figured out that it was easier to stay inside an' keep to myself. Besides, how will Stevie find me if I go out?

"Baylor, you need a whole bunch of everything. When was the last time you went to the grocery store?" Dottie hands us each a hot mug of coffee.

"Oh, I can't remember." What does it matter? Nothing tastes good anymore. "Some of the ladies from First Baptist take turns shoppin' for me."

"Why can't you do it for yourself? It ain't like you're a cripple."

Bill nudges his wife an' gives her that "leave him alone" look.

"Whatever…your pantry is bare as Mother Hubbard's. Tell them ladies you need more than Wonder bread an' cereal."

"Will do."

"So…what you been doin' with yourself?" Bill asks me.

"I spend a lot of time on the computer."

"You? The man who fought havin' a cell phone? The man who's never even used an ATM?"

"Things change, I guess. Or somethin' happens that changes em' for ya."

"Do you still hear from that Mr. Lloyd?" Dottie asks. "He seemed like a real nice fella."

Is she kiddin'? "You never liked him. How come all of a sudden he's a 'nice fella?"

"In the beginning. I didn't like him in the beginning. But he hung in there. Then by the time he finally left, I liked him…some."

"He's one of the reasons I got the computer. His wife runs that organization, WE'LLFINDYOU."

"I seen her on 'Dateline,'" Dottie says.

"She's helped find hundreds of missin' kids—some adults, too."

"An' Vince? Is he still so…so…"

"Angry? Is that the word you're lookin' for, Bill?"

He glares at me then. "That's the perfect word to describe that man. He was mean sometimes, too. I was glad when he finally went back home. We had plenty of help, we didn't need no outsider comin' in here tryin' to tell us how to look for one of our own."

All these years I thought I knew the both of 'em. But now as I look at Bill Nelson an' then his wife, it hits me. I've changed places with Vincent Lloyd. I'm the angry outsider now an' Vince is the nice guy.

We email every day. We talk on the phone. He's become my best friend. He's saved my life and done more for Stevie than anyone—even his own mother—has. And to think I almost told these self-righteous busy-bodies what happened last night.

CHAPTER TWENTY

VINCE, CALL ME NOW!!

Short an' sweet. There ain't no need for more. I aim the arrow at SEND an' press. I've learned a lot of things over the past few years. One of em' is that everythin' in a computer stays there, just waitin' to be found. Every pervert an' his brother can git all over your business. I just hope my phone ain't bugged.

The basement holds the cold around me like a death grip. I'm still wearin' my new fleece jacket, the green one Bill an' Dottie gave me. While I wait for the phone to ring, I walk in a circle, thinkin' of how I'm gonna tell Vince.

The floor's them ugly tiles I keep meanin' to carpet over. Brown flowers on a pink background. Why would someone ever lay somethin' so hideous? When Jean an' me bought this house, she never seemed to notice, though. Which ain't like most women I know who fuss an' decorate, always wantin' to spend every Saturday afternoon pickin' out curtains or furniture. But then, I ain't never met another woman who hated her own kid, the way Jean did.

As I study them ugly flowers, I realize maybe it's a good thing I never did buy a rug. That summer when all them volunteers was down here, trackin' in mud an' what-not from all parts, it woulda got ruined.

Stevie's posters are too much to look at everyday an' now there's only one, clear across the room from my desk. Well, to call it a desk is a joke. It's one of them metal tables, the long kind that they use for pot lucks at the VFW. Someone donated it, I guess an' forgot to come back to pick it up. Same thing for the computer. It's old but works good enough for what I need.

Then I stop dead in the middle of the room an' have to laugh.

How did I manage to hold it all in when Dottie an' Bill was here? Guess I have a flair for actin'.

I start pacin', into my sixth lap around when the phone rings. The metal chair pinches my ass as I sit down. "Hello?"

"Baylor? It's Vince."

"Thanks for callin' so soon. Hope I'm not interruptin' nothin'."

"Not at all…in fact I was gonna call to wish you Happy Birthday. It's today, right?"

"Yeah, an' I don't need to be reminded no more."

"Sorry. So what's going on?"

"Somethin' happened." I wondered if he can hear my smile.

"Good or bad?"

Nope, he can't.

"Stevie was here last night."

Silence.

"He was here, Vince. Swear to God. 'round twelve thirty."

"Are you sure?"

"Course I'm sure. Don't ya think I recognize my own son?"

"Maybe it was wishful thinking. Or a dream? Sometimes when I'm just waking up in the morning, half asleep, I imagine things."

"Nope. He was here…in the flesh"

I give him a minute to digest it all. Hell, I'm still havin' trouble gettin' it through my head that my son's alive an' I've had a whole day to think about it.

"Why didn't you call last night, Baylor? Where's Stevie now? Is he still there? Have you called the police?"

"No! Vince, listen to me. No cops; don't even tell Kathy. Promise me!"

"Why?"

"He'll get hurt. Please, Vince, promise."

"Okay, okay, but you have to tell me exactly what happened. From the beginning."

"I will; you deserve to know everythin'. But let's do this in person. It don't even feel right tellin' ya this much over the phone. How about tomorrow? Can ya come down?"

"I have to reschedule some things, but tomorrow's good."

"I'll see ya then."

"It might be late."

"I'll be here." Where else would I be?

Then Vince starts to laugh, just a little, an' I realize it's a sound I never heard come outta him before.

"Baylor, if this is true…"

"Oh, it's true, alright."

"I'll see you tomorrow," Vince says right before he hangs up.

I switch off the lights an' head upstairs, all the while thinkin' about Dottie's cake. There's sure to be some left-over coffee, too. But when I check the pot, it looks to be filled with mud. That woman may be able to bake, but makin' a good cup of coffee is surely not one of her talents.

Way in the back of the cabinet, over the fridge, I find a bottle of Jack Daniels an' pour myself a nice tall one. Then I take the glass an' cake into the livin' room for my own private party. Have to think back over last night so I remember every little detail to tell Vince.

I was downstairs, in the basement, workin' on the computer, like I do every night. Sometimes Kathy'll send me some emails she got, people writin' they'd seen Stevie or knew someone who knew someone who's talked to him. So many crackpots out there, so much shit to sift through. Keep the faith, have hope, think positive—I hear all the right words from all the right people but no one can find my son.

An' after three years, I started to give up on myself. Guess mothers have that built-in kinda instinct more than fathers ever do. Maybe they're born with it. I didn't get none of them feelin's women are all the time braggin' about. No miracles from God, no signs, no dreams. If Stevie's been tryin' to send me a mental message, I ain't received it. Course I want my son to be alive, more than anythin' in this world. But I can't "feel" that he's safe or alive or…dead. I can't feel nuthin' 'cept so much fear that my stomach's all the time churnin' with it.

So that was my state of mind as I sat on a wobbly metal chair in a cold basement last night. I had the little TV in the corner on and listened to a game while I hunched in front of that infernal computer screen. Hour after hour, staring into it, lookin' for my boy.

Then floorboards above me creaked an' I could hear the back door close. We've been havin' some break-ins in the neighborhood the last few months. Kids reach their teens an' get bored. Small towns breed small time thieves. Most of em' are happy just doin' drugs or lookin' for somethin' to sell to buy drugs.

I grabbed the baseball bat in the corner an' crept up the stairs. When I jerked the door open, there was this man standin' with his back to me. I slowly reached around the door an' flipped on the lights. He was headed for the hall an' froze in his tracks.

"Hold it! Where the hell do you think you're goin?"

The guy turned around, slowly. He was about my size, six feet, smaller build. His hair was shaved off an' he didn't look scared when he saw me. That's what struck me as the strangest thing about him.

"Dad?"

I had that bat raised over my head, ready to swing an' crack his skull if I seen even a hint of a gun or knife.

"I think you got the wrong house."

"It's me, Dad…Stevie," he whispered.

When he rushed toward me I started to swing. But before he flipped the lights off,

I recognized that scar across his forehead. He was four when I'd put him on that damn metal slide. It took four stitches to close up the cut an' I kicked myself for years afterwards for bein' so stupid.

I lowered that bat, still not movin'. But he did. He grabbed me into a strong hug. "Dad, please don't be mad at me. We have to keep the lights off. It isn't safe."

I didn't hear the bat hit the floor, all I heard was both of us cryin'. "My God, Stevie. Thank you, Sweet Jesus." An' we cried some more.

"Why would I ever be mad at you?" I managed to ask when my voice come back.

"Oh Dad," he said it over an' over, "Dad, Dad. I've missed you so much."

"Why isn't it safe? Are you okay?" Then I took a good, long look at my boy.

There was a full moon that night an' it lit up the kitchen. Light also come in from the livin' room. I could see how wounded his eyes were. His arms were thin but strong. I held his face in my hands an' kissed him on the cheek. He stood even with me, no more the kid who'd left my home. I wouldn't have recognized him in a crowd and it made me feel ashamed. This was my son! His teeth, the front ones that had always seemed too big for his mouth, had somehow adjusted. He was a man. In three years, the whole world had changed for both of us.

"Sit. I got some of them cookies you like." I thought that maybe if we did somethin' normal, like eat or drink, that he'd relax more.

He didn't want to let go of me an' clung to my arm as he sat on the kitchen chair.

"I can't stay, Dad."

"What?" I pulled out a chair and sat opposite so our knees touched. "What do you mean?"

"If he finds out I'm here, I can't come back. I'm takin' a big chance, Dad. But I had to come to say Happy Birthday. I had to let you know that I remembered. Maybe now you can be happy."

"I'll never be really happy until you're home, safe with me. Don't you know that, Stevie?"

"It's John now. I'm John. You have to call me that or I can't come back."

He got so agitated that I woulda agreed to anythin'. "I'll call you Dorothy if it'll make ya stay."

He grinned. "I have to go now."

"No," I held his hand as he stood up. "Tell me what's goin' on. Ya can't just come here…after all these years…I have to know why. Where are ya livin'? Who are ya so afraid of? We'll go to the police—"

"No, if you do, other kids will get hurt. This is so much bigger than you can imagine. You have to let me go so I can protect them."

"You're not makin' no sense, son."

"Just remember that I love you, Dad. I'll always love you."

"Don't leave." Then I was the one who wouldn't let go. "Stevie, don't leave me."

He walked to the back door an' peeked through the curtains, with me all the while hangin' onto him. When he was sure the coast was clear, he turned an' we stood there huggin' an' blubberin'.

I thought about holdin' him against his will. I could tie him up, call the cops an' we'd catch the people he was so afraid of. But my boy is eighteen now. How could I do to him what strangers had done? How could I force him to stay? He'd hate me for sure.

Then he looked me square in the eyes. "You can't tell anyone I was here. No one."

"But…"

"Promise me, Dad, or I can't come back."

"When? When can you come back, Stevie? I promise. Please try to come back."

Then he ran out the door, across the back yard an' the night swallowed him up.

CHAPTER TWENTY-ONE

Vince calls when he pulls out of his driveway; says he'll arrive 'round dinner time if traffic ain't too bad. This time of year the weather holds pretty steady, so I figure he'll get here close to six.

I open the freezer to see what's in there. Some broccoli, fish that's almost two years old, an' ice cubes. I slam the door shut. Tryin' the cabinets I end up with vegetable soup an' a can of tuna. Lucky there's some bread. Good enough. That still leaves me with six hours to fill.

I straighten up the livin' room—that takes ten minutes. A shower, some lunch an' I'm so restless I think of goin' for a walk. But what if Stevie calls an' I'm not here? I been scared stiff to leave my house for years. Now, knowin' for sure he's out there, that any day he might come back, it's worse. How can I ever leave? No, stay put, I tell myself. Be patient an' wait.

It's almost seven when I see Vince parkin' in the driveway. I was glued to the picture window for hours, til I seen a little girl across the street pointin'. That's all I need—for everyone to think I'm some kinda pervert.

I want to rush out to greet him, but then we'd be openin' up a whole nuther can of worms. So I sit here, watchin' him turn the engine off. The security light over the front door switches on, it's been gettin' dark earlier this time of year. I can see him just sittin' there, gatherin' his stuff up, reachin' into the glove box for somethin'. What the hell's takin' so damn long?

Finally, he gets out, walks to the back of his car an' grabs a duffle bag outta the trunk. Then he stands, just lookin' at the front of the house. Is he puttin' off comin' in? I got the curtains open. I know he can see me wave.

"Git in here, it's colder than Christmas out there!" I yell, holdin' the door open for him.

"Where I come from, this is a heat wave." He slaps me on the shoulder as he walks into the room. "Are you getting soft on me? Want me to buy you some of those old man sweaters? You know, the kind with ducks or moose all over 'em?"

"It's good to see you, too," I say, "even if ya are a smart ass. Hope ya can stay awhile."

"I was planning on it."

He walks by me, down the hall, toward the guest room.

I follow.

"I made some soup an' sandwiches."

"Great, I'm starving. I only stopped once, for gas an' coffee—no food."

While I get out the plates, I can hear him washin' up in the hall bathroom. Then he comes out an' sits at the counter. His hair looks a tad longer but other than that, he's the same as he was that summer we first met. I sure as hell don't look the same. Haven't bought any new clothes in years an' dropped so much weight, everything I own hangs on my bones, limp an' loose. My hair, what's left of it, don't need much trimmin'. But when it does, I just grab a pair of old scissors an' cut it myself.

"That looks good," he finally says.

"It'll fill ya up, that's all I can promise. I got iced tea, soda, water…"

"Tea sounds good."

I thought we'd feel comfortable with each other…but we don't seem to. All the years of letter writin', phone calls an' emails have gotten us accustomed to the distance, I guess. Now bein' in the same room makes me feel guarded.

But my friend Vince is not a man to tip toe around. No, I'm convinced that if we was standin' in front of a minefield, he'd stomp right through it. "I sat in traffic replaying everything you said. I don't even remember the drive, and now you want me to sit here patiently while you play the good host. Baylor, what the hell's going on?"

I fill two glasses from the pitcher of tea in the fridge. Have to admit I'm takin' pleasure, savorin' my secret for a few extra minutes. Oh sure, I want to share it with Vince—every detail of it. But for a few minutes more it's just mine—and Stevie's. Then I sit down, more relaxed an' happy than I've been in three years.

"Stevie was here, Vince. Honest to God, standin' right over there." I point to the door.

"You talk…I'll eat," is all he says. Then he picks up his tuna sandwich an' waits for me to start up again.

So I begin at the beginnin', tellin' him every detail. The faster the words stream outta me, the faster he chews. Couple of times he stops to take a swig of tea, then he starts in on the soup, all the while his eyes glued to mine.

I stop to take a bite of my dinner but he wouldn't let me stay quiet for too long. He urges me on an' I'm beside myself sharin' the news.

"My boy's safe, Vince. He's alive! Stevie's healthy, from what I could see. He looks older but strong. He's a man now. Even if he come home he wouldn't need me…" Then it hits—right in the heart—for the first time. And as suddenly as happiness came—it's gone.

Vince puts the spoon down, wipes his hands on a napkin an' grabs my arm. "Stevie will always be your boy, Baylor. He'll always need you. We have to bring him home—"

"No! There's danger here, Vince. He wouldn't—couldn't—say what, but he's scared. I don't wanna spook him. An' we can't tell no one, 'specially the police. You didn't tell Kathy, did ya? Please, God, tell me ya ain't told a soul."

He shakes his head fiercely. "You told me not to and I didn't. But it was hard, Baylor. I feel awful about keeping such a big secret from her. We've gotten a lot closer the past year; I wouldn't want to ruin that."

"I'm not askin' ya to, Vince. We'll tell her everythin' as soon as we figure out what to do next. But please, please promise that this stays between us til we're sure we can keep my son safe."

"Of course." He stops to lean back a second. Kinda take a break from all I'm throwin' at him. "Now tell me the words again. What did he say? Exactly…the exact words…if you can remember."

"Oh I remember. He said 'he.' Like 'if he knows I'm here.' He said other kids are in danger. I been beatin' myself up, tryin' to figure out what kinda situation this can be puttin' other kids in trouble."

"You think there's a serial killer out there? You read about it all the time. The quiet, nice man next door. That guy who looks so normal and then all of a sudden..."

"Ya mean like you an' me?"

I don't know where it come from. Figured all my laughin' time was over an' done with. But it hits us at the same time. Both of us are thought to be that guy now. That good ole boy who goes to all his kid's soccer games, the one neighbors trust an' love. Everybody so sure we just went crazy one night an' up an' murdered our own kid.

An' so we laugh. An' once we get started, we can't stop. We look like two lunatics. When we're done, things are easier between us.

"Okay, so this is what we know for sure: Stevie's alive."

"Yep. Definitely."

"He can't come home which means he's not safe."

"Yep."

"Other kids are in danger."

I nod.

"He's in a place where he's able to go outside and let's assume it's not that far away."

"Well, maybe he was passin' through."

"He's eighteen now which means he's considered an adult and if you tried bringing him home against his will, you have no rights."

"I thought of that."

"Have you thought that maybe this is something like a cult? That he got involved with some sort of fanatic?"

"Nope. No way. Stevie ain't no follower. He's always the leader an' the only times we butted heads was when he questioned my rules. That boy hated abidin' by anyone's rules."

"Do you think he'll come back? Or maybe call you?" Vince asks.

"If he didn't catch hell for comin' this first time, I'll bet my life he'll try to do it again."

"Baylor, we need the police—"

"Listen, Vince. We have to do what Stevie wants. We have to believe what he says about danger."

"You're right. We can't chance him getting hurt. So what's the answer? I'll do anything you say."

"Let's wait an' see if he contacts me again."

We sit in the basement, plotting. I made coffee an' we work on the stale birthday cake.

"Well, I've got two days I can wait with you. Tomorrow we'll get a couple of security cameras so next time Stevie comes, we can see if someone's with him. If he's driving, we might be able to get a plate number. Anything'll help."

"Ya know," I say, "If he knew I told you any of this he'd never trust me again. I'm takin' a big risk here, Vince."

"Believe me, I would never do anything to put your son in more danger than he's already in. I couldn't save my own daughter and I truly appreciate the chance to help save your child. I'll do anything, Baylor. Anything…"

Oh, I've hear the stories 'bout Vince an' all he went through when Gabriella was murdered. But it ain't til that moment, sittin' next to him, that I truly feel his pain. So deep, like lookin' into a well. And I vow never to question my friend again. Because besides me, there's no one out there desperate to bring Stevie home more then Vincent Lloyd.

PART FIVE

STEVIE

CHAPTER TWENTY-TWO

"Lift her up; she can't get in there by herself. Are you stupid in the head?"

"Okay! Okay!"

"Don't use that tone with me!"

"He scares me," she whines, shaking so much her teeth click like those plastic joke ones.

"Shh. If you keep cryin', you'll just get Mister more angry." Stupid seatbelt. Her arms clamp around my neck and I can feel she's wet her pants but it's too late to do anything about it. Maybe he won't notice. Who am I kiddin'? Mister notices everything. "You have to let go of me now."

"Hurry! Come on, Herder, move it! If I have to do it myself, you'll be sorry."

"Please. You have to let go of me," I tell her.

"I want my Mommy!"

"We're takin' you to your Mommy and Daddy." I buckle her into the car seat.

"Him, too?" She points to the baby in the back.

"Him, too."

"You're nice."

I tell the little ones that they have to pretend they're kittens or puppies. Just be nice, don't say nothin' and let him pet you. That's his way of tryin' to be human, I guess. Lettin' us know that he has a heart underneath his stink. But this kid is real stubborn.

We're all belted in and I ask what I always ask, "Why can't I drive? I'm old enough, even if I don't have my license…"

"Who the hell cares about you being legal? It's trust I'm worried about, Herder."

"So if you don't trust me, why do you let me out at all?"

"Look at yourself; you're a man now."

"Isn't that what you wanted?" I'm almost as tall as him an' I see him lookin' at me funny sometimes, like he's scared.

"A trustworthy helper is what I wanted. Someone with a good heart to match mine, is what I wanted. But I got a frightened boy who turned into a frightened man. Sometimes I think I should just send you to heaven."

"Where are we goin'? None of this looks familiar." If I change the subject real fast, he gets confused.

"Kentucky—The Bluegrass State."

"I'm hungry!" she cries from the back. "And I'm thirsty, too!"

"Shut up or I'll dump you by the side of the road."

"Nooo!"

"And then the bears and lions will rip you apart and eat you up. Nothing will be left, not even yer bones. That's what happens to bad little girls like you."

"Why do you have to say things like that?"

He's quick. His big hand strikes fast like a snake, an' he smacks me across the face. "Don't you ever talk to me like that, boy!"

The little girl is quiet now. I rub my cheek.

"Why are you always making me hurt you?"

I look out the window.

"I asked you a question!"

I shrug.

Then he grabs my shoulder, his fingers dig right through my clothes and I can't help but cry…just a little…'cause it hurts so bad. I'm embarrassed in front of the girl who watches us with those big eyes of hers.

"I don't know. Sorry."

"That's better. Now, how about we stop at that bakery over there? Bet you're hungry, I know I am."

When he stops, I stay put. If I leave him alone with the kids, there's no tellin'. As he walks around the van, he holds up the keys and rattles them at me. Struttin' like he's someone special. It's no use lookin' for a phone or radio; all his vehicles are stripped down to the bone.

"Can I come sit with you?" she asks.

"No, sorry."

"That baby sure sleeps a lot."

I'm a robot. I'm like this android, made to take care of humans. But if I call the police—they die. If I run away—they die and I've failed at my job. But if I stay and herd them to their new home, everyone lives happily ever after. Well...almost everyone.

"He's got a big box!" She wiggles her feet and claps. Funny how hunger makes her forget about bein' scared.

Mister tosses the food at me and starts the engine.

"I want to eat now!" she shouts.

"We're going to have a picnic," Mister tells her. "Be patient."

By the time he pulls into the woods, the sun's comin' up. The baby's still sleepin' so we leave him in the backseat.

He holds the donut box with one hand, the other grabs a gob of her hair and he pulls her along the narrow trail. Then he stops in front of an old bench that's spattered all over with bird crap.

"This is yucky," she complains.

His cheeks puff out, like a blowfish. "Ingrate!" He twists her hair until she screams. "That's what you get. You force me to hurt you. I'm trying to make a picnic for us and you're spoiling it. It's your own fault."

"Why don't we sit in the grass?" I ask, hopin' he'll be agreeable. "I'll go get a blanket." Before he can stop me, I run back to the van.

The baby's still sound asleep. I put my hand on his chest to make sure he's breathin'.

By the time I get back, Mister is sittin' on the bench, eatin' a chocolate donut. The little girl's just watchin' him, her thumb in her mouth.

I spread the blanket across the grass. "There, how's that?"

"Good." She plops down, crosses her legs and holds out her hands. "I want one with sprinkles."

Mister comes over, holding the box like it's full of gold. "What do you say?"

"Please."

"Good girl." Then he squats down and takes out a donut with white icing and chocolate sprinkles all over the top. He holds it just out of her reach. "First we give thanks."

"But you didn't give thanks…"

I bow my head and start sayin' the prayer Mister taught me that first night and nudge her to repeat after me.

"I said please, now give me my donut," she demands.

Mister is on top of her like a mad dog. He pushes her down and jams the donut, whole, into her mouth. Her eyes get so big. She's chokin' and kickin'. His hand looks like it belongs to a giant as he holds it over her mouth. "There, isn't it good? Isn't this what you wanted? Happy?"

If I put my hands on him, he'll kill her for sure. "How 'bout me, Mister?" And I laugh. "I'm hungry, too."

I reach for the donuts that he's forgotten all about. "Good, there's a sugar one…my favorite."

He hates when I take without permission. And he's off the girl and in my face. "You gave thanks?"

"You heard me. A minute ago, remember?"

"Right. Yes, you did."

While he calms down, she sits up, spitting and choking. She knows now. She knows not to cry, or sass. She'll never forget the crazy she saw today and she'll be different from now on. I've seen it happen to all of 'em.

PART SIX

VINCENT

CHAPTER TWENTY-THREE

"No, he seems well enough. Come on, Kath, you communicate with Baylor practically every day."

"But it's always just about finding Stevie. That's why I'm worried, Vince. I get news when Dottie calls but that's only once a month or so. She says it's gotten so he doesn't even leave the house anymore. Maybe you can get him out. Or at least talk him into therapy."

"I'm not his wife—or mother. I'm here to listen and just be a friend. That's all he seems to need until we find his son."

She breathes heavy when she's angry and I can tell she's irritated.

"Why didn't you call me last night when you got in? Why didn't you pick up any of the messages I left? I was worried sick."

"I got in late and we had some dinner and talked the rest of the night. Caught up…you know. Give me a break, Kath, it's been three years since I've seen him."

"So, how does he look?"

"Thinner. Grayer, older… same as everyone."

"Is the house in shambles? You can always tell a person's mental state by the way they keep their house."

"Everything looks fine. Even the bathroom's clean—not as clean as you'd get it, but clean. Now stop with the worrying."

"I just wish I could do something for the poor man. It's like his son was eaten up by the universe. No witnesses, no clues, no sightings. After all this time we can't even tell him if Stevie's dead or alive."

I feel like a heel keeping the news from her. What would it hurt if I tell my wife? But how can I betray Baylor's trust? I know from personal experience what it feels like to have almost every friend turn away. I can't do that to him; our unique bond has to be honored.

"People don't just disappear, Kath. Someone knows something. I have a feeling this is all going to be over soon."

"I'm just afraid of what the ending will be."

From where I stand at the kitchen sink, looking out the window, I see the day's going to be bright and sunny. Everything looks fresh. Missouri's such a green place.

"I gotta go, hon," I finally say. "I hear the man himself downstairs."

"I just got an email from him. Said he's coming up to fix you breakfast."

I laugh. "Ahh, technology. Let's outsiders know what's happening inside a man's house before he does."

She doesn't comment. Her computer and cell phone have become more valuable to her in the past five years than most people we know.

"Okay, I'll try to coax him out for some ham and eggs. There used to be a good place near here."

"Thanks. And call me tonight?"

"Will do. Love you."

"Me, too."

My phone has just hit the counter when Baylor rounds the corner.

"That wife of yours is quite a lady. We've been on that dang computer for half an hour. I almost broke down an' told her 'bout Stevie bein' here."

"Me, too."

He gets anxious. "But you didn't, did ya? Please, Vince, tell me—"

"No, Baylor, don't worry. I didn't say a word."

"Thank you, Jesus. Cause if someone was to find out—"

"Do you think I'd ever do anything to jeopardize Stevie's safety?"

"No. Course not. You been a real good friend to me. Better than some I known my whole life." Then he slumps into a chair.

I study him. The years spent coping with the terror of his situation have curved his spine. Fear has turned him into himself—literally. And he reminds me of an old warrior, strapped inside heavy armor, vowing to wear it until his quest is completed. Baylor Kracher is weary. How sad that when he finally gets to see his son, learn his boy is safe, he still can't get relief.

"Hey, how about some breakfast?" I finally ask.

"There're some eggs in the fridge," he says. "Let me see—"

"No, I'm taking you out. Is that café still down the street?"

"Myrtle's?"

"Yeah. They had the best French toast. Made from homemade bread."

Baylor doesn't say anything. I can tell he's trying to think of an excuse to stay home. But I'm not giving up.

"I can make French toast."

"You need to get out, my friend." I walk over to him and put my arm around his shoulder. "Take it from someone who's been there. You can't sit here, roll up in a ball and die."

"But what if Stevie—"

"I'm betting that if he comes back, it'll be in the nighttime. He'll wait for the dark so no one will see him."

Baylor nods.

"We'll be gone less than an hour."

"But sometimes I get this feelin'. Like I can't catch my breath... like I'm dyin'..."

"Anxiety, that's all. You'll be fine."

"Ya think so?"

"I haven't lied to you yet."

Myrtle's is this comfortable, worn-old looking place where old men wearing denim overalls and flannel shirts gather around their usual table drinking coffee all day. They even have personalized mugs. Big white porcelain ones, like officers drink out of in old war movies. They're greeted by first names as soon as their feet cross the threshold. I learned all this last time I was in town. The menu is simple: burgers, grilled cheese sandwiches, soup of the day and fried chicken. Their specialty is dessert. Cream pies so big one man can't finish a slice by himself—even if he's hungry. And the apple pie is spectacular. Breakfast is served all day and usually costs around three bucks. The decor is plain: brown carpet, wooden chairs padded with blue vinyl. Tables are covered in blue and white checked plastic cloths. Pictures all look homemade. Wooden geese are everywhere, standing in the corners, hanging from the ceiling and nailed to the wall. The first time I walked into Myrtle's I immediately picked-up on the town's attitude toward outsiders. Be pleasant and helpful but don't trust anyone you haven't known your whole life.

The few customers at the counter spin around on their seats and stare. The old men act as though they don't notice us enter, but it's obvious they have from the way they chatter and point. Small town or large, I recognize those looks. Distrust that can too easily be revved up to hatred.

"Well, Baylor Kracher, it's good to see you out among the living," a waitress I recognize from three years ago says. "What brings you here?"

"Same as everyone else, I guess. I'm hungry."

"And Mr. Lloyd… are you hungry, too?"

I'm surprised she remembers my name. "Starving. I've been dreaming about your French toast."

"Sit anywhere. I'll get a menu—that is if ya'll need one."

"Naw, thanks Bootsie, we know what we want," Baylor says.

We walk to a table in a corner. The place is pretty quiet. Even though any diner in Chicago would have been crowded at this hour, most people in town have already eaten breakfast hours ago.

"Nothin' ever changes 'round here," Baylor says. "Bootsie's been head honcho since they opened. Let's see…" he rubs his chin, like it'll help him remember, "…that musta been round eighty-four. An' Betty over there, she's Bootsie's sister. A couple of cousins work here, too. Once someone finds a place they fit in, they stay til they die."

"Do you find that comforting?" I ask. "Living in the same place, knowing the same people your whole life?"

"Never thought about it. That's just the way it is."

Bootsie comes over, holding two coffee mugs in one hand and a pot in the other. Without asking, she sets the cups down and pours. "Ya, know," she says, not looking up at us, "some folks are uncomfortable havin' you two here."

"Like who?" Baylor asks. "Just point 'em out."

"What's the problem?" I ask. But I know.

"Well, for starters, there are those who think you hurt your child, Baylor."

"So be it. But Mr. Kracher here, is my friend and if anybody got—"

"They got a problem with both of you." When she finally looks up, I can see a weak smile across her red lips. "But I ain't one of 'em. I have only compassion in my heart, Baylor…you know that. Stevie went to school with my Bobby. I fed that boy more after-school snacks than I can count. We all miss him, that's for sure.

"It's just that nothin' like this never happened here before, Mr. Lloyd. We're not like folks up in St. Louis or Chicago where people are killin' anyone who looks at 'em cross-eyed. There's only a hundred of us in this town an' we stick together. So you can imagine how frightenin' this has been...for us and our kids."

"You think this has been a picnic for me an' Vince?"

"I can't even imagine the hell you're in. But you remind us, Baylor. Just when we start to forget an' feel normal—safe—we see you an' get scared all over again."

Baylor looks confused. This is my fault. If I hadn't talked him into leaving his home...

As I sit here wondering what to say or do, Betty shouts, "Oh, hell no!"

Bootsie turns. "What now?" she shouts back.

"It's her."

CHAPTER TWENTY-FOUR

Laura Bonetti doesn't miss a beat as she struts across the room. A cameraman scampers behind, pointing his lens at our section of the restaurant.

"I heard you were in town, Mr. Lloyd."

She has the advantage; Baylor and I are caught off guard.

"May I sit down?"

"I think these gentlemen would like some privacy while they eat their breakfast. Am I right or am I wrong, Baylor?" Bootsie stands defiantly, hands on hips, never taking her eyes off Bonetti.

If Baylor loses it, what'll I do? This is all my fault, I keep thinking.

"Right as rain," he says in a calm, even tone.

Bonetti ignores both of them and asks me, "Can I speak to you for a few minutes, Mr. Lloyd?"

My stomach churns, all I can do is shake my head no.

She's just a bully, Daddy. Don't be scared.

"You have no right—" Bootsie starts.

"This is a public place, isn't it?" Bonetti shoots back.

Bootsie hesitates a minute but it's just enough time for the reporter to push in closer.

"And I'm a customer, like everyone else."

"But you haven't ordered…"

"My money's just as good—"

"Stop badgering her," I finally say. "Is that how you get a story, Ms. Bonetti? Forget about courtesy and simple kindness. Like when you interviewed me and my wife years ago? Interrogate, accuse, bully. You don't need one single piece of evidence, do you? You helped ruin my life and then… moved on. "

"Yes, I…"

"And do you realize that you've acted as though I'm a stranger, every damn time we've met here in town? Your tactics aren't going to work here, Ms. Bonetti. We're all on to you, now."

"I—I—"

"Now if you're hungry, take a seat, preferably on the other side of the room. You're certainly entitled to order a meal and eat it. But that's all you're entitled to." Even though I'm getting angrier by the second, I can't help smile at the cameraman who's obviously enjoying my tirade. "And leave a big tip. I'm sure you have a big fat expense account." By the time I'm finished, I'm standing, jabbing my finger in the air surrounding her face.

One of the old guys slowly puts down his fork and starts to clap. His friends join in and then the waitresses. A customer walks in the door at that moment and after looking around the room, decides to leave. That seems to signal an increased volume in the room.

"How about a nice piece of cherry pie?" Bootsie asks. "Outta the oven an hour ago. Nice and fresh," then under her breath she adds, "like you."

The cameraman turns off his equipment. "Sounds good." He walks to a table by the window and sits down.

Everyone in that room watches Laura Bonetti, waiting for her next move. "Think I'll join him," she says meekly. "I take my coffee black. Please," she tells Bootsie.

I have to admire her. That woman has more confidence or is just more calculating than anyone I've ever met.

Now it's my move. I can either storm out of Myrtle's or sit here, feeling angry and uncomfortable. Baylor seems amused by the whole scene.

I force myself back into my chair. Bootsie shrugs and heads back to the kitchen.

"You okay?" I ask my friend. As I start to apologize for making him leave the tranquility of his home, he tells me to stop.

"I'm a grown man, Vince. I can handle myself. It's you I'm worried about now. Ya gotta work harder at passin' the test."

"What test?"

"Life's one big test…haven't ya learned that yet?"

"Guess not."

"Ya got a good heart. What happened to Gabby was too horrible to even think about. So…stop thinkin' about it."

"You, of all people, know it's not that easy." I can't believe what he's saying to me.

"Easy? We both know what hell really is. But we all got choices, Vince. You can be bitter or forgivin'. Destroyed by a death or thankful for a life. It's all how ya think about things. Look how Kathy handles—"

"I'm not Kathy. And you and me? Our situations started off the same, that's true. Each of us trying to find our child. But, unless something goes very wrong, you'll never be in my position. And I pray you don't have to—"

Baylor holds up his hand, signaling me to not say anything more about Stevie.

By the time we finish our breakfast, Laura Bonetti and her crew of one have left Myrtle's. Funny, the incident seems to have served as a bonding experience between the town and us. As Baylor and I stand at the register, paying the bill, people stop for a word or a slap on the back.

"We showed her. Hang in there, Mr. Lloyd."

"Stupid bitch thinks she can waltz in here, pretty as you please, and call the shots. I don't think so"

"Hey Baylor, you an' your friend there, stop bein' such strangers."

On our way back to the house, we spot the News 4 van parked across the street. "Guess she's talking to Dottie and Bill," I say.

"Well she'll have a hard time doin' that cause they don't live there no more." He laughs. "She don't know everythin', huh?"

"It's turning into a real nice day. Let's enjoy some of it."

"Good idea." Baylor winks.

I walk up the bottom steps and sit down on the top one, positioning myself so I'm facing the van.

Baylor follows.

When Laura Bonetti exits the house across the street, we both wave.

PART SEVEN

BAYLOR

CHAPTER TWENTY-FIVE

Maybe callin' Vince was a mistake. Course I know I should be gettin' out of the house; I ain't no dummy. But while we was at Myrtle's, endurin' all that crap, Stevie mighta called an' I missed him. He don't know 'bout the cell phone—I never had a chance to tell him that night. Truth is I was so glad to see him, it was the last thing on my mind. But I did have the sense to add Call Waitin' onto the old phone years ago, so I'd never miss nothin'. I'd get a dozen phones if I could, but each year the bills get more outta hand...not that I'm complainin'.

Oh, at first there was donations—so much money I didn't know how to handle it all. Jefferson Bank set up an account to help sort things out. An' my pay checks come regular while I was on leave. When they stopped all together, folks said I should get back to work—mostly to forget an' move on—but I just couldn't. For every kind-hearted volunteer there was extra food to buy. Everyday...cart loads. Even though they never expected to get paid, they did need to be fed...it was the least I could do. Then they stopped comin' an' the house got real quiet. 'cept for the phone. So I got one of them answerin' machines. Funny, back when things was normal, I never needed one. Stevie used the phone more in one day than I ever did in a whole week. Who did I have to call? Now it's always somebody wantin' somethin' even if it's just to spread some crazy rumor.

Things'll work out, though. I'm even more sure of it since I seen, with my own two eyes that my son's alive. I just have to be patient.

"Are you sure you're okay? I can stay longer if you need me."

Even though Vince an' me been gettin' on just fine, I need to be alone. I have this feelin' that Stevie wouldn't come near the house with a strange car parked out in front.

"I'm fine…just fine. You have a wife back home who's gettin' anxious to see her man, ya know. She said as much in her last email." I mighta been stretchin' the truth a bit. "Besides, there ain't really nothin' for you to do here."

"I know. Guess I was just hoping you'd hear from Stevie while I'm here. I need… some…"

"Proof? Like maybe I'm goin' a little nuts an' made up seein' my son?"

"No. I was going to say, I need something good to happen for one of us. That's all, Baylor. Really."

"Calm down, Vince, I'm kiddin'. You've been the best friend I ever had. You an' Kathy are real good folks."

"So…will you let me know if you hear from him again? Get word to me somehow? You really should get Caller ID put on your phone. That way you can—"

"Track him down? Call the police to go get him? Force him to come back here? I can't do that. He's a man now. He's healthy—far as I could see. An' he said there's others that can get hurt. He was so set on that, I have to believe him. Waitin' is all I can do now. Wait and be here when he calls or comes back for help."

Vince looks befuddled. When he gets like that, I see the difference in us real clear. His little girl was such a baby when she went missin'. An' the way things turned out, well, my heart bleeds for him. But my child's a boy. A boy who was raised in this place where kids still run wild.

In the summer he used to get himself dressed, make his own breakfast an' run out the door, lookin' for his friends. I wouldn't see him 'til suppertime. An' if I couldn't find him, a neighbor knew where he was. We all took care of each other.

Vince an' his wife come from the city where people are always afraid. They don't want to know their neighbors; kids are taught to be careful an' quiet an' stay in the house. How can this man, comin' from such a different place, understand me?

"Don't look at me like that. I'm not sayin' I won't do everythin' in my power to save my son. I'm just goin' about it different from you, that's all. I gotta look at the big picture. I gotta consider what the rest of his life will be like if I humiliate him—you know, make him feel less of a man."

"Do what you gotta do," he says. But I can tell he don't agree with my way of thinkin'. An' who says he has to?

I stand up—he stays on the couch. It's still early an' I figure he can make it home before dark if he gets started right away. "As my daddy used to say, 'don't go away mad—just go away.' " Then I hold out a hand to help pull him off his ass.

I stay by the door, long after Vince drives off. The sun's hot an' feels good on my face. Some dogs bark back an' forth to each other. Down the block, the Garza kid's mowin' his lawn. I mull over the past few days, wonderin' if Stevie's feelin' the sun, at the same time I am. When the phone in the kitchen rings, I jump; then run for it.

"Mr. Kracher, Medora Prescott is calling. Please hold."

I pull over a chair.

When she finally comes on, she sounds like she just got done laughin' at a good joke. "Baylor? Are you still there?"

"I'm here, Miss Prescott."

"Why so formal? I think we've racked up enough hours to call each other by our first names, don't you?"

"Sure. I guess. So, what's up, Medora?"

"I heard that Bonetti woman was bothering you. Caused a scene in some diner down there?"

"It weren't nothin'."

"Well, you keep forgetting that you have a lawyer out here and I love to swat pests like her. But you have to keep me updated. Understand?"

"When I can't handle somethin' on my own, I'll call."

"No, you do nothing on your own now. Between the reporters and nosey busybodies, we have to keep you out of harm's way. That's what I get paid to do—be your protector." She has one of them voices that sounds younger than she really is.

The first time I seen her, back when Chief Stoffel took me in for questionin' about Stevie's shoes, I guessed her to be younger than me. But the last time I seen her, when we both went on the news to talk about the second anniversary of Stevie bein' gone, she looked even younger. I guess she got somethin' done at one of them plastic doctors.

"The Lloyds and I have worked together for years and they've asked me to take special care of you. I can be there in less than an hour—night or day—remember that. "

"It just seems silly for you to come high tailin' it down here. I've known most these people my whole life. I know how they think better than you. I can talk to 'em better…"

"You've told me all this before, Baylor. But you have to remember: everything you do now will get blown out of proportion because the world is watching you. You're under a microscope. If this was twenty years ago, you'd have everyone's sympathy, but now…oh my God, there have been way too many cases of parents killing their children. And word travels on the internet faster than the speed of light. You're convicted, tried and hanged before there's even a trial. We don't want that to happen to you. Especially if they find a body…God forbid…you'll need me by your side…"

Can't remember what she said after that. Stevie's alive. That's all I need to know.

While I'm waitin' for her to run down, I start feelin' sick. "Medora, I think I gotta go lay down."

"What's wrong, Baylor?"

"I'm not sure." It feels like a metal belt bein' pulled tight across my chest.

"I know you used to have anxiety attacks. And of course the stress you've been experiencing the last few years…"

"I'll call ya back." The phone drops outta my hand. Unsure if I'll make it down the hall to my bedroom, I head for the couch. Everything'll be fine if I can just lie down. But then I trip on somethin' and the next thing I know, I'm on the floor.

"Are you there? Baylor?

CHAPTER TWENTY-SIX

All I can think about is my son. Lord Jesus, make him appear now so I can tell him how much I love him, how proud I've always been of him an' how very sorry I am for the way his life's turned out.

The pain's takin' my breath away, surgin' through me like electricity. I try to go with it, not fight what's happenin'. Can't concentrate on what Medora's screamin' from her end.

"Hold on, I'm calling someone; I'll stay with you until an ambulance arrives. Baylor? Can you hear me?"

I keep wonderin' if the last thing I'm ever gonna see in this world is the dirty plaster on the ceiling above me. I try to roll over, make it to the window, at least catch sight of a piece of the sky. It's all I can think about—somethin' as silly as just seein' a cloud. I moan, the pain's so great an' I sound like an animal.

Then I make it to my knees an' crawl along the carpet. My brain's scramblin' don't know where to go. There's a pool of sunshine and I fall into it.

So lonely. Never felt so all alone. Even the Angel of Death would be a welcome sight. "Please, God," I pray, "I'm not afraid to die, just want to hug my boy one last time."

The front door's propped open and I see her lookin' at me. She rushes into my house then falls down to her knees. At first I don't recognize her; she ain't wearin' her business jacket. An' instead of bein' so sure of herself, she looks more like a scared little kid.

"Why…you here?"

"Please, don't get angry. I heard Mr. Lloyd left and thought we could talk…"

"No! Call Vince. Tell him…"

She looks too eager. But what can I do? Stevie's got to know what happened to his father.

"Please…"

She bends down, puts her ear close to my mouth. "Tell him what? What should I tell Vince, Mr. Kracher"

"Stevie."

"What about Stevie?"

I gotta trust her…might be my last chance…

"Mr. Kracher!"

She shakes me an' it feels like I'm bein' pulled back up outta a deep, dark hole. But I want to stay down at the bottom an' feel cheated. When I open my eyes, I see Laura Bonetti an' hear sirens. I'm so afraid.

PART EIGHT

VINCENT

CHAPTER TWENTY-SEVEN

Been on the road about half an hour when my cell beeps. Traffic's backed up along I-55 and finally comes to a complete standstill. Blue and red lights flash ahead; the highway's down to two lanes; it's a sure bet I'm going to be sitting here for a while. I glance over to read the text message: CALL ME! NOW!! Luv U Kath.

"It's Baylor," she starts before I have a chance to even say hello.

"What do you mean? I just left him. What happened?"

"You're not in Kimmswick?"

"Kathy, for God's sake, tell me what happened."

"He had a heart attack, Vince. Medora called me. She was on the phone with him when he started having pains. She tracked him down at the hospital."

"Dammit!" I hit the steering wheel. "He was fine this morning." She's crying. "Kath, where is he?"

"Vince, Baylor died in the ambulance."

"Oh no…no…that can't be right…"

"Sweetie, there's nothing you can do now…"

"That poor guy, all alone. Someone has to help…settle things for him. Take care of…who'll tell Stevie?"

"Come home, Vince. Let's just be together now and figure this out tomorrow."

"No, you come down here. Please, Kath, I need you here."

"Let me call the airport…"

"It's an hour to O'Hare, you have to be there at least an hour early, then we have to drive from Lambert…just get in the car. It'll be easier. Pack a bag and hurry. Please."

I expect the front door to be unlocked; I'm used to it being that way.

For years I've preached to Baylor about evils in the world. And for years he's given me a list of reasons why the door had to remain unlocked. The first and last were always: "Stevie might not have his key, then how will the boy get in?" He'd go on about living his entire life unafraid, familiar with his neighbors, settled in this small town on the river and he wasn't going to change—"not for no one— no how." But the strangest reason was that Baylor thought whoever took Stevie might come back, and he wanted to make it as easy as possible for that devil to get in so he could beat the truth out of him. I never understood that one and told him so. But he was stubborn and I'd have to periodically remind myself that I'm here to support him, not reform or criticize. This is his house, his town, his life. I'm the foreigner.

The door doesn't give when I turn the knob and that's the first thing that feels wrong. A small magnetic box containing a spare key is stuck to the bottom of the door. I remember when he pointed it out, I laughed at how obvious it was, out in plain sight like that. He said he intended it to be that way so Stevie could find it. Everything always because of Stevie.

When I walk through the door, small things jump out at me. Several pillows belonging on the couch are in the middle of the floor. The coffee table has been pushed aside; magazines are scattered. But the strangest thing is a pair of sunglasses in the corner. I walk over to pick them up. They're some fancy designer brand— obviously belonging to a female—certainly not the property of a small town EMT. I'd bet my life they weren't there when I left the house this morning.

Clutching the glasses, I slump into a corner chair, overwhelmed. My poor friend. Where will they take him now? I have to see him. No…can't handle it just yet. Should I call Medora? My hands start to shake. What am I supposed to do now?

I call Kathy and when she doesn't answer, I leave a message: "Just remembered you don't know where Kimmswick is let alone how to get to the house. So call me when you're south of St. Louis. There's supposed to be rain tonight but not until later. I love you… and thanks, Babe."

In the kitchen, next to the phone, is an old address book I've seen Baylor use often. Before leafing through it, I check for messages on the machine. There are none; and I'm glad. What right do I have to walk into a man's home and invade his privacy this way?

But you're his friend, Daddy. Baylor liked you a lot.

"Yeah, I know."

I leaf through the book until finding Dottie and Bill's number. But after dialing the first three numbers, I stop. What can I tell them? I need more details. So I hang up. Then I call the police station. They put me through to Chief Stoffel.

"Yeah, I heard about Baylor an hour ago."

"Could you tell me where they took him?" I ask.

"Last I heard he was at the morgue. Sit tight; I'll call ya right back."

"Thanks, Chief."

After I hang up, I pace. Should Kathy and I stay in the house? Would that be… disrespectful? No, Baylor would have insisted. Maybe there are relatives somewhere I don't know about. Finally I realize that all I can do is follow the Chief's instructions and wait.

Then in the quiet, sitting in Baylor kitchen, everything hits me. Three years' worth of memories, anger and frustration overtake my heart and soul. And I feel that familiar burning behind my eyes.

It's okay to cry, Daddy.

I cry for Baylor and his son. I cry for myself and Gabby. Sure I know it's selfish but I allow myself the luxury of a good shot of self-pity. When the phone rings, I almost don't hear it because of my wailing.

"Chief Stoffel here, Mr. Lloyd."

I can't say much except, "Yeah."

"Because I've known Baylor since first grade, I'll do the identification and paperwork to get his body released. Do you know if he had a preference about what should be done with his…remains?"

"No, we never talked about it, why would we? Isn't that something you'd know, being such a close friend and all?"

"He wasn't feelin' very kindly toward me after I had to take him in for questionin' that last time."

"I don't know what to tell you, Chief."

"Okay then, I'll have him taken to Tidderman's. It was where his Mama and Pop were laid out. I think he'd like that."

"What about a ceremony or memorial? I don't want to overstep my…"

"Let me contact the Nelson's. They're the closest thing he had to family…besides Stevie, of course."

"Please tell them I'm here."

"Will do." I can hear him sniffle. Then without another word, he hangs up.

When Kathy pulls into the driveway I'm in the basement. Don't have a clue how many times she rang the bell; I'm too involved, sitting in front of Baylor's computer.

Then I hear pounding. "Vince, it's me!"

I rush up the stairs.

"Oh, sweetheart." She hugs me. "I'm so sorry."

"I know." I hold her tightly. "Shit. This is all so unfair."

"I'll miss him," she says, kissing my cheek, "so much. I just can't believe it. He's …dead."

I want to change the subject, or at least redirect it. "What do you think we should do now? Should we go to a motel or stay here tonight?"

"I haven't thought about it." She looks confused by my question.

Taking her suitcase, I put it near the couch. "It must feel strange. You've known Baylor for years and never even seen where he lives."

"It does." She pulls her sweater tightly around her.

"I'll go make some coffee while you relax. You look cold."

"I want to see Stevie's room," she says abruptly.

"I…I've never seen it. Baylor always kept the door closed."

"In so many of his emails he said he wanted me to know his son better and if I ever came to town, he'd show me Stevie's things. He was so proud of him. I think Baylor would like it that I'm here. Don't you?"

I really don't know what I'm feeling. Maybe some jealousy? It sounds crazy but part of me doesn't like the fact that my wife knew something about my friend I didn't. "Sure."

As we walk down the hall, I look at Kathy. She seems peaceful. I'm feeling guilty. Am I under any kind of obligation now that Baylor's gone? Moral, real or spiritual? Should I tell Kathy that Stevie's alive? Would Baylor want me to?

CHAPTER TWENTY-EIGHT

Stevie's bedroom door is open. An overhead light's on making everything feel stark in the early evening shadows. Kathy stands next to me, both of us hesitant to enter.

"This is so sad," Kathy finally says as she walks over to the small twin bed covered with a frayed, navy blue spread. "Look at all these. They must be from every holiday he missed."

Packages cover the middle of the bed. Some large, some larger—nothing insignificant for Stevie. The boxes are wrapped, tied with colorful bows and ribbon. Shiny Santa faces printed on paper, birthday wishes written in silver letters. There are several Easter baskets and two Fourth of July themed boxes filled with fireworks.

Sliding doors, attached to a small closet, have been pushed aside. I walk over to look at a shirt hanging in the middle. Navy blue seems to be his favorite color. Slippers have been tossed on the floor, looking like the boy just stepped out of them,

Baylor must have come in here after I left. Did seeing his son's belongings trigger the heart attack that killed him? Or did Baylor come into Stevie's room often? I'd never seen him even touch the doorknob, let alone walk inside.

"Remember how the police trashed Gabby's room?" Kathy asks in almost a whisper.

"I do."

"I tried putting things back, making it pretty again, ya know? But it wasn't the same. I hated going near that room after..."

"It was hard for both of us. That's why we moved."

"I know."

It feels strange the way we stand here, keeping our distance, afraid to touch anything. Almost as if we're in church.

"Don't you think it's weird that there aren't any posters on the walls?" she finally asks. "Don't teenage boys have posters? Glamour shots of bikini models? Centerfolds from Playboy?"

"He was only fifteen."

"How old were you when you got hold of your first Playboy?"

I smile. "You're right. But I had the decency to hide it under my bed, away from my parents."

"Okay then how about cars? There are a lot of Nascar fans in Missouri. Or movies? My brother had his walls plastered with movie posters: Star Wars, The Terminator, Spiderman—stuff like that."

I look closer at the wall above his desk. "Aren't even any marks where something like that would have been."

"Maybe Baylor was one of those men who're fussy about putting holes in the walls."

"No, there are pictures hanging all over the house."

"Huh, you're right."

"So what do you think this means?" she asks me.

I turn to see if she's kidding. "Why are you trying to turn something so insignificant into a big deal?"

"Not a big deal. I just think it shows what kind of kid he is—or was—that's all."

"Well," I run my finger over the smooth surface, "I'd say Stevie is disciplined, a serious kid who doesn't like silly things. Have you noticed he doesn't have a game system, either."

"Maybe it's packed away somewhere."

"Now I like that." There's a framed photo on the desk. "Happier times." Stevie, all smiles, standing next to his father. The boy had a front tooth missing and a dozen freckles scattered across his nose. They were outside; Baylor wearing a vest and one of those goofy fishing hats. Stevie held up his catch for the camera, looking so proud, his father's arm around his shoulder.

"I remember Baylor bragging what a good athlete his son was." Kathy stands in front of baseball trophies lined up on the windowsill.

"Looks like there was a computer here." I point to a tangled nest of wires in the corner.

"Cops love confiscating computers. I suppose Stevie was on

Facebook—all kids are. But a lot's happened on the internet since Stevie went missing. Maybe we should…"

The doorbell rings.

We just stand there, looking at each other like we've been caught doing something illegal or…immoral. Then, without a word, we each spring into action. Kathy shuts the closet door. I flip off the light and together we leave Stevie's room, closing the door behind us.

The bell rings three more times before I get there.

"I was just getting ready to hunt for my key," Dottie says. "Baylor never locks the door."

"Hey, Vince." Bill pushes past his wife and grabs me in a strong hug. "Can you believe this? How ya holdin' up?"

"I don't know yet. How about you?"

I manage to get him off me but before I can step back a few paces more, I'm surprised by the tears spilling down Bill's cheeks.

"Now stop it, Bill. You'll get us all goin'." Dottie dabs at her eyes and then turns to Kathy. "You must be Mrs. Lloyd, I'm Dottie Nelson; I'm sure Baylor mentioned us."

"Yes he did—many times. And please, call me Kathy."

"When Dwayne called, I couldn't believe it. This is too tragic. Too, too tragic. I'm just glad that Baylor died with hope in his heart. He was always sure his boy was alive and he'd see him one day. Well maybe today's the day. Maybe they're together now, up in heaven."

"Who's Dwayne?" Kathy asks as we slowly make our way into the middle of the room.

"Our Police Chief. Dwayne Stoffel? We all went to school together. Him an' Baylor were like brothers. Well they used to be, anyways."

"Oh, sure. Don't think I ever knew his first name."

Dottie bends over to pick up the pillows, arranges them on the couch with care. Then she gathers up magazines. Kathy helps. Bill and I watch.

"So, are you folks spendin' the night?" Bill asks. "The memorial won't be for a couple of days."

"Memorial?" Kathy asks as she sits. "Who's arranging that?"

"We are." Dottie sits down next to Kathy and pats her knee. "There really isn't anyone else to do it. Stevie's the only family left and he surely can't. Baylor was so alone, poor man."

"So he discussed all this with you?" I ask, remembering the many times Baylor told me how much the Nelsons intruded and infuriated him. "When I spoke to Chief Stoffel, he didn't know anything."

"Well, we have to go talk to Carl, over at the bank, first. But I'm sure he'll okay anything we decide."

How could I have forgotten? "Is that Carl Allenton?"

Dottie looks surprised then nods. "Sure is. I take it Baylor told you…but why?"

"There's a safety deposit box. He signed me on and sent the key." Where had I put it?

"Really?" Dottie's irritated. "Ya hear that, Bill? Wonder why we never knew about this safety box."

"Why were you going to see Mr. Allenton if you didn't know about the box?" Kathy asks.

"There was an account set up—for Stevie. We was hopin' some of that money could be used to settle Baylor's affairs, ya know? It don't seem right whatever's left is just sittin' there…gatherin' dust… when it could be used for…Baylor."

I try not to show my indignation. "Look, Kathy and I will go to the bank tomorrow morning and talk to Mr. Allenton. I'll get into the box, maybe there's a will or some instructions…"

"And you have the key with you? You just carry it around with you? All the time? Along with your house keys and car key?" Dottie demands to know.

"No. It's at home. But I'm sure that due to the circumstances and with my signature being on record…it'll be okay."

"This is a very small town, Mr. Lloyd. Don't forget that for one minute. Everyone knows everyone and all their business. Maybe we should go along with—"

"We'll be fine," I insist. "And as soon as I find something out, I'll let you know."

Bill seems more hurt than his wife, which surprises me. He abruptly stands up, smoothing the front of his plaid shirt. "So that's how it is. Come on Dottie, looks like it's time for us to go."

"No need to hurry off." I can't believe it but I feel bad. "We could go out for some coffee. Is anyone hungry?"

"Too late to eat. Besides, there's nothing open on Monday." Dottie hurries to her husband's side.

"I'll call you tomorrow," I say as we walk them to the street.

"Whenever you get the time." Bill slams his car door.

After they drive away Kathy asks, "Do you have their phone number?"

"No."

"That's too bad."

CHAPTER TWENTY-NINE

"Baylor's dead? I can't believe it. First Steven goes missing and Baylor has to suffer with the loss, and now he's...gone? Never getting any closure? Just passing away like that, all alone. Man, I can't even begin to understand how that must feel. I have two kids of my own." Carl Allenton nods toward an ornate gold frame propped up on the corner of his desk. "Teresa and I, that's my wife, thought we couldn't even have one but when the good Lord blessed us with two? Ours not to reason why, as they say."

Kathy sits next to me as we listen to Mr. Allenton. I'm anticipating having to make the drive back to Chicago, tearing the house apart to look for the key Baylor sent me. But I'm hoping small town rules are a little lenient or Kathy's charm might work for us as it has in the past.

"So, how long did you know Baylor?"

"Almost four years. I came down to help search for Stevie. We managed to stay in touch."

"And I run an organization that searches for missing children." Kathy smiles.

"Like that John Walsh guy?"

My wife nods.

"Well, how about that! And you're here today because...?"

I explain about the safety deposit box. Tell him I'm signed on. Before I can elaborate, he gets up.

"Gimme a minute; I'll be right back."

We watch him walk past the tellers, all three of them. Today's obviously some sort of local spirit day because each is wearing a bright yellow sweatshirt with the name of what I assume is a local team. Allenton takes his time, chatting with customers, until he finally stops in front of a wall decorated with portraits of past bank presidents. There are a dozen or so. Then he makes an abrupt right.

"How are you feeling?" Kathy asks and gently rubs my knee.

"Anxious. And sad."

"You must be so tired. I know I am."

Neither one of us had slept well at the small motel in town. The mattress was hard and wrapped in plastic that rustled every time one of us moved. Truckers came in off the highway all night long; the temperature was either too hot or too cold if we turned the air conditioner on. But still, it was better than trying to sleep at Baylor's. That just seemed wrong somehow.

"Here ya go," Allenton comes up behind us. "Everything's in order." He hands me a small key. "I'll take you over and get you signed in. Mrs. Lloyd, you can wait here, if you'd like or over there." He points to a sofa. "There's coffee and it's much more comfortable than here."

Turning to me he says, "If there's anything else I can do—just ask. And when you have all the arrangements made, please let me know. I'm sure my staff, along with my wife and myself, would all be happy to attend. We can also post any information on our community board. We'll all miss him."

I shake Allenton's hand and follow him to the back of the room. As Kathy walks toward the Mr. Coffee, she's greeted by each teller.

"That was easy."

"Life in a small town does have its advantages," I say.

"Think we should move here? It might be a nice place to retire. You know, like when we're really old?"

"Just get in the car." I hold the door open for her. After she's seated I hand her the envelope I've taken from the bank. It contains everything that was in Baylor's safety deposit box.

"You were so fast that I didn't even have a chance to drink my coffee," Kathy says as she buckles in.

"There wasn't any need to inspect everything in there when I can take my time later."

"So where to, now?"

"Baylor's. We can get comfortable and see what we got."

"Maybe there's a name of who we can call...something...

anything. I don't know if we're helping or stepping on toes. The Nelsons seemed insulted that we're even here. Maybe we should just go home."

"Relax," I tell her. "This is what Baylor wanted."

PART NINE

LAURA ANN

CHAPTER THIRTY

Last night I had the dream—the same one I've had for years. Always the same. The biggest story of the century falls in my lap. Plop! But I always drop it—literally. One time I fumble, like it's a greasy football. The crowd boos me and I try so hard to catch it that my feet bleed. Another time it evaporates. Floats down from above, shimmers all around me, sent by the angels. And then it's gone. But each time I have that dream, I get a little closer to grabbing the prize.

Year after year, miss after near-miss, never good enough or strong enough. But now every condition is right. I'm ready and I'm not going to let anything ruin it for me.

I close my eyes and see his face. He didn't look the least bit frightened. I'd be scared to death. Maybe with each year that passes, a person gets used to the idea of dying.

His friends probably started going AWOL, that's how my dad always said it was. "Old age is like suddenly waking up on a battle field, everyone dropping around you. No rules, no order. Confusion. Should you just lie down and wait for the fatal hit, or try to fight off the inevitable?"

Maybe that's what Baylor Kracher felt. Especially after all he'd been through looking for his son. Was he finally giving up? Passing over the confusion to me?

"Find Stevie," he whispered as I stood there at the door. I didn't do anything wrong when I pushed it open further and walked inside; he asked me to come in.

"Are you okay? Mr. Kracher?"

He was clutching his chest, sprawled out on the floor, rocking back and forth in pain. It was all over his face how much it hurt.

"Baylor!" a woman screamed from his phone, beside him on the floor.

Without thinking, I hung it up. I should have called for help but...

Then I walked over to him, grabbed a pillow from the sofa and put it under his head. Why did I do that? They always tell you not to move anyone in distress. Why didn't I call for help?

As I reached down to lift his head, he grabbed the front of my blouse. Strong for a man his age, in pain and all.

"You're a reporter; you can find him."

"We've all been trying," I lied. I'd been observing, not lifting one finger to actually find the kid.

"Listen to me," his voice was getting weaker and I knew that there wasn't much time. What kind of a cold-hearted bitch was I to let this poor man die?

But I was curious...

He yanked me down to the floor. "He's alive."

"We all hope so." What was I waiting for? Was I really this monster? Had I really become so hard that I couldn't feel anything? But how the hell was I expected to relate to a guy old enough to be my father?

"I've seen him. Call Vince."

My heart raced. "Where? When? Are you sure it was him?"

"He was here. You have to find him."

Wouldn't it be something if what the man said was true? If I could track down this kid...the biggest story ever...award winning journalism...

His hands went limp. I pressed my ear to his chest. Still breathing.

"Mr. Kracher," I yelled, "can you hear me?"

His eyes sprung open.

"Does anyone know that Stevie was here? That he's alive?"

"Vince knows...made him promise...not...to...tell anyone."

Shit. No way in hell would Vincent Lloyd give me the time of day. I couldn't let him know I knew.

Then I heard a siren just when I was getting ready to call 911. Honest—I would have called for help.

I couldn't very well hang around until the ambulance arrived.

In that small town I stuck out like a red-headed wart. If I was lucky enough, no one had seen me come into the house in the first place. And if anyone had, I'd say he was alive when I got there, which was the truth.

Oh, God, what if it wasn't his heart? What if he'd been wounded by an intruder? Everyone knew how much Kracher hated me. He'd made himself heard for three years. Complaining and protesting police methods; several time he'd even called me out by name. No, it was best to just leave and shut up.

By the time I got home, it was all over the news. Baylor Kracher dead at age 50 from a massive heart attack. Natural causes. I told myself there was nothing I could have done for him.

Death bed confessions—always believed. But why? If I had murdered someone, swore I was innocent for years, why would I suddenly change my story? Wouldn't I want everyone to remember me as this nice, innocent person who wouldn't harm a fly? Why would I go into that great unknown with everyone I'm leaving behind hating me? No...I'd stick to my lies. But that's just me.

So it took me awhile to decide what to do.

Kathy Lloyd and I had been cordial years ago when Gabriella first went missing. But when fingers started pointing at Vince, neither one of them returned any of my calls. Understandable. Then when Mr. Lloyd showed up in Missouri, befriending a man who some believe killed his own son, I called her. Hoping for a statement about Baylor Kracher's possible involvement but feigning interest in her missing children's organization. I never once told her I still believe her husband hurt Gabby. I have no evidence. Nothing has ever been found to link Vince to any crime. But it's always felt wrong that those two should be so chummy—Kracher and LLoyd. Birds of a feather as they say. Unfortunately, it's not my job to tell anyone what I believe or think. I'm just a face and voice.

"Hard cold facts, that's all we need from you," a producer told me on my first audition. "Stop trying so hard to be a person."

Lesson learned.

CHAPTER THIRTY-ONE

"No big love-fest there," Ken says to Tracy, sitting on the edge of her desk. When he sees me come around the corner he stands up like he's just been caught setting a fire.

"You two splitting up," I ask, "again? Why can't you both make nice and—"

I know how much Tracy hates it when I tease her about Ken. That's why I do it.

"There has never been anything between us. I've told you that over and over." Ahh, sweet indignation of a twenty-year-old.

"We were talking about Baylor Kracher."

"And who was he in love with?" I ask, forcing him to say what I already know.

"I was just saying that there would be no mourning when you heard the news. It's not as if you even liked the guy."

"True, but it is sad."

"Sam can cover the funeral. That way you won't have to make the drive," Tracy says.

I haven't even thought of the funeral.

"When is it? Have you heard anything?"

"From who? He didn't have any family—except for that ex-wife of his in jail," Ken says. "Oh...and Stevie."

Tracy picks up a pile of pink message slips. As she hands them to me she points. "Three of those are from Mrs. Lloyd. She's been calling for an hour."

"From Chicago?"

"No, she's in Kimmswick...with her husband."

"Another one of your fans," Ken can't help adding.

"Huh." I unbutton my jacket and head for my office. "Ken,

come back in an hour."

When is he going to wise up and learn that I can see his reflection in the large glass-covered, abstract hanging on the wall?

"Will do."

"And I'd appreciate it if you stopped rolling your eyes at me," I complain, closing my door.

I hang my jacket up on a padded hanger and kick off my shoes. What should I be feeling? I wonder. I haven't done anything wrong. Why then am I so anxious at the thought of speaking to Kathy Lloyd? Reluctantly I dial her number.

She picks up on the third ring. "Miss Bonetti?"

"Hi."

"I assume you've heard about Baylor Kracher...considering your line of work, you probably were one of the first to know."

"Yes, it's very sad. When did you hear about his...passing?"

"Last night, from a mutual friend. She was on the phone with Baylor when he started having chest pains."

Should I tell her I was with him when he died? Should I tell anyone? Who can I trust?

When I don't respond, she continues. "What I'm calling about is to ask if you can come to the funeral on Thursday morning. With a camera crew."

I'm stunned and after a confused moment I say, "That's the last thing I would have expected you to ask, Mrs. Lloyd. The very last thing in the world."

"We want to keep Stevie in the news—his father would want that more than anything else. I became good friends with Baylor as did my husband. We'd like you to do a recap of the entire story—from the minute Stevie went missing to this very moment. I find, working with other agencies, that it helps jog the public's collective memory. A person often comes forward, years after an incident like this, with some new information. But please, don't come with any kind of negative attitude. No editorializing. Can you do that?"

"Sure. What time and where?"

As she tells me the details I frantically write them all down.

"Will you and your husband be available for an interview after the service?" I ask.

I'm surprised when she tells me, "Of course. We'll cooperate any way we can."

"Mrs. Lloyd, while I have you on the phone, I'd like to ask you two things."

"What are they?"

"In all the years since Steven Kracher's disappearance, have you had any reports of a sighting?"

"At first there were hundreds, which is normal. But as time passed, the calls stopped coming. Which is also normal."

"And there hasn't been anything recently?"

"No. Why?"

Certainly she'd tell me if she's seen Stevie. She'd shout it across the internet. There'd be interviews and reports on every channel. Good news travels a little slower than the bad stuff but it would be out there. No, I think, Kathy Lloyd doesn't know that Kracher had a visit from his son. But is it possible her husband knows and for some reason hasn't told her? Or was Kracher just delirious with pain and imagined it?

"What's the second thing?"

"Why would you call me when...you've made your feelings very clear about your dislike for me?"

"I've done my research, Ms. Bonetti. You're the top anchor right now, at the top rated station. Stevie and Baylor deserve the best. I don't have to like you."

Ken struts into my office wearing those old jeans that he thinks make him look young and hot. They don't. When he'd first been hired I thought he was cute. Always some hair out of place—in a Robert Redford way. Always a pout on his lips when he was concentrating. And just enough stubble on his cheeks to give off that I-don't-give-a-shit attitude. But after years of listening to his adolescent stories, I've come to realize he's nothing more than a sloppy, overgrown frat boy who thinks his last year of college was the best part of his life. No ambition, no goals. And undeniably one of the truly talented camera guys in the business.

"You wanted to see me?"

"Baylor Kracher's funeral is Thursday morning at ten thirty. The Lloyds request our presence—"

"Whoa, hold on a minute. They want us there? I thought they hated you."

"This is about a missing boy—"

"And a pushy reporter."

"And three parents who've been through hell."

"When did you become so...so soft and cuddly?" he asks as he plops down, keeping my desk between us.

"I have a heart."

He laughs. But when he sees my expression, he stops. "You're not kidding, are you?"

"Do you really think I'm such a bitch? And before you answer that, think a minute. I want the truth—nothing but."

"For real?"

"I'm a big girl; I can handle it. Just tell me what kind of a person you really think I am."

He leans back, stares at the ceiling. Shifting in his chair, he finally says, "You're good at your job. You seem to have no other life except for your job. You're a sexy woman who knows how to get what she wants. And you want to get your story before the other guy does—no matter what you have to do."

Wow, he nailed it. That's almost exactly how I see myself. But shit, I think my ambition is a good quality, one to be admired.

"And you think I'd do anything—short of murder of course—to get what I want?"

"That's kinda harsh. You're way too hard on yourself," he says gently. "Ya know, when you're not trying, sometimes in a rare moment, you can be almost nice."

"Gee, I don't know if I should laugh or cry."

"Is this what you wanted to see me about? Free therapy?" That flip attitude of his pops up and I know it's the wrong time to confide in him.

"Oh God, no! The Lloyds want an in-depth report about Steven Kracher. We'll need some of the first footage you shot and then the most recent. Get a nice mix—his home, the spot he was last seen at, school, friends, you know. I'm going to talk to the Head Honchos about getting us an hour air time—maybe more. We'll try for Thursday night. I'll do the voice-over."

He stands up. "I better get started. We only got three days."

CHAPTER THIRTY-TWO

It's been raining almost every day for weeks. Sometimes only for an hour, sometimes all night. But the serious stuff started rolling slowly down the Mississippi five days ago. Big dark clouds, making the day feel like night. Tornadoes freight-train through several suburbs, leaving only splinters and glass where beautiful homes stood. Levees up north are breaking, unable to hold back the extra water caused by all the snow we had last winter. Volunteers come from nearby to help citizens of dozens of small towns up and down the Mississippi and Missouri rivers. Dump trucks haul tons of sand, unloading it in vacant lots where neighbors and strangers gather to fill yellow plastic bags that will later be used to sand-bag against the oncoming torrent. Roadblocks are set up across streets that have flooded. The temperature rises to the high nineties by noon each day and lowers to the mid-eighties at night. The weather has been the big news in St. Louis…until the day of Baylor Kracher's funeral.

"Good atmosphere," Ken says as we drive south.

"What do you mean?"

"Nice and gloomy for a funeral."

"And you think I have no heart?"

"I'm just sayin'…"

The white van is plastered with the Channel 4 blue and green logo. I hadn't thought about how conspicuous we'd be at the cemetery. "At least we caught a break in the weather," I say. "But this humidity is doing evil things to my hair."

He adjusts the rear-view mirror. "I'm thinking of moving to Vegas. I've had it with all this water."

"What about the heat? It must feel like living inside an oven out there."

"I heard tell they have this new-fangled thang called air conditioning," he says in a Jethro Clampett accent. "Got it cranked up so high that icicles grow right off yer nose."

"Smart ass. What about the change of seasons? Wouldn't you miss that?"

"Probably. But it's not just the weather. I guess I'm getting burned out."

I've never given his work much thought, other than how it compliments my own. "How long have you been doing this?"

"Ten years in St. Louis at Channel Four, five in New York with a documentary crew. We did shorts on war orphans and a full-length feature on AIDS that was up for several awards. Before that I followed my father around. He was a correspondent in the middle east for CBS."

I had no idea. "Wow."

"Yeah, enough death and disease to last me five lifetimes."

"So this Steven Kracher story has gotten to you?"

"Maybe it's my last straw."

"What if I know some good news?" I blurt out. Not thinking first, not thinking at all. But there it is—out there. Then I back-track. "I mean, what if I know something that…"

"I have the feeling you've been trying to tell me something for days. So what is it? Spit it out."

"Turn here," I tell him. "Then go left."

"I guess I'll have to be more patient," he says as he puts on his turn signal.

"We'll talk on the way back."

Ken just nods.

Tidderman's Funeral Home isn't in a quaint Victorian house like I imagined. Located in an unremarkable, square, red brick building, it stands at the end of a run-down residential block. The lawn is thick and recently mowed. I can tell from the sweet fragrance surrounding the area. Flower boxes filled with plastic geraniums rest outside the small windows. A carport flanked with additional parking space takes up the adjoining lot. And a tasteful sign—white lettering on a black background—hangs over the front door.

"Park in the corner," I tell Ken. "We may be invited guests but we don't want to be obnoxious about it."

As I climb out of the van, I catch sight of Vincent Lloyd walking toward us. A woman, I assume his wife, follows close behind him, her steps clipped. Both are dressed in black.

"Here we go," I say, under my breath.

When he smiles I'm thrown off. Every time I've encountered Mr. Lloyd there have been bad vibes and jabs thrown by each of us. But I realize we're playing the game by his rules now.

"Ms Bonetti." He holds out his hand.

"Mr. Lloyd." I nod and shake his hand. Professionally…not friendly.

"Miss. Bonetti, I'm Kathy Lloyd," she says as she stands beside her man.

"At last we meet." I smile, trying too hard.

She stares back.

"This is my cameraman, Ken Newhouse."

Ken gives a wave as he adjusts his lens. "Are we doing some background stuff before we go in?"

"Oh no," Kathy says, "you won't be going inside. We'll do an interview here, in front if you like, and at the cemetery, but Mr. Tidderman says they have a strict rule, No Press, especially with cameras, are allowed inside."

I wonder how many times the Press has wanted to do a story inside the small- town funeral home. Maybe a local jock and his girl had perished on the way to prom, driving drunk. But I can't remember big news ever coming out of Kimmswick, Missouri until the Kracher story. "Of course. I understand."

Kathy Lloyd looks at her watch. "We have about half an hour before the service begins. Why don't we film over there on the lawn, and then you can meet us at the cemetery when we're done?"

"Good idea," I say.

The four of us go to stand in front of the artificial flowers which will come off nicely on TV. The grass is soggy from all the rain and my four inch heels sink slowly into the mud as I make my way to the flagstone walkway.

"I'll do a voice-over at the beginning while we show footage taken throughout the years. We'll talk about friends and family who have been looking for Stevie for years. Then we'll insert this piece about his father."

They both nod while Ken gets into position.

"Are you ready?" I shout to him.

"Ready when you are."

I smile slightly for the camera. "Baylor Kracher, father of missing teen, Steven Kracher has died of a massive heart attack. He was unrelenting in his search for his son, always believing that he would find the boy someday."

Out of the corner of my eye I see Lloyd reach out to squeeze his wife's hand. "We're here in front of Tidderman's Funeral Home in Kimmswick, Missouri, where friends have gathered to pay their last respects. Mr. Kracher's death came as a total shock to this small community and they will miss him greatly. But who will continue the search for Steven Kracher now?

"With me are Vincent Lloyd and his wife Kathy who run the organization they founded after their own daughter, Gabby, went missing and was later found murdered. It was through WE'LLFINDYOU that Mrs. Lloyd met Mr. Kracher but it was on a more personal level that Mr. Lloyd and the Missouri father became friends."

Lloyd seems shaken after my intro. I guess it will always startle him whenever he's reminded that his little girl is gone. But I have to give him credit, no one but I, the person standing so close, will ever notice.

"I met Baylor when I came to help look for Stevie, in the first wave of volunteers. I heard about his story on TV back home—I live in Chicago."

"That was very kind of you," I say, "coming all that way for a stranger. Especially since you were dealing with your own problems." I don't mean to jab at him, I just can't help myself. There's just something about the guy…

"Vince has always been like that," Kathy speaks up, saving me from myself. "And with all the bad press he got—we both got—after our daughter was found, he knew what Baylor would be facing."

Man, this broad's tough! I like Kathy Lloyd more than ever as she stands here, defiantly staring me down, brandishing her oh-so-white smile.

We tape for another five minutes until the sky grows dark, filling rapidly with clouds that look ready to burst.

"I think we have enough here," I finally say. "If you could give us directions to the cemetery, we'll head over."

"You go on in," Lloyd tells his wife. "I'll take care of it."

"Okay, honey. She hugs him. "It was nice meeting you, Miss Bonetti. You too, Ken. We should be there in about an hour." Then she turns and goes inside.

The three of us walk toward the van. Ken opens the back and starts putting his equipment away. Is this a good time to talk to Lloyd in private, I wonder. Without his wife here?

He writes the directions down for Ken. They talk a few minutes, pointing and laughing. While they shook hands good-bye, I start to climb into the passenger's seat.

After putting my seat belt on, I glance up into the side mirror and see Lloyd walking back toward the home. Then he abruptly turns.

"Ms. Bonetti," he shouts to me.

I open my window and stick my head out. "Yes?"

"Stay there a minute, I have something for you."

Ken's buckling up. "Another admirer? Why, Ms. Bonetti, whatever are we to do with you?"

"Shut-up."

I jump down to the ground and head over to Lloyd's car. He bends to get something out of the glove compartment.

"You might need these," he says, holding a pair of sunglasses out to me. "The rain has to let up sometime."

I take them, turning the frames over in my hand.

"They are yours aren't they?" he asks, leaning against his car. "Where did you get them?"

"Think about it. You'll remember."

I stand there, confused, watching him walk away from me.

Then I remember taking them off in Baylor's living room.

PART TEN

STEVIE

CHAPTER THIRTY-THREE

"Forty days and forty nights it rained. So don't you dare be complaining to me, Herder!"

It's hard, tryin' so hard all the time, never knowin' what crazy shit Mister's gonna pull. It beats me down from always tryin'.

At first I believed everything he told me. Like how he was savin' them kids, takin' 'em out of bad homes—puttin' 'em in good ones. An' even though I was scared, I felt like I was doin' important work...savin' lives.

But now I'm not so sure whose side he's on—God's or the Devil's.

We're somewheres in Illinois; he's been plannin' two days for this Jubilation. That's what he calls it when he's bringin' a child to their Jesus parents, the ones that God intended for them to be with. But when we pull up in front of the big house no one's home.

"We'll just leave the young un' here; the Lord will protect him." He gets out of the car and comes round to my side, yanks the door open and jerks the little kid off my lap.

"But he's only four," I tell Mister as I run after him. "He could die out here. What if he wanders off?"

That's when he gets all red an' loud. "Are you questioning me? You telling me you don't have faith in our Father?"

"No. I'm just sayin' maybe we should wait till someone comes home."

Mister drops the boy onto the grass and punches me. When I fall to the ground, he starts to kick me but I catch his foot and trip him. I'm surprised at my strength.

We wrestle, I see the anger changin' to hatred. Even in the dark I can see his eyes glowin' like he has Satan eyes. So I grab that little kid an' run back to the car. If it weren't for me, Jimmy'll die out here all alone. No doubt in my mind. None at all. I'm his Protector.

Lightnin' cracks the sky an' Mister gets in the car. Takin' that dirty kerchief of his outta his pocket, he wipes the rain off his face. "We'll wait here," is all he says.

"I wanna go home, now," Jimmy whines.

"This is your home," Mister tells him an' grabs the boy outta my arms. "This is the home God wants you to live in. Isn't it grand?"

Then the little boy screams. "No! I want my own house." He kicks Mister an' hurls himself at me.

"Trust in the Lord, He knows what's best."

"No, you stealed me from my Mommy! Take me back!"

"The thief does not come except to steal, and to kill, and to destroy. I have come that they may have life, and that they may have it more abundantly. John ten, verse ten."

No Bible verse can make Jimmy feel better. "Maybe we should just take him back," I say. "How much longer are we supposed to wait for them other folks?"

"Oh no you don't, I make the plans here. I tell you what to do; you don't tell me a thing. Always remember that, Herder." He pulls my hair, jerking my head back against the seat. "You may have strength in your muscles, but I am far stronger here," he points to his head. "than you'll ever be."

"I know."

We sit there. One hour, two hours…maybe three. All the while Jimmy clingin' to me. The rain turns on an' off, but it always starts up again. The clock in the car ain't never worked, so I have to guess. It feels like midnight.

"This is all wrong," Mister finally says.

"We can have the Jubilation tomorrow."

"Too late for that now. We've had the boy too long. Something went wrong."

This has never happened before.

"Sacrifice now."

I see the blade. It's long and jagged. Is he gonna kill me or Jimmy? I can't wait to find out and grab for the door. Have to get away from that knife.

He reaches over to lock the doors an' that's when I notice he has a piece of newspaper in his hand. He mashes it into my face while Jimmy cries.

"I prayed him dead and I can do the same to you, so you best listen to me, boy."

I see Dad's name—something about a funeral. Then I unlock my door and run. All the time, holdin' on tight to Jimmy.

Mister starts up the car.

"Are you taking me home?" Jimmy asks and squeezes his arms around my neck, his little legs clamp my waist.

"I'm gonna try." I can't tell him I don't know where his home is.

I see a house all lit up. I can make it, easy.

Mister pulls along side of me as I run. Steerin' with one hand, he opens his window then waves the knife with the other. He's laughin' at us.

Have to think. I have to stop an' think what to do.

Mister stops the car between us and the house. "If they don't get you for kidnapping, they'll certainly haul you in for attempted murder."

"I never hurt no one! Never!" I shout.

Suddenly that crazy SOB plunges the knife into his own shoulder. Blood creeps down his arm like a giant spider, gettin' longer an' longer.

An old man peeks out from behind a curtain then cracks his front door open. "Git outta here or I'll sic my dog on the two of you. Ya got a minute to be gone an' then I call the police." The dog growls, he's real anxious to have at us.

"I bet the cops will be mighty interested to hear how you attacked me, Herder." He says it in a soft voice, to my back, an' with the rain an' Jimmy cryin' the old guy can't hear.

"Now what'll it be?" the old man shouts. "This is a respectable neighborhood. We don't want trouble."

I'm so confused, and scared almost as bad as the little kid. Is my Dad alive? Who'd believe me if Mister tells the cops I stabbed him? Him bein' a man of God like he is. An' I seen his friends, they're all creeps. What would they do to Jimmy? He ain't never talked about no sacrifice before.

No, I have to go back to find out about Dad an' keep Jimmy safe.

"Okay, okay, we're goin'!" I shout to the old guy.

"An' don't come back." His door slams.

Mister holds the car door open for me.

PART ELEVEN

EN MASSE

CHAPTER THIRTY-FOUR

"I don't recognize half these people," Dottie told her husband. "Vultures is what they are. And did you see the cameras out in the parking lot? That horrible Bonetti woman has the nerve to come here, to a private service…"

"It was announced in the papers," her husband said. "Public welcome. Besides, Baylor would have liked this."

"Are you crazy? Baylor was a private person. All he wanted was to be left alone and take care of Stevie. Sometimes you say the craziest things, I swear." Dottie got up from her front row seat. Reverend Lindstrom was finished. It was time to have one last look at her friend before he got put into the ground.

Bill fell into line behind his wife. Leaning down to whisper in her ear he told her, "From what I hear, he even wrote his own obituary. I'm not sayin' that's the right thing to do, I'm just sayin' it's what he did and it sure as hell worked. The papers are gonna be full of Stevie's story. It'll keep him alive a little longer. And Baylor would have done anything for that."

"Including dyin'? I don't think so," she snapped.

Vince and Kathy moved forward, slowly. "This is the first time I'm going to be close enough to touch Baylor," she told her husband. "Do you realize that? I've known him for years, heard his voice, shared his pain, emailed dozens of times a day. I felt so close to him and yet I couldn't pick him out in a crowd. I feel like I've let him down."

"I don't think I can do this," Vince told her. "That doesn't even look like the guy I knew."

"You'll be okay. We'll get through this together."

Was it the unbearable sadness that pressed so heavily against his chest? Or was it guilt corroding his stomach? I have to tell her about Stevie when this is all over. Tonight. I'll tell Kathy everything, Vince promised himself.

Taking a deep breath, he looked around the room at the large crowd, trying to distract himself. Funny how many of those in Tidderman's Funeral Home Vince recognized. He was glad to see they out-numbered those he didn't know. It made him feel part of the small community. It made him feel close to Baylor Kracher, knowing his friends, his favorite places, his history. But that knowledge would certainly come back to hurt him at his unguarded moments. He'd learned that from Gabby. Remembering would make him miss his friend even more. Maybe he'd stopped therapy too soon. Maybe he should go back when he got home. But who knew when that would be?

Almost there. Should he touch him? Would he break down? Not here. Not now. Then Vincent Lloyd was standing in front of Baylor Kracher's casket.

The simple dark wood was dull, a matt finish, no fancy hardware, nothing shiny or ostentatious. Solid and natural—like the man inside. The lining was white, model number six-twenty-three, just like Baylor had pre-arranged. Chief Stoffel had been right sending Baylor to Tidderman's, it was exactly what he had wanted. The papers he left in the bank box were full of instructions. Even the suit he was wearing had been hanging right where he'd written it would be. And shoes. The bottom portion of the casket was closed but Vince knew Baylor was wearing shiny new wing tips on his feet. "Can't walk around in Heaven bare-footed," he'd once said, "it wouldn't be respectable."

But there'd been no tie. Probably an oversight, Vince figured. Can't expect the poor guy to remember everything. Kathy had suggested maybe that was the way Baylor had wanted it. But Vince disagreed and went shopping, returning with the black and gray striped number, the most expensive one he could find. A gift between friends. And that's what got to him the most—seeing that tie.

Vince reached down and rubbed his friend's shoulder. "I'll miss you."

No one stood behind Vince, he'd made sure of it. All the others that had filed past the casket before him were outside now, waiting for the hearse to be loaded so they could follow it to the cemetery.

Vince patted the breast pocket of his tweed jacket. "And don't worry," he told Baylor, "I got your letter right here and I read every word of it. I won't let you down."

The ride to Heavenly Garden Cemetery wouldn't have been so long if they could have gotten there on a major highway. But because of its remote location, in the middle of acres of cornfields and a mile off a partially paved road full of potholes recently filled with rain, the caravan of mourners moved along slowly.

"It was nice that Chief Stoffel didn't come in his squad car," Kathy said. "Or is he even allowed to use it for personal business?"

"I don't know." Vince studied the road.

"Good thing the rain let up," she tried again. "I bet this is a horror to drive in the dark. And if the wind kicks up, it must be even worse."

"Guess so."

"Can I ask you something?" Kathy asked.

"What?"

"Why did you have to talk to that Laura Bonetti? You know, before the service?"

"I had to return her sunglasses."

Kathy pulled down the visor to check her make-up in the attached mirror. "Why would you have her sunglasses? I don't understand."

"I found them in Baylor's house the day he died."

"How could you be sure they were hers?"

"I wasn't absolutely sure, but I had a pretty good idea."

"Why?"

"They were some fancy designer frames. You know, those two Cs? One forward, one backward."

"Chanel? Yeah, I'd say it was almost a sure bet that none of Baylor's friends would own glasses like that. But did you stop to consider that maybe—"

"I was right. They were hers." He smiled, looking proud of himself.

"I guess I'm dense," she said, "but...so what? She could have been there to interview him. Or to tell him about some new development."

"Kathy," he said, reaching out to squeeze her hand. "They weren't there the whole time I was staying with Baylor. Laura Bonetti never came to the house while I was there. It's simple logic that she arrived sometime after I left to come home, and when I returned after talking to you."

A bolt of realization streaked inside her head. She swore she could feel it. "Are you telling me that you think something happened after you left to trigger his attack? Like maybe she did or said something that physically hurt him?"

He nodded.

"So how did she act when she saw them?"

"Guilty," he said. "And I'm going to find out exactly what she knows."

"When?"

"She'll be at the cemetery to finish her report."

"You can't cause a scene there. No Vince, promise me that you'll be cool until Baylor's in the ground. You owe him that."

"I owe him my best effort. I owe him a clean reputation and his son home safe. I owe him everything I've owed myself. Don't you see, Kath? When Gabby was gone, I caved. I let you and myself... and our daughter down. Now I can fix things for Baylor the way I couldn't fix them for us. And Kath..."

"What?"

"Nothing. I'll tell you later."

CHAPTER THIRTY-FIVE

Laura Ann Bonetti adjusted her sunglasses, wondering what she would say to Vincent Lloyd.

"They'd better hurry," Ken shouted. "It's gonna rain."

"Again?" she said wearily.

Ken checked his watch. "How long does a funeral take?"

Was he dumb or just trying to get to her? "What do you want me to say, Ken? I don't know. It depends on—"

"Here they are!" he pointed. "Should I start shooting now?"

"Yeah. Be sure to get a long, slow shot of the hearse out front."

First they'd stopped at the cemetery office to find the exact spot where Baylor Kracher would be laid to rest. "Plot number fifty-seven," the Director reported, showing them a large map on the wall of his office. "The Kracher family is in the Rose Section. It's a beautiful, peaceful place surrounded by rose bushes and meditation benches."

"The Kracher family? Who does that include?" she'd asked.

"Oh, there's a dozen of 'em. William Kracher, the grandfather, bought up that piece of land back in the fifties, right after his mother died. There was a spot for Jean, Baylor's wife, but he came in here when she got sent to prison and took her name off the list."

"Is there a place for Steven?" she'd asked.

"Sure. It was set aside for him when he was born."

After that they'd driven out to the Rose section and waited. Floral arrangements, moved from the funeral home to the grave site looked fresh. More roses, red and pink. A large wreath of white chrysanthemums with a blue ribbon draped across it stood on an easel. The gold letters spelled out: Beloved Friend. She didn't recognize the name on the small card attached. Lots of lilies. So pretty but their fragrances comingled, scenting the air with that sickly sweet smell she always associated with death.

After all the cars had parked along the private road, six men gathered, waiting behind the hearse. She assumed they were the pallbearers. Lloyd was there, Chief Stoffel, Bill Nelson and three men she recognized from seeing them involved with the search for Stevie, years ago.

When the casket was lifted to the shoulders of the men, they walked it to a white tent that had been set up over the open grave, waiting to be filled with Baylor Kracher and all his grief. Put to rest at last, she thought. And as she watched the procession, she wished Baylor a pleasant journey to the other side.

There wasn't much for her to do until the ceremony was concluded. It would be vulgar to intrude so she told Ken to stop filming until the Lloyds were finished.

A light, warm drizzle started. She was prepared—always—and took a small umbrella from her tote bag. Ken threw his jacket over the camera. The group was much smaller than it had been at the Funeral Home. The minster's black robe flapped in the breeze. Soprano voices lifted in a final hymn and then each well-wisher filed by the casket one last time. Several women plucked a single blossom from one of the displays and laid it gently on Baylor's casket. Laura could see men dabbing at their eyes, the wind brought sounds of crying and sniffling over to her. So much sadness.

Kathy Lloyd made an announcement that there would be a luncheon at the VFW. Laura made a mental note to ask about who had arranged it. As people started walking slowly back to their cars, Mr. and Mrs. Lloyd approached her.

She'd never noticed what an attractive couple they were. Her with all that long blond hair, falling in loose curls. Laura had to search Kathy's hairline for the finger-length scar that creased her forehead. Either plastic surgery or dumb luck had left the trail of a bullet undetectable by anyone who didn't know the woman's history. And those blue eyes, so clear, so determined, covered with a pair of flattering glasses. Mr. Lloyd with his tanned skin, a good head taller than his wife. Dark, angry eyes that melted when he looked down at her. They certainly complimented each other.

"Thank you for keeping your distance. I was surprised; it was such a thoughtful thing to do," Vince said.

She ignored his jab; this was certainly not the time or place to start up with him. Instead Laura just smiled and nodded.

"I think we should do the interview from here," Kathy said. "It's more dramatic. And the rain's let up."

Laura was taken aback at Kathy Lloyd's showmanship. Of course it would be better to film a story about the death of a grieving father right next to his grave but she'd never suggest it—these two already hated her guts. "Ken, we're ready."

The three of them stood there quietly while Ken adjusted his focus. "Ready when you are!"

"Give me a minute." Laura collapsed her umbrella, shook it off and shoved it back in her bag. Setting the bag in the grass, she ran her fingers through her hair, trying to air it out a bit. Her raincoat had deep pockets and she took out a compact and lipstick. When she was pleased with her appearance, she tucked the small mirror away and reached in the other pocket, pulling out a small microphone. "Okay."

"We have to be at the VFW in twenty minutes, so you have ten here," Ken told her.

"That's fine," Laura said. Then turning toward Vince she asked, "Tell us about your friend, Baylor Kracher."

Where should he start? There was so much he wanted to say and so much that should remain private. It seemed everyone was put on pause while he fought to find just the right words. Thank God for his wife.

Kathy stepped forward. "We met Baylor three years ago when his son went missing. My husband drove down from Chicago, where we live, to help with the search. I got involved through an organization I began when our daughter…"

He wasn't really sure what she was saying but when Kathy was done, he was ready. He spoke for two minutes straight, figuring some editor would scrap what he didn't like. He hoped he got everything in.

The three of them talked for a total of eight minutes before the lightning started.

"That's enough for now!" Laura shouted to Ken. "We'll finish up later."

He nodded and walked his equipment back to the car.

"Are you coming to the luncheon?" Vince asked the reporter. She was caught off guard, which pleased him.

"I didn't think I'd be...you know...welcomed with open arms. I'm not the most popular person in town."

"I wanted to talk with you about finding your glasses."

"I figured you would. But now's not good. I've got to rush this film up to St. Louis in time for the six o'clock news."

"You have everything you need?" Kathy asked.

She nodded. "For now. We can always do an up-date and hit the story about your organization again."

"Sounds good." Kathy started to turn, to get out of the rain, but wasn't finished. "Miss Bonetti," she said, grabbing the sleeve of Laura's coat. "If you do anything, and I mean even the slightest thing, to discredit Baylor or his son, I'll raise such a stink. I'll campaign to get you fired. But I won't stop there. I'll keep tabs on you. I have thousands of followers on my Facebook page and website—it'll be easy. Volunteers are out there night and day looking for lost children. We'll make your life miserable for as long as we can if you do anything to ruin the chance of one family being reunited. Understand?"

She could stand up to her, point out there were witnesses hearing her threats. But she didn't want to fight. "I understand completely."

"Good." And with a big smile plastered across her face, Kathy nodded and ran for cover.

Vince shook his head. "My wife can get a little dramatic sometimes."

"Lucky you." Laura pulled out her umbrella, and kept up with the man's long strides as they walked to their vehicles.

"Come to Baylor's house tomorrow evening around seven," Vince told her. "We have a lot to talk about. Like what you did to bring on his heart attack."

She shook her head violently. "No. I didn't do anything. He was already..."

"Already what?"

"I'll see you tomorrow."

"Just you. And no cameras!"

CHAPTER THIRTY-SIX

Things. So very many things that fill up a house and a heart. Thousands of tiny, incidental, forgettable items taking up space. Paper clips, scraps of paper, half empty bottles, slivers of soap. Dozens of valuables handed down through generations or recently purchased. Pieces of art, jewelry, silverware, all occupying space in a life and a building. As he packed up Baylor's belongings, Vince kept thinking about Gabby's doll. To an outsider the bald ballerina, missing one leg, would be considered garbage. But to him it would forever be his most valuable possession.

It hadn't been a birthday or holiday. And the rule was that nothing costing more than twenty dollars was to be bought unless for a special occasion. That was the agreement Kathy and Vince had made when their baby girl was born. No spoiling her—make rules and stick to them. But she had wanted it so badly and...

The day was cold. He'd promised her hot chocolate as they walked the two blocks to her favorite diner.

"And maybe could we have some French fries? Huh, Daddy?"

He'd wrinkled his nose, teasing. "Gross. French fries and chocolate? Icky."

"Please, Daddy. Please?"

"We'll see."

He held her hand tightly. They were both wearing gloves but he could still feel the warmth of her little fingers through the material. He was so happy.

"Why can't there always be snow on Christmas? It's supposed to be snowy so Santa's sleigh can slide across the roofs. Right, Daddy?"

"Right."

"I hate it when it snows after Christmas. It's all wrong that way. Don't you think so, Daddy?"

"I guess." He enjoyed the lilt of her voice but knew she was just chattering which freed him from paying close attention to what she said.

Then suddenly she stopped, dead in her tracks, jerking him back a step.

There in the window of the small doll shop was a pink-haired ballerina doll. Standing on her toes, her slippers made of pink leather. The white net tutu was covered in tiny crystals and sparkled in a small spotlight aimed down at her from above. The bodice was lavender satin. A tiny crystal choker was wrapped around her graceful neck.

"Isn't she beautiful?" Gabby stood transfixed, hypnotized by the elegant miniature dancer. "Better than Cinderella. Or Ariel."

He knew that in a moment she would be begging him to buy the doll for her. Craning his neck he finally spotted a small price tag, discreetly tucked under the ballerina's feet. Fifty-nine-fifty. More than he had ever spent on a toy for her. "Yes, honey, she's very pretty."

"She's so sparkly. I bet she's magical."

Holidays were over. No special presents—Kathy would kill him. Be consistent.

Then she reached up for his hand and pulled him toward the restaurant.

"Don't you want to go inside and look at her? Close up?" Why had he said that?

"No."

He bent down to look into those big eyes. "Why not?"

"No big presents until my birthday. I know the rules. And I got so much from Santa…"

She was breaking his heart. Being so very grown-up. So serious and logical.

"Well I want to look at her," he said and headed for the door.

"Me too!"

Gabby skipped joyfully into the shop, her eyes ignoring the display of puppets and rag dolls. She walked right by the Barbies. As he lifted her up to get a closer look at the ballerina, he could feel her heart racing. And seeing her like that was worth anything.

When he bought the doll, she gently kissed that pink hair, careful not to disturb the crystal tiara on top. It wasn't until years later that he realized he had just lived one of the best nights of his life.

As he went through Baylor's effects, the lack of an emotional connection to anything he touched made him feel like a ghoul. To him, most of the things in the house were junk. Some would be tossed, some would be given to charity. Who was he to make the decision? That rubber fish could have been a gag gift from Stevie. A joke they shared, no one else appreciating the significance of the cheap piece of green rubber. That souvenir plate from Washington DC might have been purchased while Baylor was on his honeymoon or Stevie was on a school trip...he didn't have a clue. It may have been his friend's final wishes that he do the physical labor but that didn't make the job any easier.

"I don't think I can take much more of this," Kathy said, wiping her hands as she came into the living room.

Vince turned toward her. "What do you mean? What's wrong?"

"What gives us the right to touch his things?" Dropping to the couch, she rubbed her forehead. "It's almost like we're desecrating his grave. I feel terrible."

He went to her. "I was feeling the same way. But it's what he wanted..."

"That damn letter. It has to be as long as a book, the way you keep quoting from it. The funeral arrangements, the luncheon, bank account numbers. I know you said I could read it but I didn't think there was that much to it."

"There wasn't," Vince told her. "Not in the letter. But other papers—"

"Like what?" Kathy straightened up and stared at him, her face shiny from the sweat she'd worked up packing boxes and moving furniture.

Now was the perfect time to tell her that Stevie was alive. What was he waiting for anyway?

But when the phone rang he welcomed the interruption. "It might be important," he said.

"Go."

Should he let the machine pick up, he wondered, walking into the kitchen. Remembering the message with Baylor's voice on it he knew he couldn't take hearing his friend. He reached for the receiver. "Hello?"

"Dad?"

"Stevie?"

"You're not dead! He said you were dead."

"Stevie, my name's Vincent Lloyd. Don't hang up. Just listen."

There was no response on the other end. But, thankfully, there was no sound of a hang-up either.

"Your father told me that you're alive. He told me that you came to see him."

"Where is he?"

"Stevie, listen."

"Is he alive?"

"I'm so sorry."

"Who is it?" Kathy whispered, seeing the look on her husband's face.

He held up hand, signaling her to wait a minute. "Are you there? Hello?"

A dial tone wailed.

"Vince, are you okay? Who was that?"

"That was...Stevie."

She stood there stunned, her mouth open.

When the phone rang again, she grabbed the receiver. "Hello."

"Mrs. Lloyd? This is Laura Bonetti. I was wondering if it would be okay if I came to see both of you in about an hour?"

"That's fine."

"Okay then."

Kathy slammed down the phone. "What the hell is going on? Tell me!"

"He was here, Kath. Baylor told me weeks ago. Stevie came to see him one night."

Kathy ran her fingers through her hair—a nervous habit. "So why didn't you tell me when you first found out?"

"He made me promise not to tell anyone."

"Including me? Come on, Vince, you could've said something when I first got here, or when we were alone. On the way to the funeral? On the way back? This morning? You've had a dozen opportunities."

"I don't know. Things have been happening so fast. I can't get a handle on all of it."

"All of what, Vince? Stop playing the victim here. Baylor died of natural causes—nothing mysterious about it. That's just what happens when a person doesn't eat right or exercise. That's what happens from the stress of losing a child. You should know that better than anyone."

He grabbed her. "Calm down. You have every right to be angry but will you just listen to me for a minute?"

She pulled away from him. He recognized that look. She'd had enough.

"When I came back to the house, the day you called me about Baylor, the first thing I saw were those sunglasses on the floor and right away I knew Laura Bonetti had been here. I was confused."

"Wait a minute…have you talked to her about Stevie? Please Vince, please don't tell me that you told her—"

"No! No, Kath. But I do think she was here when Baylor died."

After a long minute she said, "Okay, let's say she was. I still don't see what that has to do with Stevie."

"What if she was the last person he saw? That maybe he knew he was dying and told her…his secret?"

"Why was it a secret, Vince? I still don't understand."

"Because Stevie's in danger. If we try to help, we might get him killed."

CHAPTER THIRTY-SEVEN

"So what do we do? Try to trick her into telling us what Baylor said? Or find out if he even spoke to her at all?"

They were in the bathroom, sharing the mirror. Kathy stood in front of the sink, finishing her make-up. Vince stood behind her, combing his hair.

"Just let her do most of the talking. We'll know when the time's right. And be nice—no, just be polite."

"Aren't I always?" She gave him an exaggerated smile. .

When they were ready he went to the living room to clear off the couch so they could all sit. She went to the kitchen to make iced tea, hopefully find something to snack on.

Why was she so nervous? Laura knocked instead of using the door-bell. It somehow seemed less intrusive.

Vince held the door open. "Come in." How should he address her? After all these years had they graduated to first names? Did he want to give the impression he wanted them to be friends?

"Vince, let me tell you again how very sorry I am about your friend."

"Thanks."

They stood there, awkwardly silent with each other a moment. Then she asked, "Is Kathy here?"

"She's in the kitchen."

As if on cue, Kathy walked in with the drinks and cookies. "Laura, you're so very punctual. Always the professional, aren't you?" She spoke with a definite attitude which sent the reporter into defense mode.

"Look, I never did anything to intentionally harm any of you.

Did you both see the piece I did last night? On my six o'clock spot?"

"Very nice," Vince said.

"Can I sit down?" She motioned to Baylor's chair.

Kathy handed their guest a glass of tea. "Let's all do that."

Taking a glass to Vince then grabbing one for herself, she sat next to her husband on the couch. The three remained silent. The only sound in the room came from ice cubes clinking against glass. No one knew where to begin or even who should.

Finally Vince just blurted it out: "You were here when Baylor died, weren't you?"

Everyone was surprised when she said, "Yes."

"Were you the one who called 911?"

"No," she said after a long, deep swallow. "There was someone on the phone with him and I guess they called."

"Medora," Kathy said, "His lawyer, Medora—"

"Prescott...I know. I've spoken to her several times. I saw her at the cemetery. She's not very fond of me."

Vince snapped, "Can you blame her? Can you blame any of us? You circle like a buzzard, Ms. Bonetti. You hover and wait, looking for bones to pick clean..."

"Literally," Kathy added.

"Okay, so I knew you were in town." She looked at Vince. "You're not the most popular person around here, either, Mr. Lloyd. The world has gone electronic; everyone wired up to catch the latest gossip. Your reputation preceded you. And people judge. That's the trouble with the system. Downloaded facts, sparked with human emotions, screw everything up. And, unfortunately it's also the business I'm in. If viewers didn't want my slant, the news would be written and read by robots."

"Maybe we'd all be better off," Kathy said.

"Maybe," Laura agreed.

"Look," Vince said, "I don't give a shit what you think of me, Ms. Bonetti. I just want you to tell me what, if anything, Baylor told you while you were here."

"I know that Steven Kracher is alive. I know that he came here to see his father. I also know that he said there are others in danger. He wanted me to find his son and the very last thing he told me was, 'ask Vince for help.'"

"And why didn't you?" he asked.

"To be honest," she said, "I was trying to decide what to do with all this information—figure out if it was even true. Or was Baylor hallucinating while he was dying. If I went to someone for help, would they leak the story to the tabloids? Did I want to be the one to break the news? You tell me…Kathy…what would you have done?"

She was surprised when the question flew at her, out of nowhere that way. "I…I guess I would have talked to Vince, felt him out. I don't know," she finally admitted.

"You've had days to think about it. So…what are you going to do?" he asked.

"One thing's for sure, we can't do anything to put Stevie in danger—at least no more than he's already in. We'll never get that boy home safely if we fight each other," his wife told him as she reached for an Oreo piled on the small plate in front of her.

"Can I have one of those?" Laura asked.

"Sure."

Vince watched as the women chewed. Was he crazy or were they? Setting his glass down, he massaged his temples.

It's okay, Daddy.

"She's in my head, all the time, talking to me."

"Who is Vince?"

"Gabby. And it's nice having her with me like that. But Stevie's different. I didn't know him; he's a stranger. And yet there's this drive I have to find him. I need to make this right. And then it'll be—"

"Right with Gabby," Kathy finished. She leaned forward, putting her arms around him. "I hear her, too, Vince. Every day. And I talk to her all the time. It makes me feel like I'm not such a horrible mother because I didn't keep her safe."

Laura sat stunned. The couple seemed to have forgotten she was there. As their real life melodrama played out in real time, right in front of her, she felt her heart breaking for them.

It was Kathy who first realized how unintentionally they had revealed so much. And suddenly, she didn't care. To hell with all of it. Stevie was the only thing that matter now. "Miss Bonetti… Laura…look, here's all I know…" She took a chance and laid everything out for the reporter.

"So, you're the least informed of the three of us," Laura said. "No judgment—we have to talk honestly between us."

Vince was still skeptical. "How exactly are you going to play your role, Laura? Are you the concerned friend? Or are you the hard-nosed reporter hungry for her story?"

She laughed at that last comment. "You have me confused with Lois Lane, I think."

He stared at her, stone-faced.

"To be honest, Vince, I wasn't sure how I'd play this until a few minutes ago. I've always just reported what I've seen, hard and cold. Then I go home. Next morning there are different stories to cover, different people to interview. I've never been sure how my words personally affect anyone."

"So you'll keep what you know to yourself?" Kathy asked. "We have to be able to trust you."

"I know." Laura nervously rubbed the knees of her jeans. "If you remember, I did call you when Baylor was taken in for questioning."

"True," Kathy said. "But that could have been to get information out of me. I was never quite sure why you did that."

Vince stood up. "Medora will draw up a contract," he said. "And you'll sign it. All stories that you do about Baylor or Stevie must be approved by me first or..."

"What?" Laura asked.

Before he could answer, she said, "Okay, I'll sign whatever you need. What about the police?" she asked. "Should we take what we know to the cops?"

"No," Kathy snapped. "You've seen what they did to Vince and me. With my connections, we can move quicker and easier without the authorities."

Vince pointed toward Laura. "And if the cops get tipped off, we'll know where it came from. And so help me God—"

"I understand," she told them. "We'll do this our own way...just the three of us."

CHAPTER THIRTY-EIGHT

Partners with the Lloyds? Was she crazy? What if they'd made up the whole thing—telling her Stevie had called right before she got there? Some coincidence! But why would they make up a story like that? What did they have to gain? Everyone had a motive. By the time she pulled into a parking spot in front of the condo, she'd had an hour to wrestle with her doubts and questions…resolving nothing.

The crazy red-headed woman from 1C was coming out as Laura was going in. Her hair was one big mass of ketchup colored tangles; she walked with a cane and was forever whistling. Not a melody or familiar song but a bird-like, incessant, whistle. Three notes then a hum…three notes then a hum…

"Oh, you scared me!"

She was always out of breath or frightened or in need of help and Laura was always trying to avoid the woman. Some people just took up more than their share of space in the world. Their movements and gestures so exaggerated that others were forced to shrink and get small. Did they even know how obnoxious they were being? Yes, Laura had decided, and they enjoyed the attention.

"Sorry, Mrs. Teal."

"Since you're already here, Laura, do you think you could help me get a few things out of the car?"

"Can't it wait until tomorrow? It's after ten and I've been going all day…"

"It'll only take a minute and I'd do it myself if I could but…" She held up her cane and pushed out her bottom lip.

Shit, it would take less time to just give in than to stand there making excuses. Laura exhaled a frustrated breath, hoping her neighbor would notice. "Okay."

Mrs. Teal limped to her car, a shiny new Cadillac, and opened the trunk. Inside was a microwave oven and two large shopping bags, both packed to bulging. Laura grabbed the bags after watching the chubby woman hoist the oven up on her left shoulder.

"Could you close the trunk?" her neighbor shouted, hobbling toward the front door.

"Got it."

Mrs. Teal's apartment was on the first floor in the back. And even though there was an entire cement floor and several units separating them, Laura could hear the woman whistling in the morning. But this would be the first time she stepped a foot into her personal space.

She had been curious from the day Mrs. Teal had moved in. And from the looks of her and her overblown personality, Laura was sure she would find a hoarder or crazy collector. Almost daily the elderly woman seemed to be hauling and unloading. Like an ant going frantically back and forth, back and forth, moving something from one place to another.

But the living room was homey and spotless.

"Here," Mrs. Teal said pointing to the table, "you can just put those things here."

The dining area took up part of the living room and appeared spotless as well. A large, round, oak table was surrounded by four chairs, each with what looked to be a handmade, patchwork seat cover.

"Can I make you a cup of tea? Or coffee?"

"No thanks. I've really got to…"

"I guess it is pretty late for caffeine. I don't sleep much, so it doesn't matter what I eat or drink—or when. I have to keep reminding myself that people are sleeping while I putter around down here. Like when I'm vacuuming or running the dishwasher. Can you hear me cleaning? Have I woken you up?"

"No, but I do hear you whistling in the morning, when I'm getting ready for work."

"Well, I'm sure a person like you would march right down and complain if I was bothering you."

Of course Laura realized how petty she sounded. But this

woman had been making her crazy for months. And even though she was tired and annoyed having gotten pressured into helping her neighbor, she still couldn't help asking, "What kind of a person do you think I am?"

"Just like the commercial for your program says: 'hard hitting, no nonsense and direct.'"

She was flattered. "I'll take that as a compliment."

"And that's just how I meant it, dear. I watch you every day. I watch all the true crime programs…"

"I don't think you can call the News, 'true crime.'"

"Sure you can. The stories are true and most of them are about crime."

No use arguing.

"Come and sit. I've been dying to talk to you about that missing boy. The one in Kimmswick? I've followed the story from the very beginning. All the characters, all the way up to that special when poor Mr. Kracher died. You did a nice job."

"Oh, you saw it?"

The woman nodded. "Hey! I have some coffee cake. Come on… one piece won't mess up that figure of yours. And I have milk if you still want to pass on coffee."

As she looked at the woman's toothy smile, she felt a little less hostility toward her. "It all sounds good, even the coffee. But I can only stay for a little while."

Mrs. Teal clapped her freckled hands together. "Good! Now you just sit on the sofa there and I'll get everything ready."

"Can I help?" Laura asked, hoping the woman would say no.

"No, I got it. You just relax."

While Mrs. Teal scurried off to the kitchen, Laura surveyed dozens of photos on the walls and those in fancy little frames propped up on the end tables. Children—probably grandkids. A man—maybe a husband. Faded pictures taken at graduations and birthday parties. Several looked like vacations, a house on the lake, funny hats and more kids.

"So how many children do you have?" Laura asked as she took the cups and plates from the tray Mrs. Teal held out to her.

"Mr. Teal had two, from a previous marriage. We never had any together—biologically—that is. But throughout the years we raised fifteen foster kids. And now some of those children have children. Last count, there were fifty-two."

Okay, she thought, so the woman's a saint. But I still don't like her whistling.

While they ate they chatted about Stevie and Baylor. Mrs. Teal did most of the talking. She seemed genuinely concerned about the missing boy, even had several theories concerning who had taken him and where he was now. It was obvious to Laura that the woman was very passionate about young lives and had even gone so far as doing something to help. The more animated the red-head became, the more Laura envied her. She was so alive. Had made a real life for herself.

"Have there been any sightings?" Mrs. Teal asked after they had been chatting for half an hour.

She couldn't tell her—anyone—the truth. "No. Nothing."

"I pray he's not dead." Tears as big as marbles welled up and ran down her rosy cheeks. "But you hear about kids being found. Even after a lot of years have passed. Like those girls who were prisoners in that horrible man's backyard. Boy, that was something, wasn't it? I mean, the poor boy could be alive and just trying to get found."

"You never know."

When they were finally talked out, Laura thanked her neighbor and went to the door.

"No, thank you for the help. John, one of my foster kids, is in the Army and says it makes his day getting something from home. And Jeannie just moved into her first apartment; she'll love the microwave."

Laura had always thought that someday, when the timing was just right, when she was established in her career and a lot older, she'd get a sign. And she'd know. She'd be overwhelmed with the urgency to help someone or join a cause. Like Mrs. Teal, helping all those children.

As she walked up the two flights of stairs to her own apartment, it hit her like a hammer. She'd been getting signs for years. Running into Vincent Lloyd while he searched for Stevie. The very same man she had interviewed years before, when they both lived in Chicago. What were the odds that she'd meet up with him in the middle of nowhere like that? And tonight, listening to Mrs.Teal talk about her children. Why had she avoided the woman for so long but tonight been receptive? Baylor's last words that she had, by chance, been in time to hear. Stevie calling just a few moments before she visited the Lloyds.

If the universe was trying to tell her something it wasn't speaking in a whisper. It was shouting.

CHAPTER THIRTY-NINE

"Do you really think we can trust her?"

"We're way past that," Vince told his wife. "She's in this now—same as us."

"Are you serious?" Kathy looked at him in amazement. "How in the world is she the same as us? We're not going to turn this whole thing into a front page story. Neither one of us is looking to get famous by telling everything we know about Stevie. Can you say the same for that woman?"

"I can't think about that now," he said, trailing behind her to the kitchen. "The minute she left here, everything went to a new level. That's just the way it is."

Kathy slammed a cabinet door shut. Then she grabbed him. "Vince, look at me! Baylor's out of this. At least he's safe. But there's three lives here—yours, mine and Stevie's—that can all be ruined. Don't you remember what we went through...before? It nearly killed us. And if we screw this up, Stevie could die. How can you just accept—"

"Accept?" He pulled away from her, afraid his rage would somehow physically hurt her. "If you think I take any of this lightly... It's all I can do to...to even act like a human being most the time. I suspect everyone I meet, I don't trust, I don't believe and I don't sleep. What do you want from me, Kath? How about if I blow my brains out? Would that make your life easier? Not having to see me? Not hearing me? Is that what you want?"

Each word seemed to hit her like a bullet, nicking her heart, piercing her resolve, finally bringing her down. When he was through, she lay crumpled on the yellow tiled floor, curled in a ball, jerking back and forth.

Her collapse stopped him cold. Gently he folded himself up, set-tling behind her, reaching his arms around to hold her. If only she'd cry, make any sort of noise he could understand. "Ah, sweetie," he said softly, kissing the back of her head.

Deadly quiet, he kept thinking. We can't end like this. Silent and helpless. "I'm so sorry. Tell me what to do and I'll do it. If only we knew what to do."

Twenty minutes passed. They must have fallen asleep like that, on Baylor's floor. She finally broke his hug and rolled around to face him, look into those sad eyes. "I'm sorry, Vince; I'm exhausted from being so sorry. Do you think everything will be fixed if we find Stevie? What if nothing changes? I'm so scared nothing will ever change."

"All we can do is try, and trusting Laura…it's a step. It's something."

She got up and brushed herself off. "I guess."

Strange how well she'd slept, how energized she felt. Seeing the world from the floor last night, literally having nowhere to go but up. Onward and upward, keep the faith, she thought, hang in there— all those cheerleader-rah-rah platitudes she'd heard her whole life and hated, suddenly felt comforting.

Vince was snoring in the guestroom they'd shared the night before. She'd always been the early riser and after making coffee, went downstairs to check her emails on Baylor's computer. She made a note, on one of her many lists, to bring it back to Chicago, before the police confiscated it. Would they do that now? He'd died of natural causes, no crime, nothing to hide…and yet she wanted his files and emails away from this house.

She considered the WE'LLFINDYOU website a living organ-ism, constantly growing, weaving itself into other factions of social media. It started off crudely, she'd constructed it herself, instruc-tions in one hand, pecking keys with the other. Then an interview on "60 Minutes" generated so much interest that within hours she was overwhelmed with requests for speaking engagements, offers of help from volunteers around the world and pictures. Thousands of pictures started arriving, back in those days they came in enve-lopes with long letters from distraught mothers or fiancé's, sisters and aunts—everyone knew someone who'd just evaporated...disappeared. Donations followed. Loose change in boxes, cashiers checks, money raised by children in elementary school to help find a classmate. Husbands so desperate for reasons why a wife would leave or a daughter would walk away. Surely they had been kidnapped. Please help! You're my last hope. Don't ignore me like all those other do-gooders have. You know what I'm feeling. You've been there.

A bigger and better website was set up by a computer technician who's ten year old son had never come back from the store five years ago. Maybe this would be the project he needed to feel useful. And when emails then Facebook, Twitter accounts and IMs erupted, Kathy was desperate for more help. Smartphones with cameras led to more pictures and videos being sent. It took her a year to get organized. But just when she thought she had a handle on things: the Tablet, the Nook, Kindle, magazines and newspapers in one convenient place, more people watching viral videos, more outrage, anger. Then a teenager in Austin, Texas lost his kid brother at a mall.

Tyler Wilcox, sixteen, had just gotten his driver's license. Jeremy, five years old, had been foisted on him by his mother who had to work late. Grudgingly the teenager took his brat brother with him. When a girl smiled at him from behind the counter at Donut World he gave Jeremy a dollar and pointed him toward the arcade. That was the last he'd seen of the boy. Now he was so depressed he didn't want to live. He hated himself. But when he saw Kathy Lloyd on TRU TV, he felt better. Could he please start a branch of WE'LLFINDYOU in his town and work with her? Then came the mother in Tampa, a sister in Reno, until there were two hundred chapters. Now when she started her day it took longer to read the posts before she could actually do some work.

Flicking on the computer, she wasn't prepared when Stevie's picture came into focus as Baylor's wallpaper. The background, a bright turquoise, he looked to be about ten years old, all decked out in a red Cardinal's baseball cap and white jersey with the familiar redbird on the front. Such a big, carefree smile. But those eyes. She leaned forward to study his eyes. An old soul she thought. This is a boy who knows about life...knows things without being told.

After settling back in the oversized chair, she went to the official

WE'LLFINDYOU website. There was no music, she'd never wanted anything cheerful or sad to strike the viewer. This was life—raw and in-your-face. Just photos. Colored ones, black and white, small, old and yellowed, some computer enhanced. A collage made up of dozens of eyes and faces, updated daily. Click on a picture, learn about a person, a name an age, last place seen, rewards, contact numbers. Every day it grew.

She checked for new emails, answered each one, trying to reassure every sender that their message had been received and recorded. She worked with search groups, the National Guard, local police departments and lawyers. With one twitter she could organize a search party anywhere in the world.

That done, and after convincing herself not to feel guilty, she tried to hack into Baylor's emails. First try with the password STEVIE, she was in.

"What'cha doin'?" Vince stood at the door, hair mussed, wearing his pajama bottoms.

She jerked her chair around. "You startled me."

"Sorry." He walked to the desk, stooping to look over her shoulder. When he realized what he was seeing, he asked, "Find anything?"

"I just started."

"Well, let me know if there's anything interesting. I'm gonna make some breakfast. Did you eat already?"

"No, I was waiting for you."

"Well hurry. I'm starved."

While he set the table, she made toast. He poured orange juice into small green glasses and she scrambled eggs. All the while they chatted about the everyday stuff that makes up a marriage and no one ever seems to remember as important. There's a new James Bond movie coming out. He wanted to see it—she thought spy movies were passé. Did he want jelly on his toast? How did she sleep? Halfway through the meal, Vince cleared his throat and took a gulp of coffee.

"You know what we need, don't you?"

"What?"

"A plan. A deadline. Something definite for each of us to do."

"I agree."

"I've been thinking, there's no need for you to stay here," he told his wife. "You can do more good from your office at home."

"Guess you're right. But you can't live here indefinitely."

"Someone has to be here if Stevie comes back. And someone has to answer the phone if he calls. Which brings up the deadline part of this. Let's give it a few weeks…a month, maybe?"

"Now that he knows his father's dead, why would he come back? What's here for him?"

"He must think of this house as a safe place. And I did have time to tell him my name; maybe he'll try to contact me."

"But how does he know you'll be here?" Kathy was getting frustrated. "I don't have a clue how we're supposed to start searching for this kid without the police being involved."

"No police, Kath. Baylor said others could get hurt. We can't let anyone know Stevie's alive."

Did he think she was stupid? "I know. I get it."

"Tomorrow I'll call Laura. If we're working together we have to stay in touch."

Finished eating, they started to clear the table. He had this thing about stacking dirty dishes, putting things in order. Too bad his compulsions didn't include washing the dishes or cleaning a toilet, she thought as she watched.

"And I'm going back to the bank to see if I can settle some of Baylor's affairs. I don't quite understand what being his executor means."

"Call Medora," Kathy said. "She'll know."

PART TWELVE

STEVIE

CHAPTER FORTY

Now there's three of us.

Jimmy don't talk much since that night when he saw all the blood from Mister stabbin' himself like that. Jimmy's been real scared since then. He's all the time rockin' himself, suckin' on his thumb. No more cryin' for his Mama or Daddy. I try comfortin' him but he stiffens up and just stares right through me.

Then a few days ago we picked up Luke. He's still tryin' to understand what's goin' on. He's older than Jimmy—but not by much. I tell him to keep quiet. But he don't listen and cries till he makes himself throw up. After I clean him, all the time sayin' how Mister will just get meaner if he don't shut up, he cries louder, sometimes workin' himself into a screamin' fit.

A few years ago there was six of us. That was the most at one time. The girls was older, he took 'em from their own yards. Mister was a lot happier then, singin' Bible songs while he dressed 'em all pretty. But it's better when there's just boys here.

This house we're at now is on a river, but I'm not sure which one. It reminds me of home an' that makes me sad...thinkin' of Dad. When I get the nerve to call or see him, I know them poor kids are gonna suffer an' I get afraid for 'em so I always come back. But in my head, Dad's alive an' doin' okay, like the last time I seen him. I ain't gonna believe what nobody says about him bein' dead—'specially not some guy in our house I don't even know.

I tug Luke along. "Hey see that bird?" I point. "That's an eagle. They fly up the river lookin' for food in the winter."

"I hate you!" he screams, pullin' away from me. "I hate that dumb bird. I wanna go home!"

"Look," I kneel down, try to get to his level, like a friend, "I ain't gonna hurt you. An' real soon we'll take you home." I don't tell him it'll be a new home, not the one he's used to.

But he don't listen to me. I can't get mad though, cause I been there—right where Luke is now.

So scared. I cried so much my eyes swelled an' I couldn't hardly see. Like Mister was one of them movie monsters—all big an' horrific. There was no escapin' him. He ran faster an' his hands was bigger an' stronger. I didn't stand a chance even though I was fifteen.

I tried everything. Scratched, bit an' clawed—wouldn't eat nothin'. But he only laughed an' said, "More food for me." Nothin' I did mattered. I was just some nobody kid. An' Mister—he was a man of God.

Dad an' me didn't go to church regular. My crap mother, when she was around, was all the time high on somethin' or drinkin'. Never cared if I went to school let alone got some sort of Bible education. An' that's how Mister held on to me. Not with ropes or threats, an' there was lots of both in the beginnin' No, he slithered his way into my soul. He was real good at convincin' me that God wanted me to help him help those kids.

"I know you hate me now," he used to say, "but God is love— pure and bright. I'm going to pray that the light will shine inside you and you'll come to realize I love you."

I'd cry that I wanted my dad, but he'd only smile an' pray some more, always sayin' he was doin' God's work an' I'd been chosen to help him.

"Any man can bed a woman and make a baby," he'd explain. "Animals make babies because of something called instinct, not love. Some species even eat their young. Did you know that? And it's up to Man to save those innocent souls. That's the cold facts of life."

Then he'd go get that worn out Bible of his, open it up and point. "Genesis Chapter One, verse twenty-seven, 'So God created man in his own image.' See? When a man saves a life, it's really God that's doing the deed. It's not us, stealing a child from a perfect life. No, it's God saving that girl or boy from damned parents who have rutted around, fornicated because some primitive, animal urge made them do it. Understand?"

When he'd worn me down, after a few months of it bein' just me an' him, he told me how God had spoken to him one night.

"I said, 'Lord, I can't do this by myself much longer. I'm getting older and there are still so many babies who need me.' And you know what happened?"

I just sat there, waiting for the rest of his story.

"He blessed me for all my years of selfless service. Thanked me for my dedication, but it was time, He said, to find a Herder. I should be patient and He'd lead me to the chosen one."

Then he grabbed me into a sweaty hug, all the time tellin' me how I should feel special. I could smell his B.O. His smile was so big I could see all his teeth.

"Tonight we go out to save a poor child," he said, big ole tears suddenly running down his cheeks. "Poor, poor baby Jessie. Satan interfered. Got his evilness into those parents of his. Having a child without the blessing of marriage. Brought that child into the world tarnished—wrapped in sin. But we can set things right."

He was a grown-up, a holy man an' he needed my help. Some dumb kid who never done nothin' serious an' now I was gonna be like a super hero an' save people. I wanted to believe him; believin' took away all the fear and left behind some excitement. You know, like ya feel on Christmas Eve?

"How?"

"I have the address of a couple—good Christian people who will give baby Jessie a fresh start. Their love and purity will cleanse this boy's soul. And as Christian soldiers, moving onward, doing God's will, it's our duty to take Jessie to his Jesus parents."

I'd never heard of "Jesus parents" before. Never even knew there was more than one kind of parents. But then I never was good in school. What did I know?

I mostly remember the smells. Flowery an' clean. The houses were big, lots of room between each other an' the road. Grand is how Dad would describe 'em. Least ways grander than any house I was ever inside before.

A new Ford pickup was parked in the driveway an' lights was on in all the rooms on the first floor. I guess I was expectin' some pretty lady to open the door an' just hand over a baby. Stupid! An' I wondered how bad could it be for this baby in such a beautiful place. But Mister pushed me against my window an' told me to get in the backseat. "Be quiet, for God's sake," he whispered.

I done what he told me.

Mister walked real casual up the walk and rang the bell. A girl about my age answered. She looked all nervous. They stood there talkin', smilin'. Mister took off his hat, holdin' it all polite in his hands. She invited him in.

I thought about runnin' for it then. I coulda made it to the next house an' called the cops. But it was dark, I didn't know where the hell I was, an' mostly I was afraid. Not just for myself but for the baby. I truly believed that I had to save that poor kid or Satan himself would get him.

They was in there for about five minutes before he came walkin' out, holdin' a baby wrapped in a blue blanket. Mister turned toward the car but the girl yelled somethin' an' run back in the house. When she come back, she had a bag an' handed it to him.

"Here," he said as he shoved the baby at me, then the bag. It was one of them green ones people buy at the grocery store so they don't have to use the plastic ones.

Then Mister got behind the wheel, turned the key and backed down the driveway.

The baby fell asleep in my arms; I touched his hand. So soft an' little. Ain't never been around babies. An' I didn't want Mister to see me hold that baby tight so I could make him feel safe. But I woulda wanted someone to do that for me if I was him.

We went back to the house.

"What's his name?" I asked. "An' where's he gonna sleep?"

Mister shrugged, kinda confused. His eyes jerked back and forth, like he was tryin' to remember somethin'. Then he got this nice smile. I'll remember it forever. He made me feel safe. I was still holdin' the baby when he grabbed my shoulders.

"You saved him and are going to help me deliver him to his Jesus Parents. So I give you the honor of baptizing this little one with a new name."

I felt so grown up an' didn't have to think too hard. The best men in the world, next to my dad, were baseball players. "Derek. After Derek Jeeter."

"Not very Biblical, but a nice strong name. Now go put the boy to bed. I set up a crib in that back room."

I laid the baby down and looked through the bag I'd been holding the whole time. Inside was some diapers, an empty bottle and these tiny little blue socks. Did his mom make 'em, I kept wondering. The mom Mister said was so horrible an' didn't deserve this baby? In the bottom of the bag was a little stuffed elephant. I put it next to Derek so he'd feel safe. He was asleep before I left the room.

Mister didn't see me comin' down the hall. He was too busy countin' out money in his wallet. Once he told me we lived on donations from Christian people who knew we was doin' good work. If that was true, he better step up the work cause all I saw in his hands was two twenties.

After that we waited. I could see the date on the TV, when he let me watch a game, an' I guess almost a week went by. Then one night the phone rang an' Mister wrote down an address. The next night we took Derek to a house that wasn't even half as nice as the other one. A few men was standing outside, playin' music amped up so loud it made the windows of the car rattle. I tried to get Derek to stop cryin' an' almost did it but then Mister grabbed him and told me to stay in the car an' wait.

It was more lonely than ever when Derek was gone. But soon there was another kid…an' another. An' I forced myself to believe I was helpin' em'.

It makes me sick rememberin' how pathetic I was back then. Talk about stupid an' gullible. But I'm smarter now. Don't trust nobody, 'cept for my dad. Still I have to wonder sometimes, did Mister kill him?

Can't think about that now. Have to keep Luke safe till I figure somethin' out. Can't waste any time, 'specially since I heard Mister prayin' last night, askin' God to send him a new Herder.

PART THIRTEEN

MISTER

CHAPTER FORTY-ONE

"Dear God in heaven…"

"Knock if off, will ya? I ain't got no time to waste with all yer Jesus bullshit."

What did I expect, a nun? If she were saintly, she wouldn't be in prison, would she? "How are we expected to do God's work when there's interference…?

"God's work, my ass. This is about money—sweet an' simple. Now stop gettin' yer nose outta whack. Keep doin' what yer doin'. It's worked for us this long, and it'll keep workin' till I say it won't."

I should just kill her. "You'd think I would have learned by now. I don't know why I try to be decent with you…"

"Decent? Is that how you think you treated me? Any of us? Threatenin', spittin', callin' us whores and scum. You think I don't know what you did at night…to the young girls? Didn't matter if they was sick; you especially liked the ones a little touched in the head, didn't you? So don't go actin' like some holy man cause I know you—I know you real good. Remember, I've had lots of years to study you."

"Don't you ever threaten me, bitch. I can make things a whole lot worse for you. There's friends of mine still on the job. Friends who'll do anything I ask—"

"For money. You can buy as many 'friends' as you need, asshole, as long as there's money for 'em."

"Yeah, yeah, all of a sudden you're so smart about human nature? Too bad you weren't smart enough to keep your ass outta the joint. Funny how brains kick in too late, isn't it?"

"Oh, you're such a big man! You did a shit job nobody decent wanted to do."

It's no use trying to talk to her; Satan owns her soul. "So what's the kid's name?"

"Troy Whitehill."

"Fancy."

She laughs. "Some made up shit. Supposed to help him get along better in school. Can't have them bullies tauntin' him about his jailbird mama."

"How old?"

"Seven."

"Where's he living now?"

"An aunt's house, over in Clinton, off of sixty-five."

"Not too far from here, that's good. And the Jesus parents?'

"Goddammit, I wish you'd stop callin' 'em that!"

She's never going to understand. "Just tell me where to take him."

"This one don't care as long as he's far from her family."

"Why? They beat him or something?"

"Since when did you start carin'?"

CHAPTER FORTY-TWO

Herder's almost bigger than me now. Can't lose control. But what to do with him?

Have to pray on it.

I hear them in the other room—the three of 'em. It's good the two little ones being so close in age, makes them seem like brothers. Just what the new folks wanted. Sometimes everything works out as if…ordained by our Holy Father.

My arm still hurts from the knife, but it was the only way.

Herder stays to tend the young ones but from time to time sneaks off. He thinks I don't know. But I have him convinced that something awful will happen to the children if he doesn't come back. And he believes me. Good thing he does.

The ringing starts, a tone deep inside, warning me to pay attention and listen. It's God telling me what to do.

"Come eat!"

They chew, except for Jimmy. Can't get paid for no psycho kid. What's that they say about getting more flies with honey?

"Come on now. I got corn dogs and soda. There's chips—regular and barbeque. Cookies for desert. Just like going to the country fair." I smile down at the boy.

When the other two reach for the food, I stop them. "Now you know we say grace first. Especially you, Herder. You know how things are done around here."

I gently touch Jimmy's head, push it toward the table. He's like one of those mannequins in a store window. Lets me move him with no resistance.

"Thank you, oh Lord, for what we are about to receive. Always let us remember that there are hungry children around the world who have nothing to eat. And children who have no roof over their head or clothes on their body. Keep us safe here together, away from Satan's emissaries, away from those who would destroy us. In Jesus' name, we pray. Amen."

Jimmy looks up. He's got to be hungry. I hand him a corndog.

"Don't be sad, now boys. Tomorrow we're all going on an adventure."

"Back to my Mommy?" the other one asks.

"Yessir. I'm taking you both to your mommy and daddy."

"This place smells bad," Jimmy says. "Like cabbage. I hate cabbage."

"Well, after tomorrow you'll be home."

He smiles, bits of food between his baby teeth.

Herder glares at me. Soon I'll be rid of him.

PART FOURTEEN

VINCE

CHAPTER FORTY-THREE

"An executor takes legal responsibility of a deceased person's financial obligations. Like disposing of property, paying bills and taxes. If you're not up to all this, nobody would blame you, Vince. It's a hell of a lot to expect from someone who's not even a family member."

"I can't let Baylor down."

"Well," Medora says, "you can resign at any time, remember that. If you've had enough, you can always quit."

"What happens then?"

"The court will appoint a replacement."

"But the only family he has is Stevie."

"It could be an official at the bank—just until all his legal affairs are taken care of." She takes off her readers and chews on the end of an earpiece. "Do you have any idea of what his estate involves?"

"Not much; I checked with the bank. There's a small savings account—a couple thousand. His checking account had a little more. Of course there's the house and everything in it and his car—a ten year old Ford. That's about it."

The sun highlights deep wrinkles around her eyes that weren't there when this all began. But then, we were all different people before Stevie went missing.

"Simple enough. I would suggest you hire an auction company. My secretary can give you the names of a few we've used. They'll come in and take inventory, set a price for each item. They even put notices in local papers, online ads, whatever they can do to advertise the event. You might be able to include the vehicle in that sale. Of course, older things that aren't in such good condition, you'll have to haul over to Goodwill or toss out. After that's done, find a local realtor and list the house. Put all the money into an account. As executor, you're entitled to payment for all your time. So keep records, kind of like a timesheet."

"I couldn't take money—"

"Hey, stop being a martyr. You're spending your own money now, right? Spending it ever since you've been going back and forth, the way you do, between Chicago and Kimswick. Gas? Food? Motels? Not to mention countless hours and days. It all adds up." She's getting irritated. "I'm your lawyer...and friend. I know for a fact that you and Kathy are not what I'd call 'well-off.'"

"I don't have to decide anything now, do I?" Should I tell her Stevie's alive? "It's okay if I stay in the house for a while, right?"

"Sure. But why would you want to do that?"

"What if Stevie comes back? He could be out there—you hear stories all the time."

She shakes her head slowly then rises and comes around to sit on the edge of her desk to face me, get up close and more personal. "Vince, we both know that after all this time, odds are Stevie will never come home. Statistics show that if a kidnap victim isn't found within the first twenty-four hours, chances of...recovery...are slim." She reaches down to hold my hands. "Please let this go. God knows, you never deserved to lose Gabby the way you did. You and Kathy have suffered for years. Can't you see you're just making life so much more difficult by getting involved with another child like this? I'm sorry for you both...so very sorry. Please, go home, relax and maybe get back into therapy."

I look into those gray eyes of hers and know she'll never understand.

So what Daddy? We know Stevie's alive. Me and you and Mommy. We'll find him.

It's fall again. The leaves are turning. Year after year, same thing over and over, season after season, sun goes up, sun goes down. Every time I see some sweet old lady hugging her grandchildren, going on and on about how life hurries by, I want to hit something. Life crawls forward. Every second feels like an hour when all I can do is wait. How much more can I take? Then I remember.

Gabby would be twelve today.

"Happy birthday, baby."

I'm not a baby.

Kathy's having a bad day. She always does this time of year. I tried a few times sending flowers to cheer her up but that made things worse. She said they reminded her of a funeral. And it isn't as if we're celebrating anything…any more. So I stopped. Now we don't mention the date, just deal with things in our own way. But I've noticed the last few years, after the day has passed, we're able to ease back into a routine more easily.

Pulling into Baylor's driveway, I'm still surprised that it doesn't feel more like home here. Some of the neighbors recognize me and wave. But in these parts people are friendlier and wave at everyone whether they know them or not. I wave back. The pace is slower and I'm thinking that when this is over we should move to a smaller town. We need more calm.

As I put the key in the lock, I hear a phone ringing. I set Baylor's land line to sound a dozen times. That way I can get to it in plenty of time—less chance of missing a call.

"Hello?"

"Vince?"

"Yes, who's this?"

"Laura Bonetti. In St. Louis?"

"Guess it'll take a few more calls before I recognize your voice—"

"I think I got something! Of course it might be nothing. I tried calling Kathy but she doesn't answer so I sent an email and I'm still waiting for her to—"

"Slow down. Give me a minute here."

She's out of breath. "There's been a sighting. I'm pretty sure it was Stevie."

I pull a chair over and fall onto it. "Start at the beginning."

"Do you remember almost four years ago, a baby was stolen from his own home? His name was Elliott Tyler; he lived near Davenport?"

"To be honest, Laura, there's way too many missing kids to keep track of." I feel embarrassed.

"Well, when the police searched the house there were no prints or any sign of a break-in. But there was this babysitter, Debby Wallace. The police interviewed her for hours. Wouldn't let her call her folks.

I don't think she even knew she had any rights; she was only fifteen. Inside her purse they found a thousand dollars wrapped up with a rubber band. She wouldn't tell them where it came from."

"You think she sold the baby?"

"Yep. And the police did, too. But Debby kept to her story about how some man came to the door and shoved his way inside. He had a gun, but she couldn't give a description of it or of him. He grabbed the baby and told her he'd blow her head off if she screamed."

"And he didn't tie her up or hurt her? Didn't do anything to keep her from running to the cops?" I ask.

"Nope. She never even called 911 or anyone, after he left."

"So where does Stevie figure in all this?"

"The cops ran the bills and rubber band for prints. Couldn't get anything. But they lied to Debby, told her they knew she had gotten paid to hand Elliott over. Her story started to fall apart then. She admitted taking the money, but maintained she didn't know who the man was who came for the baby."

"You think that man was Stevie? You think Stevie Kracher kidnapped a baby—?

"No, no, Vince. That's not what I'm saying."

"Okay, go on." How much longer until she gets to the point? I'm going crazy here.

"So they search for Elliot for weeks, there's an investigation then a trial and Debby Wallace ends up in jail. They offer her a deal if she'll tell them where the body is or lead them to someone who knows. But—nothing."

"What about Elliott's parents? Police always start close to home when there's a crime."

"Guess you'd know that better than anyone, huh?" She pauses. Is she really expecting me to answer?

When I don't say anything she continues. "They weren't Elliott's natural parents, but kinda foster parents I guess you'd call them. The father's niece had been arrested and while she was serving time, the court gave custody of Elliott to her uncle and his wife. I remember seeing an interview with them the night he was kidnapped. They looked so …wounded. They had been trying to have a child of their own for years. Then out of the blue they got this little boy. One minute they must have been so happy and then suddenly they were on all the news shows, begging for some information."

Come on, Daddy. Don't get all upset. Stop remembering.

"It's rough."

"But then last week, Debby Wallace starts remembering. A few years in jail always seems to scare the truth out of most people. Strange how memories pop up when all the hype has died down. I see it over and over. While the police are asking and stirring up crap, it's normal to get defensive. Then comes sympathy and attention from family, even strangers that get to you on twitter or Facebook. A suspect can easily convince themselves they're innocent, especially when lawyers work up some crazy defense. But when everyone has gone home, Nancy Grace or Gloria Allred has moved on to the next sensational story, they're all alone. In a cell. No one cares what happens next. It's just them and a whole lot of time to think."

"So what did she say, Laura?"

"She said there was a kid. A boy about Stevie's age. He was sitting in the car when the man drove up. And he was in the backseat when the guy, who she still can't identify, drove away."

"Are you sure? How can she be sure of something like that?"

"Hey, it's all we have right now." Laura sounds tired, finally out of breath.

"Let me get this straight. She claims she didn't know the man with the gun. She says she didn't kidnap the baby herself. So she was paid to shut up and just hand the baby over?" "I guess, Vince. But you're missing the point. There's a strong possibility that Stevie was there and helping—"

"Or being forced to help—"

"Right. So if we can track down this man, we might find Stevie. We're getting closer. I can feel it."

"And did they ever find the baby?" I ask. "Laura, does anyone know what happened to Elliot?"

"Sorry, Vince….no. He's never been found."

CHAPTER FORTY-FOUR

"Vince, where the hell have you been? I've been trying to reach you for hours!"

"Talking to Laura—but my cell should have rung." I pull it out of my pocket to see the battery's dead. "Are you okay, hon? I know how you get—"

"I'm good, really good!" Her excitement makes me feel…happy… in a lonely, disconnected way. Like she's just won a game that I don't get to play.

"So what's happened?"

"I'll tell you my news first and then you tell me what Laura said. She's been trying to reach me all morning. Gee, I hope she doesn't think I'm avoiding her, but it was hard getting out of bed…today being…you know. And I certainly didn't feel up to looking at all my emails. But after a while I felt guilty and forced myself to take a shower. Then I had some breakfast and about a dozen cups of coffee and finally sat down at the computer. Our website is buzzing, Vince. Everyone's chatting about this story—"

"Is there news about Stevie?" I ask.

"Yep. Right after Baylor died there was this man, a retired doctor, who called the local police with a complaint. He lives in this small town in Illinois, south of St. Louis. Chester! Yeah, that's it."

"A complaint about what?" I try prodding her along.

"Well, there was a strange car parked a few houses down from his. It was dark and raining so he couldn't make out who was inside. He said it was there for a few hours when all of a sudden a man and a kid holding a toddler jump out. The little one ends up in the grass and the two others get into some sort of argument. Next thing he knows, they're wrestling around on the ground. The little boy's screaming. That's when the doctor sticks his head out, yells at them to go away or he'll call the cops."

She pauses and I wait. But the anticipation is getting to me. "And? What next?"

"The three of them got back into the car. For a while. Then the boy comes out again, carrying the little one. The doctor said it looked like the man was crazy. Shouting, waving his arms, then the kid takes off running, and the man starts chasing them with his car."

"You think that kid was Stevie?" I'm standing now, pacing.

"Not at first, Vince. But then Mr. Hodges, that's the doctor's name, found our website."

"Sorry, you lost me. How would he connect that incident with a missing child? For all he knew, they could have been a father and his sons."

"You're right. But while the man was chasing the kids, Mr. Hodges thought he saw a knife. That's when he called the police."

"Reporting that they were disturbing the peace, I suppose?"

"I love it when you're smart. Which you are all the time. I didn't mean...you know what I mean."

"I know, Kathy."

She hurries on with her story. It's good hearing her so excited, spilling over with news. "By the time the police arrived, the car, along with everyone inside, was gone. A report was filed and naturally got buried under all the usual crap."

"And I bet Mr. Hodges never heard from the police again, which probably got him a little angry."

"More than a little angry; he was pissed off big time that no one understood it was much more than a domestic dispute. He said he couldn't stop thinking about the little boy. He told me—"

"Wait. You talked to him?"

"Oh," she sounded coy, "didn't I tell you that I just got off the phone with him?"

I try not to sound irritated...but I am. "When are you gonna learn to start at the beginning? You always tell a story from the middle and work back and forth to the ends."

She ignores my criticism. "As I was saying...Mr. Hodges couldn't stop thinking about the boy and started to investigate missing children. That's how he found us. After he looked at the pictures and read some stories, he said the pieces started falling into place. It came in a flash when he saw Stevie's picture. Vince, he swears the kid that night, the one holding the boy was Stevie."

I'm stunned. "Wow."

When Kathy speaks again, I can almost hear her smile. "And I assume that Laura was calling about Elliott Tyler? It's all my people have been talking about since last night. They think it could crack open some other cases." She sighs. "Wouldn't that be great, Vince? To get Stevie back? Finally?"

God, help me feel some relief. Just for a few minutes.

But I don't.

My stomach clenches, head pounds and I sit down. "What kind of shape do you think he's in by now, Kath?"

"I can't think about that. Today we have good news and I'm going to enjoy myself."

I don't want to bring it up, not then, at that very moment, but the words come out of my mouth without warning. "And on Gabby's birthday…" Damn, why did I have to spoil the joy?

But Kathy surprises me. "I thought about that, too. Maybe it'll help us get through next year easier. You know, thinking something changed in the universe on this date? Some positive energy got flushed through our hearts."

"I love you."

"Love you, too," she says hurriedly.

We say goodbye after a few more minutes. It's Laura, Kathy really wants to talk to—compare notes. I have nothing to contribute today.

After years of false leads, endless hours spent hoping and waiting, agonizing, looking, afraid to find out the truth—desperate to know the truth. Could it all be over? Could we really bring Stevie back home?

But then it hits me.

What will he actually be coming home to? His father's gone. His friends have moved on, no one his age will ever be able to relate to this boy who has been through so much. He'll be pointed at, analyzed, interviewed and every year, on the anniversary of his homecoming, he'll be written about and interviewed probably until he's dead. What's he supposed to do with his life now? What kind of person has he become?

I feel useless. Things are happening without me. I feel lost. Again.

Are we going home, Daddy?

"I'm not sure where to go."

Should I clean out the house? Would Stevie want to live here alone? He can't live alone, he's only eighteen.

Restless and uncertain, I stand at the front window and watch leaves falling, like golden potato chips—crunching when they hit the ground. What should I be doing now?

This is a familiar road, one I've been down so often I know where all the potholes are. I try matching Kathy's level of enthusiasm when she's located a missing child. I try so much my back aches, like I'm on a rack. Is that where racked with pain comes from? And when she's depressed that another lead goes nowhere, I commiserate.

Remember what Grammy used to say about the devil's workshop?

"An idle mind is the devil's workshop." I smile, remembering.

She wouldn't like you being lazy, Daddy.

"Grammy also said that a man can't work on an empty stomach."

Eleven o'clock, always an iffy time for breakfast. Luckily Myrtles makes it all day.

"Hey, Mister Lloyd. How long you in town for this time?"

Regretfully, I'm somewhat of a regular now. "Not sure, Gloria."

She shrugs. "So what'll it be? Spectacular apple pie just outta the oven. The kind with the crumbly top? I can put a big scoop of ice cream…"

Most everyone in town has had breakfast and a coffee break by now, at this hour they're thinking about lunch. "Maybe later. Right now I need some eggs—three—bacon, toast, hash browns, coffee and orange juice."

"How do you want your eggs cooked?"

"Sunny-side up." And before she can ask I add, "White toast."

"You got it."

She smiles and when she turns to leave I notice a tattoo along the back of her leg. Some sort of writing, snaking its way down into her sox. Making a statement, I guess. It's always puzzled me why people so eagerly put their thoughts or personal philosophies out there for everyone to see. Why would they think anyone cares? Bumper stickers, t-shirts, those little stick people in rear car windows depicting the family inside—Look, we have one dad, a mom, three girls, one boy and a dog. Everyone shouting: MY KID'S AN HONOR STUDENT. HONK IF YOU LOVE JESUS. MY OTHER CAR'S A MERCEDES.

A man whose name I've never known, waves. I nod. My stomach growls and I'm happy, actually happy, when the food comes. As I eat, my spirits seem to lift a little more. By the time I finish my second cup of coffee, I feel content.

Gloria's pulling double duty today and stands at the register, ready to take my money. "How's it going, Mr. Lloyd? I mean…really. How are you?"

"Okay, I guess. Why?" I ask, shoving change in my pocket. Then I notice the fifteen year old face of Stevie Kracher smiling at me from a faded HAVE YOU SEEN ME? poster behind the register.

"I don't mean to pry, but you can't keep a secret here in town. Especially since you been coming here for years and all. I know it's none of my business, but it's just that I'm a true crime junkie. It's all I watch. Morning, noon and late night. My husband says I need a hobby and I tell him, babe, I already got one—murder and mayhem."

She's like a train barreling on through and all I can do is nod and watch.

"Anyway, I saw the program on Stevie, of course, it being local and all. Then I found your wife's website and read about the good work she does. Tell her we're all real proud of her. Will you do that? All of us here at Myrtles are proud to know her. Well, we don't know her, really but kinda…through you."

"I will."

"And I know Stevie's gonna be home real soon." She nods, thoughtfully. "Real soon."

She's a sweet kid. "Do you mind if I ask about that tattoo on your leg?"

Her face goes red. "What a dumb mistake that was. But then there are no smart mistakes, right?" Three men sit at a corner table, laughing and drinking coffee. When she's sure no one can hear us or even cares, she says, "I had this boyfriend, Travis Peterman…"

It's obvious she's getting upset. "I didn't mean to—"

"No, no, it's okay. I need to talk about it so I have closure. Dr. Phil talks about closure all the time. It's the only way to move on, you know. Otherwise, you're just one big, oozing sore. Walking around, trying to be normal, but all the time festering."

I nod.

"So Travis ends up in jail and I, being the idiot I was, pledged undying love and promised to wait forever. Even though he was only sentenced to a year. But when you're sixteen, a year is forever. Right?" She slaps the top of her head. "What an idiot I was."

"You were in love. And young." I offer her a choice of excuses.

"All of the above. Then add in a big hunk of stupid for good measure."

"We've all been there."

"So while Travis is in jail, I get this tattoo. A few lines from a letter he wrote me, probably stolen from a book. But I thought it was beautiful. Fast forward a year and I find out he's writing to four other girls while in the joint. I was gone real fast but the ink stayed. Now I have this great husband. We've been married almost two years, and even though I try to keep the damn thing covered, there are times when he sees it and a fight starts up. So, when I get next year's tax refund, I'm having it removed. I hear it's real painful but I don't care."

I reach in my pocket and pull out a twenty. "Here, put this in your removal fund."

"Thanks, Mr. Lloyd, I will. And you work on that closure, now."

I inhale the warm smell of cinnamon and nutmeg before I step back outside.

CHAPTER FORTY-FIVE

Chief Stoffel sits on the front step of Baylor's house. The wind has picked up; the temperature dropped at least ten degrees since I got up this morning. A storm's coming and I wonder why he hasn't waited for me in his car instead of out in the cold. He explains it seems more "friendly" this way.

I open the door. "So does this mean you're not here on business?" I ask.

"You know this whole thing has been hard on all of us in town, Mr. Lloyd," he begins. "We grew up with Baylor. I was at his wedding, drove him and Tammy to the hospital when Stevie was born. Many an afternoon we sat together at little league games and shared so many holiday dinners I've lost count." He looks uncomfortable with himself. "Then you come along."

I gesture toward a chair, tossing my jacket across the back of the couch. He sits stiffly, zipping his windbreaker up so tight I think he'll cut his neck.

"I just came to help. That's all…really," I assure him. "It was never –ever—my intention to step on any toes."

"I know that now."

Does he want me to apologize for being here?

His hands move to his chin to support his head. Then he starts rocking slowly. I watch him, uncomfortable with the silence. He wants to tell me something. My heart races. Have they found Stevie? Is he alive? No, if he was, Stoffel would be more animated. Oh no, please no, Stevie can't be…

Do something mundane, I won't buy into the panic. "Can I get you something?"

Then he jerks upright, as if struck by lightning. "No thanks.

I've been rehearsin' what I want to say ever since Baylor died. Been watching you come and go, out of this house, like you lived here your whole life. Everyone in town has. And there's talk." He rolls his eyes. "There's always talk in a small town like this."

"I'm well aware of that."

"And through all of it, for months an' years, you've been here. Better than any of us. A stranger who probably didn't even know this town existed until he heard about Stevie on the news. A guy who's been through hell himself, you kept on comin'."

"Like I told you, Chief Stoffel, I wanted—"

"Please, Mr. Lloyd, let me finish what I came to say."

"Okay."

"Kids go missin' all the time. And men die from heart attacks. No big news there. We all talked about how sad everything was for old Baylor and then went about our merry way. But you...and Mrs. Lloyd...don't take offense at this but you're like two old dogs, holding onto a bone, never lettin' go.

"So I want to say thanks, is all. I know I haven't been that friendly in the past, but if there's anything you need, I hope you'll let me know."

Now. It's the perfect time to tell him Stevie's alive. But I can't.

He stands to leave. "So there it is. That's all I came to say." He holds out his hand. "I hope you'll accept my apology if I've been unkind."

Our fingers lock in a strong grip.

"Of course."

The phone shrieks from the kitchen.

After four rings he asks, "Aren't you gonna get that?"

What if it's Stevie? Certainly Baylor didn't mean it to go this far, when he made me promise not to tell anyone about his son. But still... I stand frozen with indecision.

"Sure I am." I can't move. My brain screams for every part of me to RUN, ANSWER THE PHONE. But my body resists.

He knows I'm hiding something.

"Okay then," he says. "I got work to do."

I run for the kitchen after a hasty goodbye and grab the receiver.

"Mr. Lloyd? It's Benny Hodges. I spoke to your wife earlier today?"

"Sure, Mr. Hodges, Kathy told me." Hope I don't sound too disappointed.

"I'm driving up to Kimmswick this afternoon. That's where you're at, right?"

"Yes, but—"

"Your wife told me about you not wanting to leave Stevie's house—perfectly understandable. I'm retired, plenty of time on my hands. And I've got something you might be interested in. To hell with the cops. To them I'm just some old crank. I'm through wasting my time on those idiots. I've been following your story since your own daughter went missing. You're good people—you and Kathy. Now you sit tight and I'll be there in a few hours. Got my GPS all hooked up; no need for more chatter about directions; see you soon."

"Okay," I manage to say before he hangs up.

Benny Hodges is what they used to call, a "dandy." Starting with his black, cashmere sports jacket, covering a monogrammed shirt, down along his creased trousers and ending at leather, tasseled loafers, he looks more like an actor hired to play a doctor than an actual one. His smile displays perfect, white teeth; his blue-gray eyes are alert and clear.

"Vince, I'm Benjamin Hodges." He grabs my hand and shakes it vigorously. "Call me Benny."

I like him immediately. No bullshit here. Benny is the real deal.

"Come in."

He stands straight and walks quickly, then settles himself on a far end of the couch.

I sit on the other end, turning to face him. "I can't tell you how much I appreciate you coming here. But you'll have to excuse me; so much has happened today and I'm still sorting through it all..."

"Can we sit at a table?" he asks. "It's better that way, facing each other. Better to get down to business." This guy doesn't waste any time.

"Is the kitchen okay?"

"Great." He runs his hands across the top of his short white hair, smoothing down a few strays. Then a pat, making sure every strand is in its place.

After he's seated I ask, "Care for something to drink?"

"Scotch? Or bourbon would be fine."

There's a bottle, if I remember right, back in a bottom cabinet.

"Black Grouse. Is that good?" I hold it out to him.

"Great. If I have one small one now, I should be good to drive in a few hours."

I pour one for both of us. Before I can put the glasses on the table, he starts.

"I don't mean to be intrusive but it's all in the timing here. Everything in life is, actually. I've seen it too many times. Someone drops the ball and bad things happen. Disease can develop from a group of complex cells or something as simple as a cut that goes untended. And then there's this 'old' thing. You have a ways to go until you get patted on the head and told to go away—let the kids take over. People of 'a certain age' are now to be humored—laughed at." He takes his first swallow of the scotch.

I smile. "Old geezers always welcome here, Benny."

He calms down. "Sorry. You've had a rough time of it for too long and here I go carrying on about my trivial problems. Hell—that's what you've been through—literally. I've always thought you got a raw deal." He reaches out and pats my hand.

The gesture makes a comforting image. But his warmth and caring are foreign to me. My own father was a bully, a regular tyrant. Sure would have been nice to have a man like Benny around back then.

"You don't have to do this alone, son," he says. "Least ways, not anymore."

And without realizing it, those words seem to be the ones I've needed to hear my whole life. My shoulders go slack, I blink quicker, trying to banish tears welling up.

So aware of what's happening, he sits and waits. No cheap reassuring words, no slap on the shoulder. He knows it's enough to just be there. "Take your time, Vince. I got all day."

Words come out in small spurts at first, going back to my drinking. Moving to the day I came to Kimmswick, until the current of my story builds into a tidal wave. His eyes stay locked on mine the whole time. And the more intently he listens, the more I want to tell him. Even through parts he's already familiar with, chunks covered in newspapers, magazines and television interviews, he's patient. Funny, I'm thinking of Gloria as I talk. She's right about closure.

I finally catch my breath. "After Kathy told me about your

conversation, instead of being excited, all I could think about was what kind of life the poor kid will have if we ever get him back..."

"And then I burst in on you like this," Benny says. "What a day you've had! What a day." He swirls the remainder of his drink around in the glass, holding it between his manicured fingers.

"Seen more action this morning than in the last few years," I say.

"So your wife told you about me calling the police, the knife, the boy...all of it. But there's something else. Oh, I know it's not the PC thing to do, but I relate more to you, the father of a girl. I have a daughter—remarkable kid. She's into design. Our only child. And now that my wife's gone, she's more precious to me than ever."

I really, really like Benny, Daddy. He's nice.

"How long has your wife been...?"

"Passed away the year after I retired. Kept putting it off. One more year, one more year. As if a few lousy months would make our savings so much better. Money...money is an evil thing. All our plans to travel, all the places we were going to see. She was healthy and so beautiful. We managed to get to Europe for a week and... that was it."

"I'm so sorry."

"I miss her every day. But I have little conversations with her, in my head. It helps."

"I talk to Gabby, sometimes."

"Feels good, doesn't it?" His eyes glisten. "I knew we'd connect. That's why I had to come here to kick your ass."

CHAPTER FORTY-SIX

"Oh, not physically." Benny holds up his hands and cackles. "You should see your face."

I'm not sure how to react. "Had me worried for a minute."

"Well don't be. There's something you should see. I called the police, the local hotline, anyone I could think of—never heard back from any of them. Red tape is chocking up the system, I tell you. Unanswered emails, unreturned phone calls and erased voice mails." He shakes his head. "Technology gives us more ways to ignore people every day. Then throw in a handful of denial and you got yourself a nice big sinkhole. I saw it every day at the hospital. No one wants to hear bad news or believe bad things can happen in their little town. And, it's that 'old' thing again. To my neighbors I'm the cranky old man in the neighborhood. Boohoo, I won't let their kids skateboard up and down my driveway. But when Billy or Tommy breaks his leg, who do they come to for help?"

"And here I was picturing you as the kindly, small town doctor everyone loves."

"Bull! Remember me for my work, that's what I say, not my manners."

I really like this guy. "So what do I need to see?"

He reaches into his breast pocket, pulls out a plastic sandwich bag and tosses it down on the kitchen table. There's a white plastic card of some sort inside, but I don't pick it up.

"After realizing I was being ignored, I decided to investigate on my own. Since retiring, and especially after Irene passed, I needed something to distract myself and bought a metal detector. So I went across the street to where I saw the scuffle and tried to detect. Oh, I've found lots of stuff with that thing. Pop tops from beer and soda cans, a ring once, mostly junk. But I figured it was worth a try."

I pick up the bag. "Looks like some sort of work badge."

"Take it out," he says. "It was raining that night and this must have gotten mashed into the mud. The metal clip on top is what set the detector beeping."

"What makes you think it has anything to do with that night? It could have been there for a while."

"True. And after coming up with part of a retainer, a pen and one earring, I gave up and went home. But the next day I tried a different area and found this."

I rub at the rough edge, where the bottom part has broken off, and bring the card closer.

"Did you know Steven Karcher's mother—Baylor's wife—is in prison?" he asks.

"Yes, he told me." And I found some letters. Even read a few but felt ashamed afterwards. Too personal. Tammy was vicious and hateful. But I stopped myself from throwing them out. Should Stevie have them? No, what good could they serve? Yes, they were from his mother, maybe the only correspondence he'd see. I couldn't make a decision then and stashed them in a box.

"And do you remember the name of the place she's at?" Benny asked.

"No."

"Vandalia, Missouri Women's Correctional Center. She's there on drug charges. Been in and out for years."

Benny sits back in his chair. "Look real close at what's written across the top. Some of it's worn off but you can make out enough."

I have to squint, bring the badge closer to the light, but it's there: VAND LIA CORRE TIO A CENT R. "You said there was a man, a boy and a toddler that night. No woman, right?" I ask.

"Nope. She was definitely not there—I checked. You can Google anything—amazing. But it is strange, isn't it? More than a coincidence I'd say. Someone was with her boy, someone connected to the very prison she's lived in for years. Someone she probably knows."

Still examining the badge I say, "Maybe we should call Chief Stoffel, with the police here in town. He's a friend of the family. We should let him know—"

"I already called him," Benny says, his face suddenly somber.

"Vince, that man's convinced Stevie's dead. And with an election coming up, he's not doing anything to rock the boat. He's just a good ole boy in a situation too big for him to handle."

"He said that? Those exact words?" My heart races. "He told you that Stevie's dead?"

"Not in those words, no. But I do have connections in local government throughout Missouri and Illinois, even ran for mayor once. At least those folks return my calls. And after a lot of checking, it was agreed that your Chief of police has done nothing to help find Stevie. Nothing. Oh, when the cameras start rolling, he puts on a good show. But that's all it is—a show."

"Then why would he come here today?" I wonder out loud.

"He's a small fish, Vince. That story about Elliott Tyler is stirring things up. Stoffel's on the hot seat. National attention is going to be focused on this little town again. People are interested…again. Mr. Chief of Police is covering his ass, hoping you won't throw him to the wolves."

I believe Benny and I've only known him a few hours.

"If that was Stevie you saw, and I'm sure it was, he's probably long gone by now."

He catches my tone. "You know something more, don't you? What is it?"

It's now or never. "Stevie came to visit his father a few times. He's alive. I heard his voice on the phone myself."

"I knew it!" Benny slaps the table. "By God, I knew it." He smiles, so satisfied with himself. Then his smile wilts. "You know what happens next, don't you?"

"Truth is, I don't. I've been stumbling around for years. Confused, angry—"

"No more time for a pity party, young man."

I nod. "You're right."

"No more excuses, Vince. If you can't figure out what comes next maybe I'll have to kick-start your ass into action."

Suddenly he stands up; his chair skids loudly across the linoleum. He comes around behind me and shakes my shoulders. "Vince, you're going to Vandalia tomorrow. I'll stay here to man the phone. If anyone asks, I'll say I'm your…"

"Father. It's okay if you say you're my father."

Baylor had been so wounded. Sick and afraid toward the end. Kathy carries the hurt with her. She thinks I'm oblivious, I guess, but it lives in her eyes; I see it blinking back at me every day. No matter if she's happy or just watching TV...I see it. And I wonder, what does she see when she looks at me?

She can think I'm weak but please, I pray to any God that will listen, don't let her think I'm afraid.

Sadness has tarnished every corner of my house for so long that I take it for granted. I've forgotten how life used to shine. But meeting someone like Benny helps me remember.

I came to this place, picked up a stick and beat the bushes, hoping to find something...someone. That was as far as I'd planned. Offered up my sweat and anger. When that didn't work, I struggled, hoping for the best. And where had it all gotten me?

Too many years have evaporated. Too many good people gone and too many bad people still hanging on. I'm ashamed of all the time wasted, tangled up in self pity.

Benny's right...no more excuses.

CHAPTER FORTY-SEVEN

"Empty your pockets," Benny says after we've had our coffee.
"What?"

He digs down into his pants pocket and pulls out a handful of coins. "Get a plastic bag." Then he begins sorting through the money, picking out dimes and quarters. "They allow you to take coins for the vending machines. A present for Tammy, to soften her up." He grins, then shrugs. "Hey, it can't hurt."

I put our cups in the sink and get a bag. After cleaning out my jeans, I come up with five dollars and fifty cents. Together we end up with ten dollars and twenty-five cents. A pitiful gift. But I guess it's better than showing up empty-handed.

"It's about a two hour drive," Benny says, "which will leave you plenty of time to talk before visiting hours are over. I've called ahead, there's a doctor I know; he'll get you on the list. Any questions?"

"Gee, Benny, you make me feel like a kid on his first day of school," I say sarcastically. "I got this. Talked to Kathy last night, told her you'd be here for a few days—"

"At the most."

"She'll probably check up on you today."

"I like having a woman look after me. It's…comforting." He hesitates a second, probably thinking about his wife. Then he's back. "I got your cell number and you have mine. We're all set."

The metal detector doesn't surprise me. Been through them hundred of times—mostly in airports, stadium events, some schools, even a casino here and there. But when the guard hands me a towelette, I'm stumped.

"Ion Scan Search, sir" he says. "Wipe it over the front of your

"I certainly don't need any proof of your strength, Mrs. Kracher."

"So what do you want from me?" she asks defensively.

"I thought maybe you'd be curious…just a little…about your boy. You must have seen the news lately. Stories about Elliott Tyler? And his babysitter, Debby Wallace? Stevie may still be alive. As his mother, it seems only natural—"

"You don't know me!" she suddenly screams. "You don't know one holy fuckin' thing about me or my boy neither. In fact, if I recall correctly, you never met my son in your whole damn life. Ain't that the truth Mr. Lloyd? So who the hell do you think you are waltzin' in here, all holier than thou, tellin' me how I should feel about any damn thing!"

A large black guard rushes over. "Everything okay here?"

"We're fine, Roy," she says.

I nod. "It's okay."

"I'll be here," he points to the wall nearest us, "if you need me."

We both watch him walk away.

"Now," Tammy says, "if you think I believe that horse shit you're tryin' to sell me, you're wronger than wrong, Mr. Lloyd. So I'm gonna sit here, all calm 'n' lady-like while you proceed to tell me the real reason you're showin' up here. Cause you 'n' me both know Stevie's been gone quite a while 'n' you've had plenty of time to drop in on me before now. An' believe it or not, I have things to do. Better things to do with my time than to waste it conversatin' about that stupid Debby girl. Sluttiest, dumbest con I ever known."

Debby Wallace was here? Tammy knew her? Too much of a coincidence. At that moment I'm convinced Benny's right to connect the badge with Stevie's mother. Maybe I can get her to talk more, trip herself up.

"I'm the executor of Baylor's estate. I know you two were divorced but maybe there's something you'd like me to hold aside. You know, something sentimental? Everything will get auctioned off and the house will be put up for sale."

She shakes her head violently. Her hair sticks out in a short cut, so thin I could see through it. "Got what I needed from that place long ago. An' that dumb sonofabitch, too."

It's hard not to flinch when she mentions Baylor. "Isn't there something you'd like Stevie to have? He could be found, you know.

shirt, your pockets and across your palms, please."

He glares as I follow instructions. When I'm done, he holds out his hand, carefully taking the towel, then walks to some sort of machine and puts it inside.

The procedure takes a minute or so.

"Am I allowed to ask what that was for?"

"It detects traces of narcotics or explosives on your person, sir." He sounds as if he's reciting a manual.

"Cool." I'm impressed.

He cracks a smile. "It sure is." Then he walks me to another guard who points the way.

So few things in life are exactly as we expect them to be, but walking into that visitation room is like being on a movie set. Foreign and yet so familiar. It's cheerful and sunny. Molded orange chairs are set around small tables which are bolted to the floor. A family: Convict Mom, Distressed Dad and Bored Teen huddle in a corner, talking quietly. Against one wall sits an older Convict Mom, probably her Sister, and one rambunctious girl of six or seven, who screams, runs in a circle, then screams some more.

I go as far away from the child as I can.

"She'll be here in a minute," a female guard says.

"Thanks."

It's at this moment I realize I have no idea what Tammy Kracher looks like. If she's Baylor's age she'll be in her fifties. The hard life she's had will surely have aged her even more.

"So you're a friend of Baylor's is that right? Or should I say, 'was a friend?'" The remark apparently amuses her and she smiles while pulling out a chair.

She seems to have suddenly appeared in front of me and I'm startled. Up close she looks more like a seventy year old. Her skin is dry, deep trenches run along the corners of her mouth. She licks her lips non-stop which must be the reason they're so chapped.

I reach out my hand. "I'm Vince Lloyd. I knew Baylor for years. We met when I came to help look for Stevie." Her handshake holds like a vise.

When she sees my surprise, she says, "I may be scrawny, but I'm strong. Never underestimate me, Mr. Lloyd."

There's always a chance. You hear about it happening all the time."

"I truly doubt it." Not one ounce of interest or compassion in her voice. "Been way too long for that."

I want to slap her. But instead hold out the coins. "A peace offering. For the vending machines." Maybe this will soften her up a little.

She snatches the bag like it's full of gold. Her eyes light up as she examines the contents, pushing them around with her thumbs, counting. "Got a cigarette?"

"Sorry, no."

Then she notices the badge stuck among the money.

"What's this?" I can tell she recognizes it.

"Now how'd that get in there?" I snatch the bag and fish out the plastic then toss the coins back to her. A few roll out, falling on the floor.

"This was found in the area where your son was spotted." I bluff. No need to mention that no positive identification was ever made.

She's on the floor now, scrambling around for quarters.

"Isn't that some coincidence? It being from the same prison where you and Debby Wallace have been held? Weird, huh?" I ask, fishing for more information.

"I don't know from coincidence, Mr. Lloyd. What the hell do you want me to say?"

Still no questions about Stevie. No surprise hearing that her son might be alive.

"And you don't recognize this?" I hold it out to her.

"It's all tore up. Letters rubbed off, could be from anywheres. I think you're grabbin' at straws is what I think."

"I have an appointment with the Warden," I look at my watch, "in ten minutes. But I thought I'd see you first. You know—one parent to another." Where the hell did that come from? There's no appointment. I put the badge in my pocket.

"Far as I know, you ain't no parent no more. An' I suggest you refrain from callin' or even thinkin' of my Stevie as your son. You're a do-gooder, Mr. Lloyd. Tryin' to fix other people's lives. Why don't you go back where you come from and git a life of your own?"

In a strange way, her anger entertains me.

"Guard!" she shouts, "git this asshole outta here!"

I don't look back on my way out but make a point of checking Roy's work badge. It's a bright green plastic square, slightly larger than a credit card.

"Are all ID badges green?" I ask.

"Just the ones issued this year."

"Is it possible to see the Warden?" I ask at the last minute. "I won't be long."

"Office is that way." Roy points. "You'll have to check in with his secretary."

PART FIFTEEN

STEVIE AND MISTER

CHAPTER FORTY-EIGHT

Stevie grabbed Troy and ran for a dark corner of the bedroom. With his back against the wall he slid down to the floor, holding the boy tight. The noise coming through the wall made both of them anxious but Stevie tried to calm the little one.

"I hate you!" Troy shouted and struggled. "Let me go!"

For a few seconds the commotion stopped. The boys froze.

Stevie put his hand over Troy's mouth. "Shh. When he gets like this you have to be quiet. And don't cry, no matter what. He hates that."

The child clawed at the teenager's fingers. Kicking to get free he aimed for a shin.

Stevie didn't even flinch. Mister's so busy with Jimmy, he thought, we could run for it now. Probably wouldn't even notice till we're long gone. I could call the cops; flag down a car. How far to the highway? Where would I get a phone? Ain't even sure where we are. But what kind of scum would I be runnin' off, leavin' Jimmy alone when Mister's like this?

Troy kicked again, got loose and ran for it. But before he could touch the knob, the door suddenly opened, banging against the wall. Mister stood there—one hand on the door, the other holding Jimmy upright by the hair. The boy hung, limp, his eyes closed. Stevie could see a small trail of blood on the kid's cheek.

"Can't you do anything right?" Mister screamed at Stevie and lunged at Troy, catching him by the back of his shirt. "Get the car! Now! Bring it up by the door."

He could get in the car and just drive away. He could drive real fast until a cop pulled him over and then he'd bring 'em back here. But would they think he was just some idiot kid out for a joy ride?

Mister would tell 'em somethin' like that.

Stevie grabbed the keys from a rusty nail by the front door as he ran to follow directions. He expected to hear screams, shouting—something from inside—but there was only the sound of a jet passing overhead. An old trailer had been their home for the last week. It was parked next to a house with a caved in roof and green mold smeared across the chipped white paint of one of the three existing outside walls. Hidden by a circle of trees, in the middle of a large piece of land near the river, the trailer and house were practically invisible. Especially at night.

Stevie pulled the car up and sat behind the wheel, waiting for what would happen next.

Mister came outside, dragging Jimmy. The boy's shoes left a trail in the dirt as he was pulled along, his head drooped like he was sleeping. Troy kicked and punched at his captor who yanked him along by his Superman shirt. Mister kicked at the back door on the passenger's side. Stevie reached over to open it.

"Herder! Get back here and keep the both of them quiet!"

If he slammed on the gas real hard, Mister would go flying when the door flew shut and they could drive to safety. Now, he'd have to do it now.

But the man was on him before he had time to react. "Move it, I said."

Next thing he knew, Stevie found himself on the ground.

"If you don't move your ass, I'll leave without you."

Did that jerk think this was a threat? He'd be free. He'd get help. But then he looked up and there was Troy, his face wet with tears and snot, banging against the glass. "No!" he screamed. "Stevie, don't leave me!"

Stevie stood up, slapped the dirt off the back of his pants and got in the car. Troy's little arms clamped around the big boy's neck. His body trembling as he kissed Stevie's cheek. "I'm sorry. We'll be friends, okay? You won't leave, promise? Say you promise. Say it, Stevie."

"Promise." Stevie said, trying to smile.

Jimmy was stretched out next to them. His eyes glassy, staring at the torn fabric above him. Stevie shook the boy's foot. "Hey, you okay?"

No response.

"Jimmy, are you—"

"Shut up back there. And leave the kid alone. He's being punished. He's got to learn how to behave. How to honor thy mother and father. Nobody's going to want such a disobedient child."

Mister steered south. He was doing God's work. Dedicated his life to the Jubilation for years. But now he was lost. For the first time he was without divine guidance. He'd have to pray on it.

"Dear Lord," he started, quietly to himself, "help me." Before he could continue, the ringing started. Not in the head this time, but from his phone.

Mister checked the readout: ROY.

"Got a name for ya, man. A woman in Flat River. One of them career types. You seen 'em. All the time too damn busy for anything but business. Business, more important than anything. All the time writing reports, going to meetin's. Then one day, 'Oh Lord, I'm so lonely.' But it's too late. Now she's all freaked out about that biology clock."

"So what do you want me to do about it?"

"Tammy says you got a seven year old. An' career lady ain't picky. She'll take what she can get, know what I'm sayin? It'll be just her and the boy. No husband in the house. No one to ask questions. And a regular adoption—all the waitin', an' paperwork. Lady in a big hurry. Know what I mean?"

Hallelujah. The Lord truly does work in mysterious ways his wonder to behold. "Give me her address."

Sometimes it was about the money. Damn, he hated it when Tammy was right.

But most of the time it was about herding the little sheep. Keeping them safe from those who would steal their souls. That was the Godly work. Making things right with the world.

Troy whimpered. "I peed my pants."

"Don't worry," Stevie said.

"Clean that kid up!" Mister shouted from the front seat. "There's a box of diapers in the trunk." He pulled over on the shoulder of the deserted road. "Clean him up. See if there's some new clothes, too. Tonight there's going to be a Jubilation. Praise the Lord."

CHAPTER FORTY-NINE

Oh God, no. Please no…no…Jimmy can't be dead.

Stevie had never seen dead up close, never touched it with his own hands, hadn't even been to a funeral. Not one single relative or friend had died in his whole entire life. But he was pretty sure poor Jimmy was gone. Why didn't Mister take him away for his Jubilation like he done with Luke an' the others?

"Everything okay back there?" Mister asked as he steered onto the road.

What should he say? What would Mister do? "Yeah," was all Stevie could manage.

"Good. Because this is a happy time. A celebration. Today our little brother, Troy, has his Jubilation. Are you happy, little boy? Today you get yourself a God parent, a loving new Mama. What do you have to say to that?"

Troy shook his head violently all the while holding his cheeks. "I already have a Mommy."

Stevie patted the boy on the back. Then he bent down and whispered in his ear, "Pretend to be happy or you'll get the same as Jimmy got."

Troy looked over at the boy lying so still on the seat next to him. He reached out to stroke Jimmy's hair. Seeing the dried blood made him scared. His parents had warned him about bad people. And Mister was for sure the baddest. "But…I could get used to a new Mommy…I guess."

"Atta boy. You just wait and see. Everything's going to be wonderful. A beautiful life for a beautiful boy. God has a plan for us all."

"How much longer till we get there?" Stevie asked.

"Why are you so interested all of a sudden?"

"It's just that we ain't eaten today. We're all pretty hungry."

"How about you, Jimmy?" Mister asked, looking in the rear view mirror to check the backseat. "You feel like eating?"

Think, think, make a plan, Stevie told himself. "He says he's hungry, too." Why did he lie? Think of something…

"Guess we all could use some breakfast. The first place that looks good, we'll stop. Will that make everyone happy?" Mister asked.

Stevie signaled Troy to join in as he answered, excitedly.

They had driven about fifteen minutes when a weathered billboard announced:

FATTY'S DINER.
OPEN 24 HOURS.
TEN MILES AHEAD.

Have to make a plan. Think…

It wasn't just himself Stevie worried about. He couldn't grab Troy and leave Jimmy in the car with Mister. What if he was wrong and the little kid was still alive? He wasn't a doctor. And he couldn't leave both boys and save himself. How could he live the rest of his life bein' a coward like that? Mister always brought food home to them. But when they were out in the car, they hit a drive-through. No one ever left the vehicle. So why was this time different?

Think…

FATTY'S DINER.
BEST BURGER IN TOWN.
FIVE MILES AHEAD.

Mister must be slipping. First taking them all out like this— actin' like they was a real family. And then the knife. He'd left that big ole blade of his sitting out in plain sight—right on top of the diaper box. It'd been easy to slide it in his jacket pocket. But Stevie wasn't a killer.

WELCOME TO FATTY'S DINER.
ATM INSIDE.

The gravel parking lot was empty. If the place was open, workers' cars had to be in the back somewhere. An ATM sign, the only colorful thing about the place, blinked red and blue. Mister turned off the ignition and sat still, tapping the steering wheel.

Stevie knew better than to question the man. But Troy didn't.

"Aren't we gonna get out an' eat?" he whined. "I am very hungry."

"Let me think a minute," Mister told him.

A middle-aged man came out the side door and lit a cigarette. Under a wrinkled black apron, he wore jeans and a long sleeved, white tee-shirt. Having a smoke was obviously more important than staying warm or even acknowledging people in the strange car. When he leaned against the building his large stomach jutted out.

"Well, that must be Fatty himself, in all his glory," Mister mumbled.

Maybe, Stevie plotted, if I got that guy's attention I could... what? He's not even looking over here. If I rolled down the window, shouted...nahh...before I got a word out, Mister would floor it.

"Guess it's okay. No one except the cook to bother us," Mister finally said. "Come on boys." He opened the glove compartment. Looking back at his passengers he realized Jimmy hadn't moved the whole trip. "What did you do, Herder?"

"Me? Nothin'. You know better than anyone what happened to this kid! Don't go blamin' it on me!" Oh no. Now he'd done it. Mister didn't like no one talkin' back to him. There'd been lots of bruises throughout the years and a few scars just to remind Stevie to stay in line.

But Mister just sat there, staring and thinking. Growling slightly. Then he took the gun out and slammed the glove compartment shut.

"What's wrong with Jimmy? Is he gonna be okay?" Troy asked, breaking the tension. He held Stevie's arm tighter.

"He's cold. We'll warm him up and he'll be fine." Mister told him calmly. Grabbing the dirty blanket that had been bunched up on the seat next to him, Mister tossed it to the back seat. "Herder, cover him up and we'll go get some food." Looking at Troy he smiled. "Don't worry, we'll bring something back for him and after he eats, he'll be right as rain." He slipped the gun into his jacket.

Stevie tenderly wrapped the blanket around Jimmy and tried acting like he hadn't noticed. But there was only one other thing Mister kept in that glove box.

CHAPTER FIFTY

Fatty's was dingy. The carpet, worn and frayed, was a coffee spattered brown. Wood paneling coated all four walls; health department certificates stuck to the paneling by the register. Country music played in the background. Some man with a twangy, hillbilly voice sang about something no one could hear. It was the big screen TV in one corner, suspended from the ceiling that was the attention grabber. The only thing in the place that looked new.

The threesome walked up to the WAIT TO BE SEATED sign and waited. No customers littered the dining room. The only voices they could hear were the ESPN sportcasters drowning out the singing cowboy. They stood and waited some more. Troy held his crotch. "I gotta pee," he said, looking up at the big boy who held his hand. "I gotta pee real bad."

"In a minute," Mister told him. "Hold it."

Finally the same man they had seen on his cigarette break walked out of the kitchen to the front of house. Smiling a real dazzler, he greeted them.

After they were seated, Fatty handed out menus.

"Where's the bathroom? I gotta pee."

"Right there, little fella" Fatty pointed, smiling brightly. "I got a young one just about your age at home."

"Give us a minute," Mister told the man.

"Sure thing."

When the coast was clear, Mister turned to Stevie who sat wedged in the booth beside him. Grabbing the front of his shirt he pulled the boy close. "Now you listen to me. I got the car keys so don't even think of leaving. And you know what I'll say if you tell anyone about that boy out there." He jerked his head toward the car.

"You'll tell them I hurt Jimmy. I know."

"And who will everyone believe? A Man of God or a dumb runaway?"

"They'll believe you."

"Damn straight they will. Now, take little Troy here to the bathroom. You have five minutes."

The burger was the best Stevie could remember ever eating. Even Troy was happy, chatting between bites and sips of milk. For a few minutes things felt normal…and that was nice. Fatty came over to see if they needed anything else before dropping off the check.

"No." Mister smiled. "That's all, thanks."

"What about Jimmy?" Troy piped up. "You said we were gonna bring him some food. So he'll feel better. You said so, remember?"

"Is Jimmy another son?" Fatty asked.

Mister swiped a napkin over his thick mustache.

"Yeah, my brother's got a cold," Stevie quickly answered, hoping his lie would appease Mister, maybe even make him think Herder was still on his side.

"Well you just tell me what you want and I'll get a take-out ready for ya'll." The man smiled down at Troy and it seemed they would get out of there just fine. Everyone happy, no problems.

Until Troy said, "He's out in the car. Sleepin'."

The fat man looked puzzled. "It's pretty cold out there."

"Oh, I left the heat on for him," Mister said. "If you have some soup that should do it."

Fatty hesitated a moment before answering. "Vegetable okay?"

"Great."

Stevie held his breath while Mister pulled out that dirty old wallet of his. The chain attached to a belt loop rattled as he counted out enough to pay the bill.

Then they walked to the car, Mister carried Troy this time. "How about you sit up front with me? You can be my co-pilot."

"No." The boy squirmed, holding tightly to the container of soup he'd insisted on carrying. "I wanna sit with Stevie and Jimmy." But he knew what that scowl meant and quickly added, "I can sit by you later, okay?"

Mister nodded and opened the door for them. "Sure."

Fatty stood at the window. Something wasn't right with those folks. He looked for exhaust, some sign that the car had been running the entire time the family was eating. But there was none. Craning his neck, he searched for another head—Jimmy's head. Nothing.

After the three got into the car he walked out front, casually taking a cigarette from his pocket to cover his real intention. But he didn't have to be so careful. No one was paying him any mind.

Should he write down the license number just because he was having one of his "feelings" again? he wondered.

The car backed up and Fatty started to wave, trying to just seem friendly. But what he saw paralyzed his arm. He squinted to be sure.

Yep, there was no missing that big blade. Sun shined off the steel like a beacon. The big boy saw him and waved—obviously wanting him to see the knife. But the strangest thing was when the car made a right turn and Fatty could get a real good look. That's when the kid started stabbing at the little guy's head.

Fatty was too rattled to remember the license plate as he ran inside for the phone.

PART SIXTEEN

EN MASSE

CHAPTER FIFTY-ONE

"Tammy," Roy whispered through the bars. "He's gone."

She got up from the small cot, dragged her feet across the floor of her cell and went to where he stood. "What happened with the Warden?"

"That badge he showed you? It was Malcolm's. From when he worked here last. What we do now?"

"I told him to pitch that thing a million times. But, no, he said it was his free pass. Said it made him appear official."

"Looks like all it done is bring that Mr. Lloyd here pokin' around. He was in the Boss's office almost an hour. So now what?" He wiped at the sweat on his forehead.

"You think I'm gonna have a melt down? Just because some dumb fuck comes nosing around? We been through this shit a million times before."

Roy thought a moment, rolled her words around his head. "Guess you're right. But I can always go visit that asshole an' mess him up. You know, discourage him from comin' back here…"

"For a big man you got a real teeny brain, you know that?" she snarled. "You give Malcolm the name in Flat River?"

He nodded. "Just like you tell me."

"And you told this Reese woman they's comin'?"

He nodded again. "She's waitin'." He looked at his watch. "They should be there any time now."

"Good." Tammy smiled. "What about the money?"

"I'll pick it up later tonight."

"Where?"

"He'll call an' tell me where," Roy said. "Same as always. He'll call after the Jubilation."

"Jubilation my ass," she said and shuffled back to her cot.

Fatty ran back inside the restaurant. Doubting what he'd seen with every jerky step. When he finally got to the phone he was out of breath. Trying to calm himself, he bent over as his fat fingers punched in the numbers.

"911; what's your emergency?"

"I'm not really for sure. The damnedest thing," he managed to say between gulps.

"Sir, what is your location?"

"I'm off Highway sixty-seven. Fatty's Restaurant."

"Hey, Fatty, it's Melba. You okay?"

"I'm fine, girl. There's this man traveling with two kids. Maybe three. The oldest one had a knife and it looked like he was stabbin' the younger one."

"Good Lord! So where are they now?"

"Headed off north, drivin' a black car. Out of state plates but I was too shook to see from where. Didn't even get a good look at the numbers or nuthin'. Just couldn't believe what I was seein'. Shit, I'm still not sure. It was all so—"

"You done good, Fatty. How long ago was this?"

"A minute. Maybe five. They was talkin' about another kid in the car. Said he was sick. Oh God, you don't think they killed—"

"Calm down. I'll have someone come talk to you and –"

"No! They gotta go after that guy. Those kids…no it was the boy who was holdin' the knife…maybe he was gonna kill the man…hell I don't know what was happenin."

"Sit tight, Fatty."

"Hurry."

Officer Bradshaw pulled onto the highway. It had been a slow day— probably would end up that way. Fatty had this way of exaggerating things. Everyone in the county knew it. And after his last cataract surgery, those old eyes of his still weren't at a hundred percent.

"Jergens is goin' to the restaurant to take a report. You see if you can find that black car. He's for sure there are two kids traveling with a man. They don't have much of a lead. Call if you find him."

"Will do. Over." Well at least this was better than sitting behind the Fast Lane all day, writing up kids or old farts trying to skip out without paying for gas. Or parking by the four way stop to catch speeders, he thought. But not much.

Mister slammed on the brakes. All three boys jerked forward; Jimmy would have rolled onto the floor if Stevie hadn't held him back. The knife was ripped from Stevie's hand as tires chewed up gravel on the side of the road. Before he knew what was happening, the man jumped out of the car, ran around to Stevie's door and yanked him out. He tried to fight but Mister was ferocious, stronger than a bear. Then the boy was rolled over onto his back. Rocks jabbed his skull. Mister dropped down onto Stevie's stomach and pinned his arms over his head with one hand while he held the knife to Stevie's throat with the other.

Mister was growling he was so mad. Like a rabid dog, spit pooled at the corners of his mouth. Then he leaned down, got in real close and spoke slowly so the boy wouldn't miss a single word. "I've had enough of you, Herder."

Troy was too scared to watch. "We'll be okay, Jimmy. Stevie'll protect us," he whispered to the body next to him, gently patting his friend's leg.

"Leave me here," the Stevie said defiantly. "Why don't you just leave us all here."

Mister gave out a low, coarse laugh. "Oh, please, Mister," he mocked the boy, "I promise to never ever tell anyone about you and all the work I've done for you. Because I'm just an innocent little boy who was forced to do…what?..God's work."

When Mister got crazy eyes, Stevie knew better than to talk back.

Spit dropped onto Stevie's face as Mister continued. "I've been good to you, boy, haven't I? I've given you shelter, food and the clothes on your bony ass. Haven't I?"

"Yes, Mister."

"And I've had to discipline you, like any father would. You have to learn. I never spared the rod. I did what was right and good." Suddenly, like a curtain rising on the second act, Mister's expression changed. He leaned back, releasing the boy's arms, slipping the knife into his back pocket. Stevie swore he could see real affection in those dark eyes then. And it frightened him more than ever.

"Okay, now we got a Jubilation to attend," Mister said, standing up and holding a hand out to Herder. "Come on, son."

Stevie was yanked up. He could see Troy looking at him from inside the car. The little kid was so scared. Stevie waved and smiled the best he could to offer some kind of comfort. It was all he could think to do.

Carla Reese tried reading while she waited but was too distracted. Today! She was going to be a mother today. This time tomorrow she'd have a son. And she'd call him Tucker. A boy's name never changes—not like a girl who gets married. A lot of women hyphenated a string of names to sound classy. But everyone knew, the more names, the more failures. First came the family one, then the married name. After that followed more married names until they usually gave up. Embarrassed, the woman most times just went back to the start with the original they were born with. Men had it easier. Born with a name—died with the same one.

But still, it had taken months to pick just the right name for her baby. Then one night while she watched the credits roll by after the last scene of a Turner Classic, she spotted it. Tucker. Strong, honest and simple. But he'd be "Tuck" for now while he was little and sweet.

She put her book aside and turned the TV on. Finally. The day had finally come. Her guilt would be washed away with the goodness she was doing. No, this wasn't a selfish act like the two abortions had been. But when she rationalized, which she did weekly now, instead of daily like at the beginning, she hadn't done anything illegal. She'd even gotten the name of the doctor from her gynecologist. And her life was just beginning then. There'd always be time for a baby.

A year turned into five then ten and now here she was forty-five. Head of her own company, managing two branches and thirty employees, money to spare. She could finally relax a little, look around and enjoy herself. But there was no one to enjoy it with. Hell, she didn't even know what she enjoyed doing besides work. And then one day at church, she'd met Roy.

Carla walked out to the kitchen. She opened the refrigerator. Maybe a sandwich, do something ordinary to calm herself down.

No, don't eat from anxiety her trainer had shouted. "A donut doesn't help anything." She smiled, pitying the jock who obviously didn't appreciate a fresh glazed Krispy Kreme.

She forced herself down the hall, gripping a pink cell phone, checking for messages. Intending to stop at her office she kept walking to the boy's—Tuck's room. Her favorite decorating magazine had featured celebrity nurseries and she'd copied it perfectly. Except where the crib had been, she put in a twin bed, and covered it with a Disney throw. Books and toys waited to be loved, arranged on custom shelves. She'd told her neighbors, when they asked, that her nephew was coming to live with her. Sometimes she really got into it, elaborating about the accident that took his wonderful parents. But the truth would have been much better—a lot more exciting.

Everyone noticed Roy that day. Next to her, he looked like a giant. They'd talked; it had all been casual and superficial until he started telling her about his friend. Mister Malcolm, he called the preacher. He told Carla how Malcolm was doing God's work, helping poor children who were victims of an unfair system, seeing that those kids got nice homes with parents who truly wanted them. Not parents the poor things got by default. Just because their mother or father had committed a crime, why should the little angels have to suffer?

He'd been so distraught she agreed to have supper with him. After they'd ordered their meal, the big man broke down, telling her how his step-sister had hooked up with an addict. How the bum had turned her into a user and thief. And Angie, his little niece was the one who suffered the most. He'd tried so hard to get custody of the girl. But according to the judge, he had two strikes against him. One: he wasn't married. Two: he had a record. Nothing that should really count, he'd argued. Okay, a few months in juvie when he was sixteen. Stole a car—just a prank—no one got hurt. But now he had a steady job, even worked for the state. Stupid court didn't even check his work record and poor Angie got shipped off, clear across four states, to some aunt she didn't even know. A divorced, fifty year old, raggedy clerk at a dollar store who lived in a run-down, dirty place. What chance did poor Angie have now? Just because that woman shared some of the same DNA shouldn't mean she was the one to raise her sister's child when she was no better than the one in jail.

She'd asked about foster homes but he'd gotten so red in the face she thought he'd pass out. He worked in a prison, seen the products of foster care first hand, he told her. Those inmates had been tossed around in the system, shoved back and forth from home to home. They'd been beaten, starved, and raped. No, Mister Malcolm hand-picked the parents of the unfortunates himself. He investigated. He prayed on it, devoted his life to matching the right parents to the perfect kids.

What a good listener Roy had been. She cried along with him, explaining how she'd tried adopting but it either took way too long or cost too much. And between therapy sessions for her depression, living expenses and keeping her business running, she could never save enough. All she wanted was a child of her own. Someone to give her unconditional love—never judge her. And if in return, she could help out another poor soul…sign her up.

CHAPTER FIFTY-TWO

Wooden markers in the shape of crosses randomly showed up near a dangerous curve or close to the edge of a field, telling drivers that someone had died on that exact spot. Mister pulled the car next to a pink cross, planted about a hundred yards back, shaded by two willows. The name, "Abby" was printed in black marker over the chipped paint. A large teddy bear, the kind won at the State Fair, sat in front of the sad reminder. Beside the animal was a pot of plastic daisies.

"Come on, boys, we're gonna play a game!" Mister shouted happily, turning the ignition off.

Troy locked his arms around Stevie's neck, holding on with all his strength. "No! I don't wanna play with you! Stevie, you won't make me play, will you?"

"What about the Jubilation?" Stevie asked, confused. Troy clung to him like an octopus. Mister would never hurt the boy; he had to deliver him safely. But was Stevie using the kid as a shield? Was he a coward?

"Now, what fun would it be without Troy?" Mister said as he put the knife into the glove compartment. "Come on, little man." He even smiled.

Next he reached down and popped open the trunk then got out of the car. The boys could hear metal clanging. A second after the trunk slammed shut, Mister was standing outside holding two shovels. "How about a treasure hunt?"

Even if Stevie hit the man with a shovel, he wouldn't get far. So he did all he could do—he got out of the car with Troy still wrapped around him.

"Come on you two, it'll be fun."

Mister dropped the shovels next to the cross so he could pull both boys into a bear hug. "Now there's no reason to be afraid." He smiled and patted the little one's back. Then he whispered, close to Stevie's ear, a message meant only for the teen. "The gun's still in my jacket. Now put the boy down."

Helplessness was a familiar emotion, one Stevie had been forced to live with for years. "It's okay." He broke the boy's hold. Then trying to ignore the fear staring back at him he said, "Mister's never hurt you before and he won't now." It was a struggle but he managed to set the boy down on the ground.

"Here," Mister handed Troy a shovel, "the smaller one's for you. And you can keep anything you find."

Stevie picked up the other tool. Trying to reassure the boy he said, "Just like a Pirate, Troy. Buried treasure."

"See that?" Mister pointed to the cross. "It marks the special place. Dig behind it."

The weather had been typical of fall in the Midwest. One day in the eighties and the next, sixty. Indian Summer had been long enough to leave the ground soft. The digging went quickly.

While he watched, Mister played with the loose change in his pocket. Soon he would toss it in the bottom of the small hole to distract the little one long enough for Herder to gather up Jimmie. Then after leaving him in his final resting place, they would have a Jubilation. Praise the Lord!

There was no sign of a black car let alone some crazy dude and three kids. But Officer Baldwin didn't really believe anything Fatty said. Everyone knew he was borderline senile. And it wasn't as if this was St. Louis or Chicago. There was just the two of them out in the field, trying to patrol some of the even smaller towns that didn't have a force. County roads cut through corn fields, larger highways led to the interstate. Then there were gravel trails and private roads. How could one man be expected to cover all that ground? But he'd keep looking. He'd taken an oath to protect these people, even if half of them were crazy.

She saw them pull into the driveway before hearing them. Her son was here! Carla clapped as she stood at the window. What would he look like? For a moment she was nervous. Would he like her? From all the stories Roy had told her about the little guy's family, the one forced on him, she had to be an improvement.

Before they could ring the bell, she had her hand on the door knob. But she didn't want to scare the boy, didn't want anyone thinking she was strange, so she stood and waited. Even after the chime sounded, she waited. His first impression of her had to be a positive one—a loving one—not of some hysterical woman all up in his little face.

When she finally opened the door, she was surprised to see an older boy holding the little one. Roy only spoke about Mister Malcolm but the kid seemed harmless so she smiled. "Hi, come on in."

The two boys looked lost and dirty around the edges. A man walked behind the pair, solemn in his black leather jacket and out-dated suit. All of them seemed…weary.

"I'm so glad to see you." Why was she so nervous, she wondered.

"We can't stay too long, Ms. Reese," the man said. "I'm Malcolm and on behalf of the poor mother of this boy, a woman who made some bad choices but certainly should not have her innocent child punished for her deeds, I thank you. God will certainly acknowledge your kindness. And we want to thank you in advance for your discretion and generous donation to our cause."

Stevie put Troy down on a large recliner. It was the first time he'd been inside during a Jubilation. Would there be praying? Would Mister launch into one of his sermons?

"I'm Troy," the boy said, gleefully. "I have treasure," He held out his small fist and opened his fingers to reveal three quarters and several smaller coins. "I'm like a real pirate."

"You certainly are." Carla squeezed next to the boy. "He's adorable," she said to Malcolm. "Perfect."

Mister's phone rang, playing some Christian song Stevie had come to recognize when business was going on. "Excuse me; I have to get this."

Carla was glad when he stepped outside.

Take a chance, Stevie thought. Tell this lady what's going on. But then he remembered the gun. Mister would snap. Might even shoot them all. And even if he got away, how could he live knowing he'd gotten this poor woman and Troy killed? So he stood there and smiled.

"Would you boys like a soda?" Carla asked, never looking away from Troy's angelic face. "I have orange and cola."

"Orange!" Troy shouted. "We like orange, right Stevie?"

"Sure."

When the woman left the room, Stevie walked closer to the front door, hoping to catch some of the conversation on the other side.

Mister was agitated. "I've had it with this guy. He's gonna spoil our whole operation. Get back there and end this—permanently. Yes, that's what I'm saying. Do it sooner than soon. Go to Kimmswick now. Yeah, yeah, we're here at the drop off. You did real good; she seems nice. No, I didn't get the money yet. You just do your job and stop worrying about me doin' mine. Okay?"

"Here we are," Carla said, smiling, holding two glasses of orange soda. "It's okay if you take off your coats." She meant to be polite but didn't really want the big one getting comfortable. She wanted to be left alone with Tuck. They had to start their life together this minute. She'd waited too long.

Stevie started to unbutton Troy's jacket. Carla set the glasses down on the coffee table and hurried over to help. "Let me do that."

When Mister came back into the house he saw Stevie sitting where Troy had been. He was drinking a soda, his jacket thrown over a chair. "Where's Troy? Where's Ms. Reese?"

"She took him to see his new room."

"Well, don't get all comfortable here. Tell Ms. Reese I have some paperwork belonging to the boy."

"His name's Troy," Stevie said as he walked out of the room.

"Watch your attitude," Mister hissed. "Remember what happens to a smart ass."

CHAPTER FIFTY-THREE

"Hey, Benny. It's me, Vince."

"How'd it go? Did you see the Warden? Did you show him the badge? Where are you? Damn cell phones! Used to be when a person called you at home—on your home phone—you were at home. Now there's no telling where someone is when you call them or they call you—"

"I'm walking to the car. Saw the Warden and, yes, I showed him the badge. I'll tell you all about it when I get back."

"Right. Don't talk while driving. Very dangerous. Especially with these crazy drivers, all the time cutting a person off. You can tell me everything over dinner."

Vince could take a hint. "I'll bring something home. What sounds good?"

"Chicken," Benny said. "No one can screw up chicken."

"You got it."

After getting into his car and before starting the engine, Vince called Kathy. When they spoke the night before he told her all about Benny and their plan. He thought she'd try to talk him out of it, but she hadn't. And she didn't seem surprised when he told her about his visit from Chief Stoffel.

"I never liked that guy. He has mean eyes. But I didn't want to say anything."

"Why the hell not? I thought we're in this together."

She hesitated a minute. "Well...you would have said that emotions have nothing to do with all this. But I learned a long time ago, when we were desperate for news about Gabby, and later when I set up the website. There's a lot of politics going on behind all the sympathetic words and offers of help. And you'd never believe how

many egos want to be fed with money or publicity. I know you,
Vince. You wouldn't have listened to any of it. You weren't exactly
yourself back then."

He nodded as she spoke. "Well, I'm listening now, Kath."

Another hesitation. "That means a lot, thanks. Call me tonight
after you've filled Benny in; I want to hear his reaction to everything.
Right now I can feel a migraine coming on. I need to lie down."

"Okay." He started to hang up but then remembered something
you'd been meaning to tell her. "Wait, Kathy, you still there?"

"I'm here."

"Sorry for checking out on you sometimes. It won't happen
again."

Roy headed for Kimmswick the minute Malcolm gave the word to
"make that fucker gone." Oh, he done way worse before—sometimes just 'cause he was bored an' needed a laugh. But today he was
doin' God's work with a cash bonus.

Him comin' down here, buttin' his nose in where it don't belong.
Big city man! Well now he was gonna learn all about how river rats
conducted business. "Things ain't so pretty an' shiny like you're
used to, Mr. Lloyd. You need some educatin'." Roy pounded his
horn at the bitch trying to cut in front.

"Watch the road," he told himself. "No need gettin' excited.
Stay calm. You're no damn good if your temper wins. Think of the
beauty. Beauty in the world. Think of the beauty," he repeated the
mantra they'd jammed down his throat at anger management.

There was a real beauty about it all, Roy thought. Most towns
they hit didn't even have a thousand people. And them people didn't
have nothin' extra. Police departments shared a building with the Fire
Station most times an' if there was something big, too big for their
one or two man team, State Troopers were called in. But it sometimes
took those lazy bastards hours to respond. Most folks didn't even
want to talk to no cops. Most of 'em had records, knew the inside of a
jail better than their own mama's trailer. Perfect set-up.

Kids went missin' all the time where he come from. What was
the big deal? Hell, most times everybody knew where the kid
was anyway. Why make a fuss? Like that dim-wit girl. Everyone
knew she didn't just up and go for a walk, by herself, in the night.

Everybody knew her mama couldn't take no more—no one talked about it, that's all. The TV news showed her dumb high school picture for months. Every night at six an' ten. The same ole sad pimply face. Then her mama, wearin' her best Walmart dress, cryin', beggin' for help to find her little darlin'. Everyone watched…an' talked. They especially talked to news people. It was fun seein' who could get on camera the most times. But when those same folks got home they all talked about how poor, dim-witted Beth Ann was buried near the water tower, in the field north of town.

Stoffel took the call himself; Janet was out for another parent-teacher thing at the high school. "Yeah?"

"Is that any way to answer an official phone call?"

"Who is this?" he grumbled, irritated that his football game was being interrupted.

"Melba Etch. Janet's sister-in-law?"

"Oh hey, Melba. Janet's not here, try her at home."

"Are the kids okay? Is she sick?"

"Everyone's fine and I'm kinda busy here…"

"Does your busyness have anything to do with what happened out at Fatty's?"

He muted the game. "What happened?"

"Oh sure, now you got time to talk to me."

"Come on, Melba, give."

"Fatty's convinced that some kid with a big ole knife was fixin' to kill a poor little boy. There was three of 'em that come into the diner. A scary Johnny Cash kinda guy—all in black, a little boy and this teenager. Poor Fatty just about had hisself a heart attack."

"So this kid pulled a knife out? Right there in the diner?" Stoffel asked. "Come on, you know how Fatty is. How many times has he called you with some crazy story?"

Melba snorted that laugh of hers. "Member the time he said there was them crop circles? An' just last week he got all excited, convinced his back room was haunted?"

"Last Friday I was out there for his Fish-Fry. He jabbered on for more than twenty minutes, all the time tryin' to convince me that some kids was usin' that abandoned store across the road from him for a meth lab."

"Well, that one coulda been true," Melba said. "Lot of that stuff goin' on out here. But, no, the three of 'em was in their car, fixin' to drive away when Fatty seen the boy stabbin' at the other one's head. That's when he run inside an' called us. Baldwin is lookin' for 'em now. Haven't heard from him yet."

"So when did all this supposedly happen?" he asked.

"'bout an hour ago."

"Melba, this is Baldwin," the officer's voice came out loud and clear. Stoffel could hear every word. "Got some trouble out at Sal Turner's place. You know that part of his property that runs along part of Highway Eight?"

"What kinda trouble?" she asked.

"He found a kid buried near Abby Lawton's cross."

"Oh my God! I'll call the Doc. Are you okay?"

"Shaken up, but yeah, I'm fine."

Melba forgot all about her cell phone being on.

Vince had been waiting ten minutes for his order in the drive-through when his phone rang. Usually he didn't pick up when he saw the name but things were different now.

"Hey Laura, what's up?"

"Ever hear of a small town called Flat River."

"Nope."

"Well, you're not alone on that one."

"What about it?" Vince asked.

"I think Stevie might be there. Can you talk?"

Calm. That's all he felt. There'd been so many starts and stops—disappointments and excitement that he was getting numb to it all.

Two cars were ahead of him and neither had moved in a while. Three cars inched up behind, boxing him in. He couldn't go anywhere if he wanted to. "Sure. Looks like I got plenty of time."

"Good; I'll try to make it quick." He must be on speaker phone from the way her voice sounded. "I'm researching an article on child trafficking. My God, Vince, it's frightening. I've heard about girls being held and shipped overseas, but here? You wouldn't believe it. Anyway, about a week ago I get a call from a source in Flat River. This woman works for a lady, Carla Reese, who's getting custody of a child today. All very sudden. Some story about it being her brother's boy. Then Reese tells an assistant that her nephew, Tucker, is her sister's son. Everyone at the place thinks it's all very suspicious. And today there was an incident at a diner near Flat River involving a man, a child, and a teenager."

"What happened out there?" he asked as he moved up a few feet closer to the window.

"The teenager, a boy about Stevie's age, pulled out a knife when the three of them got back in the car. Fatty, the owner of the place, said he saw the whole thing through the back window as they drove away. He was really shook up."

"Do you suppose the kid was doing it to get attention?" Vince asked

"No telling what was going on. But I thought we could drive out there—you and I—to ask around. I'm on my way to Baylor's house now to pick you up."

"Don't you think this is all premature?"

"No. It only happened a while ago and I've got a bunch of photos of Stevie with me. Maybe Fatty can identify him."

Vince was letting her enthusiasm get to him. "You won't have a camera crew with you? And you haven't told anyone at your station?"

"Look, you and Kathy and I agreed we'd work together; Stevie' welfare comes first. And if we can save some other kids along the way...wouldn't that be great?"

"Yes, it'd be wonderful. But I'm not home now. I had a visit from a man, Benjamin Hodges—"

"Kathy emailed me all about Benny."

"Good. I was going to call tonight and tell you about the prison—"

"Prison?"

"We'll talk later. Just go to the house and introduce yourself to Benny. He's a great guy; you'll like him. He'll tell you why I went to Vandalia."

"Okay, see you later. Laura? Tell Benny his plan worked out great."

CHAPTER FIFTY-FOUR

Benny saw the red van drive by the first time. Watching TV near the front window, he couldn't help notice it the second time. When it slowed down, he headed for the basement. Something didn't feel right. And when it didn't feel right—it was wrong.

Roy never expected the neighborhood to be so quiet. Where was everyone? Now he stuck out like a parade float. But he knew most folks spent time in the kitchen or family room, in the back of the house, saving the living room for entertaining.

He patted the gun, holstered under his arm. Then after parking a few houses down, he got out of his car. After ringing the bell twice he knocked. Checking for anyone who might be watching, he put his mouth close to the door and spoke is a deep, low voice. "Mr. Lloyd, this is Roy Willis from the prison. We met this morning? The Warden wanted me to drop off a file. It could maybe help you."

Nothing.

Roy looked over his shoulder at the blue Ford parked in the driveway. Then he turned back to the door. "Sir, I think you should give this a look."

Benny stood beneath the living room and listened. If this file was so important the Warden would have faxed it to Vince. Was he being silly? Just another paranoid old man? Should he call Vince? While he was thinking, Benny heard wood cracking then heavy footsteps above him.

Mister counted to make sure there was five thousand dollars in the envelope. Carla was too enamored of the little boy to be insulted.

"Everything looks good. Put your coat on," he ordered Stevie.

Troy got hysterical when he realized they were planning to leave without him. "No! I don't wanna stay here." Then running over to Stevie, he wrapped his arms around the big boy's thighs. "Please, Stevie, don't leave me here alone."

Carla bent down to gently pry him off his friend. "You'll love it here, sweetheart. You'll make new friends. It's going to be great."

But Troy wasn't having any of it. "I'm going home with Stevie!" Tears covered his cheeks, his nose ran. "I don't like you!"

Mister grabbed the little guy by the hair, yanking him back so hard he fell on his butt. Carla stood back, shocked.

"I'll come visit you all the time," Stevie lied. "Maybe we can even have a sleep-over?" He looked at Carla, hoping she was smart enough to play along. He had to convince the little boy to stay here where he'd be safe. He just had to. Because now was his chance. There'd be only the two of them in the car this time. Just him and Mister. And once they got to a main street or passed something he could recognize, he'd run for it.

Laura parked behind the blue Ford in the driveway. She'd never seen the car before and assumed it was Benny's. Where was Vince?

She was too busy juggling her black tote bag, keys and the envelope with Stevie's pictures to notice the open door at first. Even when she did look up and saw it like that, she didn't think it strange. Should she knock, or ring the bell or just walk inside? While she was trying to decide, she noticed splintered wood and shards of glass inside, on the carpet.

Benny had watched Laura walk up the steps from his position in the basement. He frantically looked for a weapon—anything. Something sharp; something heavy.

She'd seen it play out a thousand times before. Some unsuspecting homeowner comes home to find the door open that he swears he locked, or a broken window. But he ignores the signs and enters anyway. That's when he runs smack into a burglar or stalker. And, if he survives, he'll regret that moment forever. So she turned away from the house and started back to her car.

Vince rounded the corner in time to see a woman standing in his driveway. As he got closer he recognized Laura Bonetti and waved. She looked puzzled. Grabbing his take-out dinner he cut the engine. Before he could shut the car door, she was next to him.

"What timing, huh?" Vince asked. "Did you just get here?"

"Well, not exactly."

"Come on, we'll have some dinner—"

She reached out and grabbed his arm. "I think someone's in the house."

"It's just Benny. I told you he was here."

"I don't know, Vince. The front door's open—looks like it was kicked in."

"Shit. Here." He handed her the bag and started toward the stairs.

"No, they might have a gun or something."

But he wasn't listening

Benny found a hammer and started up the steps. He could hear the intruder outside the basement door. Then he was in the kitchen, probably going for the back door.

Vince rushed into the house. "Benny! Where are you?"

The older man raced up the wooden steps, hoping he wouldn't have to use the heavy hammer. "He's going out the back!"

Roy ran out the kitchen door, across the patio and cut through the neighbor's yard,

Laura heard the beep of the key opening a car door and looked down the street to see a large man in a uniform getting into a red van. As he drove past her, she memorized the license number.

Realizing he'd never catch up and that Benny was okay, Vince watched the intruder escape. Nothing in the house was worth getting killed for.

Benny dropped the hammer, visibly shaken.

The sound of steel against tile made Vince jerk around. "What the hell was that all about?" he asked.

"Hell if I know," Benny said. "I made it to the basement. Don't even think he knew I was down there. But when I saw that pretty lady starting up the walk, I just about had a fit."

"Laura, she's the reporter Kathy and I have been working with."

"Hello," Laura called as she walked into the house.

"We're in the kitchen," Vince called back. "The coast is clear."

"Shhh, don't talk." She tossed the bag and envelope on the counter then rummaged through her tote for a pen and paper. Quickly she wrote down the plate number of the van. "Got it."

"What?" Vince asked.

"A description and plate number of our bad guy. Hope it wasn't just a routine burglary or home invasion. I'm praying it's a real lead to Stevie."

"He said his name was Roy Willis," Benny said. "And he asked for you, Vince."

"That was the guard I talked to at the prison today. How did he know I'd be here?"

CHAPTER FIFTY-FIVE

As they pulled away, Stevie felt good—proud even. Convincing Troy to stay behind was the best thing he'd done in a really long time. But now he was alone with Mister. Just them with two weapons between 'em. A knife sittin' in the glove box—Mister with a gun under his jacket. The knife would be the easiest to get to, he thought. But then what? Could he really stab that asshole? Get in real close? See his eyes bug an' blood shoot out?

They'd never been alone, outside during the day, like this before. Stevie thought back and realized he'd never ever seen Mister kill anyone…'cept maybe Jimmy. So why would he suddenly start now? No, he's way too smart for that. What are you waiting for? His brain wanted to know. Run away, it commanded. But his body froze, not knowing where it was.

While Stevie sat plotting and confused, watching for anything familiar, Mister stared straight ahead, looking through the windshield. Amber leaves fluttered as they drove down the back roads. Dozens of birds perched on telephone wires, chattering. A cool breeze hurried the few clouds hanging in a patch of chambray sky, along.

Suddenly a school bus pulled onto the two lane road then stopped. Its doors opened, allowing a single boy to exit. After waving to the driver he walked around the front of the large vehicle and started up a hill. From where the strangers sat, there was no house in sight. Then the stop sign on the bus went down and it drove away.

After a minute, when they were out there again, Mister shouted, "Get out!"

Not here, Stevie thought. No, this ain't a good place. No buildings, no people. Not even a rock or tree to hide behind. Only miles of fields harvested weeks ago. All he could do was hold onto the seat-belt cinched around his waist and look at his shoes. Maybe if he pretended he didn't hear...

Mister took out the gun and looked at it. "You've been a good Herder. Always so kind to the children. And I've appreciated your help with the Jubilations."

"My help?" Stevie asked meekly. "You forced me..." Instantly he regretted speaking, aware any word he said could set Mister off.

"Whether you did it willingly or not, I appreciate your—efforts." Then Mister patted the boy on the shoulder and for a minute seemed kind. "Now get out of the car," he growled.

Stevie slowly unfastened his seat belt, trying to buy some time. It was obvious now—this crazy bastard was gonna kill him.

Mister reached across Stevie and pushed the passenger's door open. Then with one sudden shove, the boy was on the ground.

Stevie lay in the dirt, waiting for Mister to open his own door and get out. Surprisingly the man moved slowly, like he had time to spare. And that over-confidence allowed the boy his big chance. Jumping up he opened the glove compartment, grabbed the large knife and stood, waiting.

It was as if Mister wanted it this way. He laughed, dangling the car keys. Stevie held his breath.

"Come on, Herder. Now what are you planning to do with that blade? Kill me right here, in front of God and the world? Out in the open?"

Stevie didn't have any answers.

"Okay," Mister continued, "let's suppose you do overpower me? Maybe even stick me with that blade. What then?"

"I don't want to hurt no one. Please, I done everything you asked. All these years. Just let me go home. I'll tell anyone who asks that I run away from home back then. Willingly. On my own. I'll make everyone believe it, too."

Mister listened to Stevie beg, even seemed to be considering the boy's plan. But that only lasted a second. Slowly he brought the gun up level with the kid's eyes. "I think the problem here is that you're too old for this job, Herder. You're not a child anymore. Why just look at yourself; you're almost a man. A child is supposed to lead them, not a pimply, raggedy teenaged boy."

He could reach out now, strike quick like a snake, stab that asshole square in the gut. Do it now before he knows what hit him.

Mister cocked the gun. His hand steady, eyes unflinching.

The silence was unexpectedly broken by the roar of an engine. The boy they had seen getting off the bus was now coming straight for them, riding an ATV.

"You guys need help?" he asked when he got closer. His smile shined with silver braces. "Everything okay?"

Mister kept the gun aimed at Stevie. "This kid's trying to steal my car," he said. "Got a cell phone? Mine's dead. I need to call the police."

"Sorry. It's up at the house." The boy looked more amused than anything.

"No!" Stevie shouted. "It's him. He kidnapped me." Stevie figured the newcomer was probably a few years younger than himself. Younger and too dumb to realize this was real. But he tried anyway. "Go get your dad."

The boy looked around then said to Mister, "You expect me to believe that this kid was just walkin' along in the middle of nowhere? Cause I sure don't see a car he come in or a motorcycle not even a bicycle. No, nothin' like this never happens out here." He shook his head. "Is this some kinda prank? Is there a camera somewhere?"

What if he said the wrong thing an' got this poor idiot killed? Stevie didn't know what to do next.

"Yeah that's what this is," Mister said. "So if you don't play along, you won't be on TV." Then he walked closer to Stevie, put his arm around him and motioned for the other one to come where they stood. "If you stand over here you'll get in the final shot."

Without one more question, the boy hopped off his ATV and hurried over to join the two.

That's when Stevie took his chance and plunged the knife into Mister's belly.

CHAPTER FIFTY-SIX

"Tom. Come in Tom,"

"Baldwin here. What's up, Melba?"

"A call just come in from out at the Dayton place on Highway Nineteen. You better get over there real quick. "

"What's up?"

"Their youngest—Franklin—said some kid and a man were parked off the road about a mile from the house. Said he saw the kid stab the guy right in front of him. Thought it was all a gag at first, that they was on some TV show."

"Damn, that's got to be the same kid Fatty reported. Is the man dead?"

"Wasn't when they called," Melba said.

"And I bet they were in that black car I've been chasin'."

"You're right on that one. Only thing, the kid took off in it."

Vince grabbed for the phone on the second ring.

"Let me talk to my dad!"

"Stevie? Are you okay?'"

Laura stood next to Benny, straining to hear every word Vince was saying as well as the person on the other end of the conversation. When her phone rang she glanced down to check out the caller. Expecting to see the usual numbers and area codes, she was surprised when Chief Stoffel's name appeared. "I gotta take this," she whispered to Benny and started for the front of the house.

While he waited for an answer, Vince wondered how he should play this. Should he tell the boy the truth and maybe spook him? Or should he lie—say anything that would get Stevie home safely?

All he could hear was labored breathing, like the poor kid had been running. "My name's Vince Lloyd; I was a very close friend of your father's."

"My dad never had no friend named Vince an' I knew all his friends. Are you a cop? Cause you gotta tell me if you're a cop or not...it's the law."

"No, I'm not a cop. I helped your father look for you and after he had a heart attack, I kept on looking. He made me promise to never give up."

"So did the heart attack kill him? Come on, tell me mister."

After all that had happened to this boy, Vince couldn't lie to him. "Yes. I'm so sorry. He was a great guy and he loved you—"

"I know all that." His voice cracked then came a few gulps like he was trying not to cry.

"Stevie? Please...tell me where you are and I'll come get you," Vince pleaded. "I'll come right now. We just want you home."

"I did something real bad. I think—I think I killed someone. But I couldn't let him take another kid. I had to—"

"I'll go to the police with you. You have to trust me, Stevie. Your father did. Just come home."

"I'm gonna try," Stevie said. "I'm on Fifty-Five now. It shouldn't take too much longer. And Mr. Lloyd?"

"Yeah?"

"I didn't hurt any of 'em."

The connection broke.

"What did I miss?" Laura asked as she hurried into the kitchen.

"That was Stevie," Vince told her. "He's scared. Says he killed someone."

"What?" Benny and Laura asked, shocked.

The three of them got lost a moment in their confusion, trying to digest what the boy had said. It was Laura who snapped them out of it.

"Well that was Chief Stoffel on my phone. Remember I told you about that incident at Fatty's this morning?" she asked Vince.

Benny couldn't contain himself. "What happened? And who's this Fatty?"

Laura brought him up to speed then told Vince and Benny what she had learned from Stoffel. "The little boy with them talked about another boy who was sick, out in the car. When they drove away

Fatty saw, who I'm assuming was Stevie, attempting to stab the little boy and there wasn't any sick kid in the back seat. Not as far as he could tell."

"I'm hoping he had a plate number or something to give them," Benny said.

"No, just the make and color. And the police couldn't find them—looked all morning."

"Good God, you'd think, in this day and age that they could—"

"I'm not finished," Laura said. "Then next thing you know a teenager, Franklin Dayton, is riding along on his dirt bike and spots a man and Stevie pulled over by the side of the road. So he goes to see if they need help. He said the man pointed a gun at him and then the big kid stabbed the man and drove away."

"What about the little boy?" Vince asked

"And the sick one?" Benny wanted to know. "Where was he during all this?"

"Neither one was in the car. I'm thinking that they were dropped off somewhere. Sold or traded. God," Laura said in a faint voice, "I hope they're still alive."

Vince didn't join in speculating. "Why would Stoffel know any of this or care? All this time he's convinced Stevie's dead."

"He's looking for a slice of fame," Laura said. "I see it all the time. Once this story hits the news, everyone involved will be hit up for interviews, book deals, public appearances… They'll be household names for a while."

"Idiots on blogs are gonna have a field day," Benny said.

Vince went to the cabinet to get dishes and glasses. "Well all we can do now is eat our dinner and wait for Stevie."

"Guess you're right. No need going to Flat River now. And I can't leave without seeing that Stevie gets home," Laura told him.

Benny opened a few drawers, searching for silverware. "And we gotta make a plan. What do we do once he gets here? Should we take him to the police or hide him?"

CHAPTER FIFTY-SEVEN

The name Carla Reese kept coming up.

First time Kathy noticed was about six months ago when a Facebook friend who lived in Flat River, Missouri, wrote to her about a neighbor, Carla Reese. She said this woman seemed too "touchy—feely" with some of the local kids. Watching her with the children made the woman so uncomfortable she'd reported Carla at a neighborhood watch meeting.

A few weeks later there was an email from the mother of a pregnant teen. Mother and daughter had been at a furniture store near Flat River, shopping for a crib, when they noticed they were being followed. Finally the stalker approached them and bluntly asked if she could adopt the baby. They were very upset by the incident, having just seen a news report about another pregnant girl who had her baby cut from her stomach and left to die.

Then a month ago a woman who helped WE'llFINDYOU from her home in Tampa, emailed Kathy that she had a friend, Barb, who had worked for a woman named Carla Reese. Many times over coffee and cookies Carla had confided to Barb how much she wanted a baby. Went on and on that she had done so much research on fertilization that she knew the numbers by heart. Freezing eggs or embryos—$15 to $25 thousand plus $500 a year for storage. Success rate: somewhere between 11% to 35%. But, she said, even though her business was thriving, she couldn't afford to try the procedure more than once.

Barb had asked about adoption. All the girls in the office had, but Carla just kept playing the "yeah—but" game. Yeah she'd thought of it, but the waiting period was too long. Yeah, she called an agency, but they had all kinds of questionnaires and reports to fill out.

Sooner or later they'd find out about her little drug problem back in college. Yeah, there were countries that had children available, but she didn't want to deal with miles of red tape or make the trip to some country where she didn't even know the language.

Suddenly, Barb wrote, out of the blue a little boy is coming to live with Auntie Carla. Some made up brother got killed and he had a made up son. Everyone knew the whole story was bogus because Carla has no siblings.

When Kathy looked up Carla Reese and her business, she was stunned to see the Flat River, Missouri address. Maybe this Reese woman was involved with Stevie somehow. She was getting ready to call Vince when her phone connected to the hotline rang.

The caller lived in Kimmswick. She'd been a "close personal friend" of Baylor's. She and her husband, Bill, knew Stevie since he was born. In fact, she remembered meeting Kathy and had dropped in on Vince a few times. Anyway, she wanted to know if Kathy was aware of all the commotion going on down in Missouri today. Quite a mess. "Well," she went on excitedly, "some boys was spotted with a strange man. One of 'em, a teenager just about Stevie's age, stabbed the man and escaped before the police came. Now everyone's out lookin' for him."

"And what about the other children?" Kathy asked.

"Strange thing…when they was first seen, at some diner, there was three of 'em. At least that's what the owner said. But about an hour later, when they was spotted along the road, there was only the teenager."

"Where did all this happen?" Kathy asked.

"Just outside Flat River."

After thanking the woman, Kathy immediately called Laura. The reporter would certainly know more details.

"Hey, Kathy, we were just going to call you."

"We?"

"Yeah, I'm at the house with Vince."

"Does this have anything to do with a boy who looks like Stevie being in Flat River?"

Laura was stunned. "How did you know?" Then she turned to Vince. "It's Kathy. She knows what's been going on here."

"Have you heard of a woman named Carla Reese?" Kathy asked.

"Yes." Laura was surprised again. "That's why I'm here. Let me put you on speaker."

Laura laid her cell on the counter; the three of them huddled over the phone. Kathy explained everything she knew.

"And she lives in Flat River?" Vince asked.

"She's got to have something to do with all this," Kathy said. "Don't you always say that there's no such thing as a coincidence?"

"I think that was Freud," Benny chimed in. "But in this case I'd say he's right. Let me go see what I can find out," he said walking quickly to the front of the house, looking for his phone.

"So what now?" Vince asked. "Think we should call Stoffel—"

"No," Laura said, "that guy's good for nothing. Let's go to Flat River; Kathy can give us the address of the Reese woman and we'll see for ourselves."

Vince knew Kathy was thinking exactly what he was at that moment. Laura wanted to get her story, beat everyone else to the prize. How stupid they had been to trust her.

"Vince," Kathy said weakly, "I don't think it's a good idea to—"

"There's a black car pulling into the driveway," Benny shouted. "Vince, you should go see if it's the boy. We don't want to all rush out and spook him."

"Go, Vince. Call me right back." Kathy hung up.

He wanted to run, but forced himself to walk casually to the door. Give the boy time. He doesn't even know me, Vince reminded himself. Stay calm.

And then he saw him. A thin teenager with shoulder length dirty hair. That was all Vince could see as he waited. The kid sat in the car, gripping the steering wheel and staring at the house. His home.

When he finally got out, he didn't run but walked cautiously, as if afraid the cement beneath his shoes might explode. He wore faded jeans with a patch on one knee. His t-shirt, a dingy white cotton thing, clung to his bony frame. All he had for warmth was a camouflage hoodie that he wore unzipped. The sole of one of his black tennis shoes flapped with each step he took.

Vince couldn't stand the tension anymore and opened the front door. "Stevie?"

"Yeah," The boy gave a slight nod. His lips were a tight line across his pale face. "I made it." Then he started to sob. Falling to his knees he pounded the ground as he erupted with emotions held in check for years. His body rocked as he cried.

Vince didn't move, wanting to give the poor kid a minute. Finally he gently asked, "Are you okay?"

"I'm fine." Stevie wiped his face with the hem of his t-shirt. Slowly he started to get up. When he was standing he brushed off the knees of his jeans and looked up at the front door. "Mr. Lloyd?" It was as if he was making a wish instead of asking a question.

The screeching made them both turn. Suddenly the red van came to a sudden stop on the front lawn, plowing into the mailbox.

CHAPTER FIFTY-EIGHT

Roy flew out of the vehicle, then came bounding across the grass, up the driveway and tackled Stevie back to the ground. Vince was so confused he didn't know how to react. Maybe this kid wasn't Stevie. Maybe he'd escaped from prison and Roy was here to bring him back?

Come on, Daddy. You know it's Stevie.

Jumping down the steps, Vince ran behind Roy, grabbing for his arms. But the man outweighed him and was at least a foot taller.

Stevie managed to wiggle out from beneath Roy's weight, shimmying backwards, kicking all the way. The big man's face, stomach, his chest, all got pounded. When he was free, Stevie came around to stand by Vince.

Benny took the stairs cautiously, gripping the hammer he'd found earlier. Laura followed behind him, holding her phone. Standing clear of the men, she called 911. After disconnecting with the police, she started snapping pictures of the struggle.

Stevie kicked and pounded his fists on Roy's back as the big man wrestled across the lawn with Vince. It looked like more of a power struggle than a fight coming from the guard. Vince battled to flip Roy onto his back, grabbing low on the big guy's legs. Roy went for the stomach, punching Vince in his guts. But it was just to get the man off him. All he wanted was the kid.

They groaned and cursed as they tumbled, until Vince finally got enough space to rear back and land a bull's eye kick on Roy's chest. The man doubled over, trying to remain standing but his knees gave out. They all heard the crack as he came down like a felled tree. Then Stevie tackled Roy backwards, slamming himself on top of the injured man's chest.

"The police are coming!" Laura screamed. "Just stay there."

That last remark seemed to strike Roy as funny and he laughed. "I work for the damn state. Who you think they gonna listen to? You or me? His mama asked me to come here. How you think I got this address?"

"I don't believe a word you're saying," Vince yelled.

"She been worried sick about her little boy. I done all this for her. Now git off me!"

Stevie didn't move.

"If this is true, why didn't you tell me any of this at the prison?"

"You was thick with her old man. She always say he's the one got Stevie stolen. She blamed him for everything that went bad."

"You're a liar," Stevie growled. "You think I'm stupid? That I didn't see you with Mister? My dad's a good guy."

Vince came behind the boy and lifted him off Roy. "We have this guy's name; we know where he works and," he nodded at the cop car coming toward them, "they'll take care of it now. You're safe."

Stevie wanted to relax, believe that things were gonna be okay, but when Mr. Lloyd patted his shoulder, he jerked away.

Stoffel got out of the patrol car. Seeing the stranger on the ground, he asked, "What's going on here? You okay, Mr. Lloyd?" Before anyone could answer, he the spotted the boy.

"That you, Stevie?" he asked, squinting, turning his head to just the right angle so he could be sure. "Oh my God, son, I thought you were…I mean we all thought…"

"Don't start gettin' all choked up here," Roy said as he got to his feet. "You gotta help me git this kid to jail, Sheriff."

Stoffel suddenly remembered the stabbing. "Were you out near Flat River today?" he asked Stevie.

"Yes, but you gotta listen to me." He held up his hands. Turning to Vince he pleaded. "Mr. Lloyd, it was self-defense. I had to get away from that creep. Mister was gonna steal more kids—"

"Self defense? What the hell did you do, boy?" Roy demanded.

"This Mister, he was the one who kidnapped you?" Vince asked.

"What was his name," Laura wanted to know. "Do you know his name, Stevie?"

"No. He just told me to call him Mister. That's all I ever called him."

"The kid's a born liar," Roy said as he reached out to grab Stevie's arm. "He's comin' with me. This is out of your jurisdiction, Sheriff. The boy has to answer for what he done."

"Don't touch him!" Vince shouted, shoving Stevie toward the house.

"That kid's a killer," Roy yelled. "An' he gotta pay."

"I'll take full responsibility," Stoffel said. "Until I find out exactly why you're here and what you want—"

Roy had his gun out so quickly it seemed to have magically appeared.

Several neighbors were gathering now. He knew he was outnumbered but if he didn't give it a try, he'd end up deader than Mister was.

A father was supposed to protect his little girl—or boy, Vince thought. But he'd let the worst thing in the world happen to Gabby. Not this time, though. He'd promised Baylor and himself that Stevie was coming home. And that's exactly what was going to happen today. Even if he had to die keeping the boy safe.

Vince grabbed for Roy's gun. Laura gasped; Benny raised the hammer he held but knew he could never use it to kill anyone.

Stoffel pulled out his revolver with a shaky hand. "Hold it. Mr. Lloyd, step back."

Vince didn't hear a thing. His ears buzzed with rage. Nothing could have changed his mind or distracted him. All the hurt and self-loathing had somehow programmed him for this moment.

Roy jammed the gun into Vince's stomach.

"Do it!" Vince said softly, looking the man in the eyes. "Please, do us all a favor and kill me."

Wildly, Roy turned and shot at Stevie. That damn boy had caused all this trouble. "You're the reason for all this. Killin' the preacher like that." How many times had he told that asshole to git rid of his damn Herder? Now look what happened.

Vince jumped to twist the revolver with both his hands, trying to get it out of Roy's grip. Bones snapped as the beefy man resisted.

"One of us gonna die here, Mister. Who you think it'll be?"

Holding the gun, Vince stepped back and aimed. Everything was so clear. The hairs on Roy's chin, his stained teeth. Clear and slow like they were moving in honey. Someone was shouting; a child was crying. Hands reached out to stop him.

The first shot vibrated through Vince's arms. The second brought every movement back to real time.

Gasps. Then silence so pure, so complete, he relaxed.

It was Stevie who made the first sound. Sitting in the grass, he began to scream hysterically.

"Oh God," Vince said, as he suddenly realized he'd killed a man.

Stevie stopped screaming and it became impossibly quiet.

"Jesus," Benny said. Vince looked at him. "I didn't see a thing," the older man said.

Vince turned his eyes to Laura who was staring at him in disbelief.

"Neither did I," Laura said.

Stevie moaned and rocked himself.

"Yes," Stoffel said, suddenly. He stepped forward and took the gun from Vince's hand. "You all saw it. I shot him."

"But—" Vince said.

"I shot him, I said!" Stoffel cut him off. People were beginning to gather around. The Sheriff lowered his voice and said to all of them, "You got that? I'm the one who shot him!"

As Stoffel went to the body, both Benny and Laura approached Vince.

"What's he doing?" Benny asked.

"He's taking the blame," Vince said.

"No he's not," Laura said. They both looked at her. "He's taking the credit."

CHAPTER FIFTY-NINE

As the EMTs loaded the body of Roy Willis into the back of the ambulance, Laura and the Sheriff compared notes.

"This Mister person Stevie talked about?" Laura asked, "is he dead?"

"Naw. From what the witness says, Stevie stabbed him in the stomach. Didn't hit any vital organs—luckily. He's gonna be fine. The police are questioning him now and after he's good to leave the hospital, they'll take him into custody. But you know they're gonna need to question the boy."

"Not today. He's been through so much; he needs to rest…in his own bed."

"You know better than anyone that the press is gonna have a feeding frenzy when all this gets out," Stoffel said. "None of us is gettin' any rest once they find out Stevie's home. Unless we can work out something here. You know—I wash your back, you wash mine? I can keep things quiet around here till tomorrow an' you can git me on your news show. What do they call it? Oh yeah, an exclusive?"

Here she was, right in the middle of a national—no, worldwide—story. After all the excitement died down she'd get a book deal. Six figures at least. Then the made-for-TV-movie, based on her best-seller, maybe she'd be a consultant for some crime show… But she'd given her word. "Sure," she told him, "we can work something out."

He winked at her. "Good. I got plenty of connections an' even a few favors I can call in. Should be able to give you all some private time."

"So you think this man is the one who took Stevie to begin with?" she asked.

"I do." The Sheriff smiled, hoping she couldn't see the doubt behind it. "And you can quote me on that."

"Let me go get a few things out of my car so I can take a few notes."

"I'll be right here." Stoffel straightened his tie.

When she was sure he couldn't see what she was doing, Laura called Kathy.

After filling in all the details she finished up by saying, "Don't worry, Vince and Stevie are fine and I think we can hold the press off for a day. That should give us time to decompress."

"How will Vince come off?" Kathy asked, "when you write up your version of all this? We both know he's not a killer. For God's sake, Laura, you know what kind of man he is."

"He was saving Stevie. It was self-defense all the way. That's what I saw and that's what I'll write."

"I'm sorry," Kathy broke down. "He could have been killed—you all could have been. I can't stop shaking."

"Me neither. And now I've got Stoffel out there expecting me to report that he's some kind of hero. You should see the dope. Hasn't done one thing to help for years and now he wants—"

"So write it that way. Make him a regular Superman," Kathy said. "It'll take some of the attention off Vince, right?"

Laura thought a second. "And Stevie. He's so confused."

"I'm throwing together some things and I'll be down there tonight. Do what you think is right for Stevie…and then us. I trust you, Laura," Kathy said. "And thanks for everything."

"We're in this together. Remember that," Laura told her. "No matter what happens."

"Hey, Tammy!" Big Mouth Lawanda shouted. "Yer kid's on TV!"

"Is he alive?" she called back. "is he okay?"

"Looks like it."

Tammy pushed her face against the bars of her cell. "Guard! Come on, let me out so I can see my baby. Oh my God, my baby's back! Guard!"

Act happy, she told herself. Act more than happy. What the hell happened? Where was Malcolm? And Roy? Stay calm. You're the happy mother, excited to have her baby home. Smile big…no…cry, that'll look better.

The guard unlocked the door and walked Tammy to the TV room. "It's a miracle," she said. "You must be feeling pretty lucky, huh? Getting your boy back—alive. And after all these years—who would have thought. Yep," she said as Tammy sat down, "Mighty lucky. Not like poor Roy."

After a thorough examination, Malcolm Barnes was stitched up then transferred to a private room, courtesy of the state of Missouri. He nodded toward the cross nailed to the wall opposite his bed. So far, so good, he thought. He was a respected member of the clergy. No jail time, no offenses of any kind—his record was flawless. Well… maybe there were a few things but nothing anyone knew about, or would believe coming out of the mouth of a dumb ass kid.

He'd asked the doctor when he could go home and got a shrug. "An FBI agent has been waiting to question you. Depends on him."

"Then send him in," Malcolm said. "Let's get this over with."

Agent Wells looked annoyed when he entered the room. After a polite introduction and handshake, making sure Malcolm felt up to an interview, he got right to business.

"Let me get this straight, Mr. Barnes. You say Steven Kracher worked for you? Willingly?"

"Yes."

"Doing what, exactly? I don't understand why a minister would have to go out and kidnap someone to work for him."

"It was more of a favor…to his mama. You see, I was working as a guard at the prison where she was serving time. Her baby boy had been entrusted to her husband—"

"The boy's father."

"A genetic mistake. Just because a man lies down with a woman, doesn't mean he'll walk away father of the year." Malcolm shook his head. "And Tammy wasn't the only one. Many inmates have their children taken away from them and placed in the home of some stranger—"

"Relative. The system places them with caring relatives. Those closest to the family."

Malcolm snorted. "No. Those people shouldn't be parents just because some judge says so. Or a burned-out social worker, over-loaded with too many cases just wants to hurry up and get rid of them. I've seen it again and again."

"But Steven Kracher wasn't a baby. He had a father who loved him—"

"And a tramp for a mother. A sinner. But she asked me to save her son from a man she believed was an abuser. A child molester."

"Those are mighty big accusations, Mr. Barnes."

"No, those are true words," he corrected. "Big words come from God. And it was He who gave me this mission."

This guy was a real nut job. One of those religious fanatics, Wells thought. It was getting late, he was hungry and Barnes wasn't going anywhere. The press had gotten wind of the story somehow. He'd passed a CNN news van outside the gate. Nothing could be kept quiet for too long with all the cell phones and amateur detectives on line. He hated the pressure, the frantic need for news updates. Everyone out there like vampires, sucking up any drop of news. He'd have to calm things down before they got out of hand.

"That's all for today," he told the preacher. "We'll talk later."

He's scared, Malcolm thought. Afraid he'll make a false arrest and have his precious career ruined. "I'm not going anywhere… apparently," he said.

Wells hated the man on sight. When he first joined the bureau, he'd listened to all the lectures, took courses in reading body language, interrogation, tried to be neutral—just work with the facts on the table. But after a few regrettable screw-ups and too many years on the job, he'd learned to trust his gut. And today his gut was screaming that Barnes was guilty of not only kidnapping Stevie Kracher but much more.

PART SEVENTEEN

STEVIE

CHAPTER SIXTY

"Dad! I'm home! Where are you? Dad!"
Please, I need for my Dad to be here. Can't trust those people out there—don't know any of 'em. An' Mister sayin' he killed Dad… They all lie—him to keep me out there—them to get me back in here.

I run to his bedroom. "Dad!"

Not there.

So I run faster. To the spare room, kitchen, backyard, basement and…finally I'm standin' at the door of my room. Why would it be closed? Bet he's in there, waitin' to surprise me. Yeah, when I open it, he'll be there an' we'll both laugh. I shove the door open an' rush inside. "Dad!"

But…he ain't here. An' where's all my stuff? At least I still have a bed but it's piled high with a bunch of presents—all kinds, Some in boxes, some in bags, every one of 'em with a card from Dad. Always kidded him how he wrote like a first grader. "I miss you, son. Here's hoping we'll be together next birthday. Love, Dad." I touch the big box it's stuck to but can't open it without him here. Santa Claus paper an' stupid Easter Bunnies. Looks like there's somethin' for every holiday I was gone. Never needed no special time—I thought about him every single day.

There's clothes in my closet. Lot of good they do me now—all too small. I check the corner for my posters. When things got real bad, I'd pretend I was racin' 'round the track at the 500, leavin' Franchetti in the dust. Or I'd be in the Millennium Falcon, cuttin' through space.

When we took each one down, Dad would roll it up an' put a rubber band around to keep it from rippin'. I was gonna just throw em' on the floor till we got the paint. Navy blue was the color I wanted. But Dad said it was way too dark for this little room an' I'd feel smothered. He wanted green. When I told him it looked like puke, we had a fight. Even while we was yellin', he kept rollin' those stupid posters up. Bein' so careful. When the walls were bare, he piled 'em in the corner of the closet so no paint would get to 'em.

I never thanked him.

Don't matter now where those stupid posters are, I guess. This ain't my house no more—not like before. It even smells different. Kinda like nobody lives here.

I go back to the front room. Same couch, same dumb glass table. Dad was all the time hittin' his shin on the edge. He hated that damn thing, threatened to just pitch it out the back door. But Mom bought it. Said it was "elegant." As if she'd know what that meant. Maybe he was hopin' she'd come back. Not me, though.

Same lamps, same school picture by the window. New carpet, blue—my favorite color. Things are kinda the same—but different. Like me. I'm a killer now.

After Mr. Lloyd tells me the truth about Dad, the cops can take me away for what I done to Mister. I deserve it. Guess I'm no good, like my mother.

"Stevie? You okay?" He comes up behind me.

I turn around. "Were you with my Dad when he died?"

He looks sad when he says, "No. He died in the ambulance on the way to the hospital. I'm so sorry."

"Do you think it was on account of me not bein' here?"

"Absolutely not. No way. Your father just had a bad heart. No one's to blame."

I know he's tryin' to make me feel better, but it ain't workin'.

He changes the subject all of a sudden. "I came in to tell you some good news. Mr. Barnes is okay."

"Who?" Why should I care about some guy I don't even know?

"The man you stabbed."

Everythin's churnin' inside my stomach, like a tornado I can't hold down. "I had to! He was gonna take that kid. He was gonna make him do bad stuff—like he done with me. I wanted him dead. I tried to stop him but I couldn't. I can't do nothin' right." I don't want to cry but I feel it comin' on.

When he gets closer, I push him off.

"Okay." He holds up his hands like they do in them Westerns. Showin' me he got no weapon. "Just listen to me. You're not in any trouble. No one's going to hurt you or take you away—ever. No one."

He means it. I can see his eyes are honest. I want to believe him... but...

"And after he gets out of the hospital, he'll be taken into police custody. He can never hurt you again. Never. Do you want to ask me any questions? Or maybe you want to be alone for a while? Are you hungry? I can fix you—"

"Damit! Stop askin' me so much!"

"Sorry."

Now what? He looks like I hit him and it makes me feel bad. But I gotta think of myself now. Can't worry about nobody else, 'specially some grown-up man.

"Your bed's all made up. Why don't you relax...I'll be down the hall. We can talk when you're ready."

He tries again, so I try. "Thanks."

They're in the kitchen, chatterin' away. I catch somethin' about this Barnes guy, somethin' about it bein' on the news. But when I come into the room, they get quiet.

"Stevie, you're up. Did you sleep well?" a red-headed woman asks.

"I guess." I can see its dark outside. "What time is it?"

"Almost ten. You've been asleep close to nine hours," the old guy says.

The blonde lady smiles as she walks toward me. She's pretty. "I'm Vince's wife, Kathy. I was a friend of your father's. He was such a good man." I can tell she wants to hug me but holds herself back.

"And I'm Laura," the other lady says. "You must be starved. Come sit, we made dinner."

What do I say to these people in my house that knew my Dad? They all act like they belong here. I'm finally home...but I'm not.

While the blonde lady—Kathy—goes to the stove, the old guy smiles. "Hi, I'm Doctor Hodges. Glad to meet you, young man." He holds out his hand and I shake it. He seems like a nice dude.

"Did you know my father?" I ask, hoping.

"No, I did not. Sorry to say. From what I hear, though, he was a wonderful man. And he never stopped looking for you. You always have to remember that."

"Then he's really dead?"

"Sorry, son. About a year ago."

Kathy brings a plate of spaghetti and sets it down in front of me then rubs my shoulder.

"I know this is all too much for you to process today," the doctor says, "and you can have all the time you need…but there are so many people who have been looking for you for so long and they want to know what's going on—"

Laura interrupts him. "I work for Channel 4 News in St. Louis. I've been covering your story from the first day you went missing—"

"Got kidnapped. It ain't as if I just walked off for no good reason. I'd never do that to my Dad."

"Oh no, we all know that. But there are people out there who don't know it and we need to set them straight—"

Mr. Lloyd interrupts her. "And you don't ever have to talk to any of them—individually. But in order to protect your privacy, we need to issue a statement. Understand?"

"I guess so."

They all look at the doctor. He nods. "First thing we have to do is make sure you're okay—physically. Good thing I'm here or the authorities would insist you be sent to the hospital. But I can examine you and write a report…if you'll let me."

"I'm not a kid. No one can make me go anywhere, can they?"

"Well…you did assault someone…" Mr. Lloyd says it like he's sorry.

"You said he's okay. Mister's okay, right?"

"We're just trying to head off any problems," the doc says. "Don't worry, there's nothing to worry about. We're all going to help you."

"So I'm not in trouble? There's nothin' I have to do this minute?"

Kathy's voice is like a mother's should sound when she tells me, "Nothing. You just relax and eat your dinner. If there's anything else you'd like, something special, a favorite ice cream or hamburger, just say the word. I'll go right out and get it."

"And if you're not comfortable with me doing the examination we could take you to—"

"I don't want to go nowhere. Not for a while. So I guess I'm okay with you doin' your report."

"Good. It shouldn't take that long anyway. You look healthy to me." The doc smiles in a nice friendly way.

"And tomorrow we'll write up a statement for the press," Laura says.

"I can read it for you—"

"Why would you want to do that, Mr. Lloyd? You ain't my dad or even a relation. I can talk for myself."

"Stevie," Kathy says, "there might be some mean questions. People can be like vultures. Picking at you, asking the same question over and over until you crack. And don't forget, Mr. Barnes was a minister. I'm sure he had parishioners and they'll try to blame you for everything he did."

"But he had a gun; he made me do stuff. When I stabbed him I was only tryin' to save that kid."

"We believe you, Stevie." Mr. Lloyd rubs his arm like it's hurtin' him. "Your father and I had long conversations about what a good kid you are. He was so proud…"

Everyone's quiet for a minute. Then Mr. Lloyd starts up again.

"No one is going to believe you'd try to kill anyone. But if it would be okay, I'd like to be there. We can talk to the reporters together."

"I don't get it. Why do I have to talk to any of them?"

The reporter lady laughs, kinda in a sad way. "Because if you don't, they'll never leave you alone. Might as well give them something now and hopefully, they'll back off for a while."

Kathy looks like she just thought of somethin'. "Why can't you record an interview here? Just the two of you. Or all of us if you think that's better. It would make a great story. And that way Stevie won't be caught off guard."

"I thought of that but didn't want it to look like I was using this situation for my own—"

"We'll be using you," Mr. Lloyd says. "to help Stevie.

They all seem happier now.

"Why don't we let the poor kid eat now?" Kathy says. "Have you thought about anything else you'd like?" she asks me. "Maybe for dessert?"

"Got any Oreos?" Mister wouldn't get any 'cause he knew I liked 'em so much.

"A boy after my own heart," she says.

CHAPTER SIXTY-ONE

Why don't I feel safe here? I'm home. I'm where I wanted to be all those crumby years. Yeah, it feels real good havin' four people—even though they're strangers—care so much about me...I guess. Before there was just me an' Dad. Neighbors too. Most were okay but some were real nosey. One time Dad an' me turned all the lights off an' hid when Mrs. Nelson come snoopin'. The more she knocked, the funnier it got. We weren't much for goin' to church neither. Just wanted to be left alone to ourselves.

I'm eighteen now. Sure don't feel like no man, though. There's a few hairs on my face but not enough to make a beard or mustache. I got to watch TV when I was...away. Is that how I should think of them years? Tell folks, for the rest of my life, that I went "away?" I know what kids my age are talkin' about. But there are way too many short ways to say things. Lots of letters now—no real words. I'd feel stupid tryin' to talk like 'em. Mister always talked formal, like he was in church preachin'. There's new music I don't know about an' movies I never seen. I can catch up...but then what?

This mornin', bright an' early, Sheriff Stoffel come by. Wanted to see me, an' after makin' a fuss, talkin' on an' on how sorry he was about Dad an' me havin' such a hard time of it, said I had to come in to be questioned 'bout the stabbin'. Mr. Lloyd was there the whole time, askin' if there was charges against me. When the Sheriff said there was, Mr. Lloyd got real mad, threatenin' to make our own charges against Mister for kidnappin'

"Mr. Barnes insists Stevie came with him of his own free will. Said the boy was helping rescue those children. Claims the boy just up and stabbed him for no good reason."

"That's a lie!"

"Of course it is," Mr. Lloyd says. "Don't worry, son, we'll take care of all this."

I don't like when he calls me "son," but it don't make me all that mad neither.

"Do you know a boy named Troy Whitehill?" Sheriff Stoffel asks me all of a sudden, like he just thought of it.

"Yeah. Is he okay?" Please say the kid's alive. Please.

"And you took him to Flat River?"

"Stop interrogating the boy. We'll bring him down—"

"Mister drove me an' Jimmy an' Troy to Flat River. He made us all go. I didn't do nothin' on my own. No way—it was all him."

"Jimmy? Where's this Jimmy now?"

I helped dig the hole. I left poor Jimmy there, all alone. I'm worse than Mister. I should go to hell for all I done. Should I tell? If I tell will they put me in jail?

"Enough!" Mr. Lloyd shouts at the Sheriff. He gits so mad his face turns the color of watermelon. "After I call my lawyer, we'll come in. Tomorrow."

It only takes a second for him to calm down. Then he says to me, "Don't answer any questions now. No more."

Doc Hodges comes in with his report. "Here. The boy's been through a lot but he's in good shape—physically. I'll take full responsibility for him."

"Hey, I'm not the enemy here. I only want the best for the kid." Then the Sheriff turns to me. "The whole town's rootin' for ya." He tries to give me a high five but I act like I don't see his pathetic hand hangin' there. This guy's ego is the biggest thing about him. I always thought he was a creep.

Finally we all end up in front of the window, watchin' the cop car drive away.

"I guess I should be going, too," Doc says.

"How can we thank you?" Kathy asks him. "If it wouldn't have been for you we'd never know about the badge and Vince wouldn't have gone to see…"

There's somethin' they don't want me to know.

"I needed a kick in the ass," Mr. Lloyd tells him as they hug good-bye. "You're one of the good guys, Benny."

I don't know how I'm supposed to act now so I push my hands

deep in my pockets an' smile at Doc.

But the old guy puts his hands on my shoulders, an' when I look up he's starin' straight in my eyes. "Now you listen to me, Steven. You haven't done anything wrong. You didn't deserve all the bad things that came your way. And you'll be fine. Oh, it might take a while...but be patient with yourself. No one's asking you to hurry. Understand?"

I nod.

"Trust these folks here. They've all been working so hard to get you back safe and sound. You can go to anyone of 'em, tell them anything." Then he grabs me in a strong hug. If I had a grandfather, I bet he'd be like Doc. I can smell the mint in his mouth that he's been chewin' on. When he finally lets go, he puts on his jacket.

The reporter lady says goodbye and for a few minutes they're all huggin' and pattin' shoulders.

Doc starts out the door but then stops. Reachin' into his pocket, he hands me a card. "Call me if you just want to talk. I'll always be there for you."

"Thanks." I'm not sure what all the numbers runnin' along the bottom are but if I need him, I'll figure it out.

Mr. Lloyd walks Doc to his car and the two ladies look sad. It's uncomfortable in the room...so quiet I can hear my stomach growl. They musta heard it, too.

"Do they still make cherry pancakes down at Myrtle's?" I ask. I need to get outta here for awhile. An' I'm real hungry. "Is Myrtle's still there?"

"Sure it is," Kathy tells me. "Let's all go—"

"Do you think that's a good idea?" Laura wants to know. "There'll be people down there, asking all sorts of questions."

Mr. Lloyd walks in then. "Who's asking questions?"

"Stevie wants to go to Myrtle's for breakfast. What do you think? Should we expose him to outsiders so soon?" his wife asks. She seems like she really cares about me.

"There's about ten reporters out in the street, waiting to catch sight of you," Mr. Lloyd says. "We can sneak out the back, I guess. But are you ready for the people and questions when we get to Myrtle's?" He's taller than me by a head; his eyes ain't as angry as yesterday. "If you think you can handle it...we'll do whatever you want."

Laura chimes in, "I can go out and talk to them. Maybe make a statement for you? Be your spokesperson? Since your parents aren't here to do it. Unless there's some relative…"

"No, you should do it. Please."

The three of 'em talk it over an' finally come up with somethin' she writes down. Then they ask if I wanna go out with her.

"I just want some pancakes. That's all."

There ain't too many cars in the lot but I feel scared. I been comin' to Myrtle's forever an' all of a sudden I don't wanna get outta the car.

"You okay?" Kathy asks. "We can leave. You don't have to go inside. We can turn around—"

"Let's just git this over with."

Reporter lady told us she'd talk to them news people; give us a chance to escape out the back. That's the word she used. "Escape." I feel like a criminal. Maybe I am.

Mr. Lloyd opens my door and stands there while I undo the seat belt. Kathy looks worried when she gets out. I'm not so hungry now. Maybe we should go back.

Finally, I force myself outta the car.

There's a big ole sign on the front door. WELCOME HOME STEVIE. The letters look like they been written in red crayon, sparkly stuff is glued in the corners. I hang back, let the Lloyds walk in ahead of me.

At first she don't recognize me, but I'd know her just by her cough. Bootsie's been smokin' three packs a day since I been a baby. After she talks to Mr. Lloyd she finally sees me standin' behind him.

"Good God! Is that you? Little Steven Kracher?" She screams it. Everyone in the place looks up, some come runnin' over to take a look at me. Bootsie hurries out from behind the counter an' hugs me real tight. She smells like cigarettes an' flowery perfume she wears, hopin' she don't smell like smoke.

After she's done, she pushes me back to have a better look. "I want you to know that we never gave up hope. None of us. Not for one day. All of us been out there day after day, month after month, lookin', just waitin' to hear some…" She can't finish her words 'cause she's too emotional. "Someone fetch me a chair before I pass out right here on the spot."

A girl I never seen before leads Bootsie to a front table. Then she reaches over to a napkin holder an' peels off a few. Bootsie rubs her face with that piece of stiff paper til I swear she's gonna draw blood.

I sit down with her. "I'm fine. See? I'm good, Bootsie. But I been thinkin' about them cherry pancakes of yours for so long. Suppose we can git an order? An' bacon?"

"Honey, you can eat pancakes until you bust." She laughs. "Now you go sit down. I'm fine. This is your day. Don't let some old hysterical woman steal your thunder."

When she gits up, she looks happy.

"Ya'll sit down an' I'll git some coffee," she tells the Lloyds. "Do you drink coffee now, sweetheart? Or do you want chocolate milk. 'member how you loved your chocolate milk? Your daddy would all the time say it weren't no good for you. But—"

"Milk would be great."

CHAPTER SIXTY-TWO

I don't wanna see Mister—but I have to. None of this'll be over till I face him. They keep showin' my picture on TV. Every channel with a story about me bein' back home an' then there's always another about…him. An' every time they mention Malcolm Barnes, it takes me a minute to figure out who they're talkin' about. If I don't think that he has a regular name, then he ain't real.

This lawyer lady, Medora, flew all the way from Chicago. She asks me a lot of questions after dinner. Asks about the little kids.

"Did you help Mr. Barnes kidnap them?"

"No. He just brung 'em home."

"And you didn't wonder where they came from? They must have been crying? I'm sure they wanted to go home. Did they ask you to take them home? Back to their parents?"

"Yes."

"Why didn't you, then? Were you tied up or locked away?"

"No. But I couldn't just pick 'em up an' run. We moved all the time. I never knew exactly where we was."

"So when Mr. Barnes was out…trolling…why didn't you run? Try to get help?"

"Cause I had to stay an' protect the ones in the house. If I weren't there, no tellin' what he'd do."

"But you just said—"

"Medora," Mr. Lloyd jumps in, "the boy's not on trial here. Lighten up."

"You're right. He's not on trial today. But there's that boy they found buried in the field, countless missing children he—"

"Saved. Stevie protected them. And Benny will testify that he witnessed Stevie running with that child. He was running away from Barnes. Benny saw a knife." Then he looks at me. "Tell her how you were threatened, beaten. Tell her what you told me."

I been buryin' stuff for a long time now. Don't want to remember how it was in the beginnin', when Mister first grabbed me.

"I can't talk no more."

"Later," Mr. Lloyd says. And when he smiles at me, I feel better. "No rush."

"Are you sure you're okay?"

Everyone keeps askin' me that. An' I always say I'm fine. But now that we're in front of the police station, I'm not so sure.

Lots of cars are parked in front an' news vans all over the place. Laura runs over to us.

"Hey, Stevie, how ya doin'?"

"Fine."

"Is your crew here?" Mr. Lloyd asks her.

"Just Ken, my cameraman." She points an' waves at a guy in a red jacket.

"Get in," Medora says. They talk about a story an' what's gonna happen when we get outta the car.

"You know it wasn't me who leaked the story," Laura says to us.

"We know," Kathy tells her.

"Personally, I think it was Stoffel."

"We talked it over last night," Medora says. "You can have an exclusive interview but it has to be done today. Right, Stevie? If you've changed your mind, I can issue a statement—"

"I won't have to answer nothin' I don't want to...that's what you said."

"I'll make it quick and painless," Laura says. Then she winks at me.

"Fine. Let's go."

It's like I'm a movie star or somethin'. People start yellin' an' wavin' microphones in my face. We get pushed around. For a minute I'm afraid they're gonna pull me away from Mr. Lloyd so I grab for his hand. When we finally shove through, we race up the stairs. A cop comes out just in time an' holds the door open.

"Show's over, folks. Leave the poor kid alone."

The Sheriff's waitin' for us in the hall, lookin' all polished up.

He done somethin' to his teeth. They look white as milk. "Ya'll okay?"

"Have we got time for a quick interview?" Laura asks him. She talks in a flirty way.

He slicks back his hair. "Sure."

"Sorry, Sheriff, we just need Stevie—"

"An' Mr. an' Mrs. Lloyd," I tell her. I'm shakin' now.

Kathy puts her arm around me. "We're not going to leave you alone, sweetie."

The Sheriff looks hurt, standin' there like a big ole Baby Huey. He wants so bad for everyone to think he's in charge.

"But if you could get my camerman? He's across the street. And while you're out there, maybe you could talk to those reporters. Keep them occupied?"

His chest puffs up. Now he's happy, him an' his plastic smile. "You can use my office, if you'd like. I'll be right back."

Then Mr. Lloyd says in a low voice, "After the interview, we have to talk to the Sheriff. Medora's here to answer his questions—protect your interests."

Lawyer Lady pulls me into a hug all of a sudden. After a tight squeeze, she lets me go. "No one's getting past this old bird, Steven. I've been at this a long time. I won't let anyone hurt you. But if you want to say something, check with me first. Everything can be twisted against you. Be smart. Got it?"

"Got it."

We walk to the office. It don't look like police stations I seen on TV. But then this ain't New York City. There's just one big room with three beat up desks an' a bunch of wobbly lookin' chairs. We stand there, waitin' for Ken.

"Stoffel's an idiot! Did you see him out there? He's working the crowd, milking his fifteen minutes." Ken takes off his jacket. "Where we gonna do this?"

"Over by the window, I guess," Laura says. "The light's better. Let's get this done before Stoffel comes back."

Ken pushes us around until we're lined up, me in the middle, Mrs. an' Mrs. Lloyd on the ends.

Laura gets a comb out of that big bag she's always got with her. Then she puts on some lip stuff. "Ready."

Ken starts countin', "Three, two one"

"This is Laura Ann Bonetti with Channel Four News. A miracle happened yesterday. The missing boy, Steven Kracher, who was abducted from his home five years ago has been found alive..."

PART EIGHTEEN

VINCE

CHAPTER SIXTY-THREE

Poor kid. Poor, sweet, innocent kid. What chance did he have with scum like Barnes out there? Kathy's been telling me stories for years, how these bastards come from abusive homes, or were abandoned. Drugs, violence, endless excuses for the monsters they've become. These men should be pitied, she would tell me.

When I'd had enough I would ask her, "You can't be telling me that you have pity for the sonofabitch who killed our daughter? How in God's name can you be so naïve, Kathy? You know the statistics better than anyone—or at least you should. These men are animals. They'll never be cured. Ever! And you want me to have pity for them?"

I'll never forget that afternoon, how she couldn't look at me. She was sitting at her desk and just stared down at the keyboard. Silently, her tears dropped, making little puddles on the black plastic. And I stood there...watching them hit. She never made one sound. Nothing. Not a sob, not a gulp. It was as if someone had flipped a universal switch and turned her off.

How often had she cried like this, I wondered. Over the years had she trained herself to weep silently while I screamed my rage? And I felt like such a bully. I put my hand on her arm, didn't say a word. What could I say? I was too embarrassed.

"No, Vince I don't have pity and I can't forgive any of them!" she shouted. When she stood up I thought she was going to hit me. I deserved whatever she dished out. There was a searing anger in her eyes. "But you know what? I don't have to be a kind, sweet caring person to do what I do. If I'm operating out of rage and hatred, what does it matter as long as we bring another child home? Who cares what I'm feeling? This isn't about me...or you, Vince."

"I know," I said weakly.

"But maybe tomorrow. Every morning I get up and hope that this will be the day I feel less hatred inside me. I need to feel some… peace. I tell myself to have pity, forgiveness, understanding. Maybe if I say it enough times, it'll happen."

I grabbed her, fearing if I let go we'd both collapse.

But I can't muster up pity today. Forgiveness? Hell no. As I stand here, listening to Laura ask Stevie her questions, I wonder how people will feel after watching the interview. Seeing the Little Lost Boy back home, safe, all in one piece. Will some convince themselves that the Big Bad Man is locked up so everyone's safe again? I'm hoping that Stevie's story will kill their innocence. Kill it forever. Cause there's a lot more where Barnes came from.

"Did you know your attacker?" she asks.

Why should he have to defend himself? The real problem everyone's going to have is that he was a teenager—a strong, healthy young man who could defend himself. He was a kid, for God's sake. But he coped.

"You've told me there were other children," Laura continues. "Did Mr. Barnes—"

"Mister," Stevie tells her. "He told me to call him Mister, so I did."

"Did Mister hurt any of these children?"

"No. He just wanted to take them to their Jesus parents. The family he thought they were supposed to be with."

Laura explains to the camera how Barnes had met Tammy in jail while he was a guard. How she heard about him helping other women who had children on the outside living with court appointed guardians. How she convinced him that her husband, Baylor, was an unfit father and Stevie deserved a better home.

"But you were older than the other kids."

Stevie nods. "Yeah they was all pretty little."

"So why do you suppose Mister took you in the first place and then kept you so long?"

I grimace. How should the poor kid know what that bastard was thinking? Should I stop this whole interview? He doesn't look upset and Stevie is legally…an adult. I'm not his father or even a distant relative. While I wrestle with my thoughts, he answers.

"He needed a Herder."

"A what?" Laura looks surprised even though she's heard this before.

"Someone to take care of the kids while he…ahh…made plans… found us places to live…stuff like that."

Stoffel struts into the room and I rush over to him.

"What's going on?"

"Shh, hold your voice down. They're recording an interview."

"Do they need me—"

"No, that's okay. They're almost done."

I hold back a smile as his dejection becomes more obvious.

Stoffel keeps harping on the stabbing. We sit around his desk, Kathy, Medora and I along with a secretary/stenographer, some woman I've never seen before. We've been here for more than two hours and my back aches against this wooden chair.

"Am I to believe that Mr. Barnes is pressing charges against Steven?" Medora asks bewildered.

"Yes," Stoffel says.

"The man who kidnapped my client? The man who beat him, kidnapped countless other children and God knows what else, has the nerve to make accusations against one of his victims?" Medora doesn't wait for an answer. "Well this is a first."

"It takes all kinds," Stoffel says.

"What about the boy in Flat River?" Kathy asks. "Stevie can't be held responsible for that."

"The lady up there, the one who thought she was adoptin' the kid, called the cops when she saw the news. Kid says his name is Troy Whitehill and has nothin' but good things to say about Stevie here. Talks like he's a regular hero."

Stevie looks more frightened than relieved.

"Don't worry," I whisper, "this whole thing is just Mister's way of trying to stay out of prison. Make himself look good"

"Did they find Jimmy?" he suddenly asks.

He says it in such a low voice that we're not sure Stoffel heard.

Medora leans in. "Don't talk about Jimmy now."

But Stevie can't help himself. "We buried him. Mister made Troy an' me do it."

It started down at his feet. They'd been running in place all day. Now his legs twitch. No one seems to notice but me. When the questioning began he rocked back and forth, every so often. Trying to comfort himself, I guess. Talking about Jimmy makes the shaking take over his entire body until even his eyes are bouncing from side to side.

Medora looks concerned. "My client is finished answering any questions. From now on you deal with me." She stands and gestures us to stand, also. "You have my card. I'll be staying in town for the next few days, so it's best to call my cell."

"But...wait a minute," Stoffel sputters.

"Call me tomorrow," Medora barks and pushes us out the door.

CHAPTER SIXTY-FOUR

Laura drives back to St. Louis with Ken to edit the tape. People all over the country are so eager to hear anything about the boy that a special report has been scheduled after the ten o'clock news tonight. Stevie can't stop shaking. Kathy gets in the backseat and when she pulls him into her arms, he offers no complaints.

"We missed lunch," I say to break the ice. "How about a burger? Stevie, got any requests?"

"No."

I pull into a drive-thru and start ordering one of everything.

When we finally get to Baylor's—Stevie's house—he rushes ahead. His key still works, I made sure it always would. The three of us follow behind, slowly.

Kathy sets the table then I put food in the middle. She asks if we should take Stevie to a doctor. "I've never seen anyone so…shattered like that."

"We'll give him ten minutes and then I'll go check on him," I say.

Medora washes her hands at the kitchen sink. "I don't know how to handle this," she says. "Do I coax him to tell us about Jimmy after we eat? Should I wait until tomorrow? Do I go home tonight or stay here? All my clients are adults…well, older than Steven. I'm not good with kids. What do you think, Vince?"

"Let's not force anything."

"Well, I'm starved," Kathy says as she bites into a cheeseburger. "Angst makes me very hungry. I should weigh a ton by now."

Maybe it was the sound of the wrappers or the smell of food, but Stevie slowly walks into the kitchen. "Did you get fries?"

"Sure did. Come eat; you'll feel better. We don't have to talk about Jimmy right now."

"Only when you're ready," Kathy tells him and smiles. "And remember...nothing you say can ever make us mad at you."

"Even if I did something really bad?"

A horrible thought flashes across my mind. What if this teenager isn't so innocent? He's not the kid he was before all this shit happened to him. I don't think I can take it if he's turned into one of the bad guys.

Medora nods. "Everything you tell me will be held in strictest confidence."

"You mean you won't tell no one?" he wants to know.

"Only after we've discussed what's best to tell the authorities. Together we'll figure it out. No surprises. Does that sound fair to you?"

"Sure." Then he hits the bottom of the ketchup bottle until a red blob oozes onto his plate. Emptying a large order of fries on top of the ketchup, he grabs a fork and starts eating.

All conversation up to now, has been about Stevie's kidnapping, his return, Barnes' capture, Baylor. I have no idea how to talk to him about...real life. He's been living such a strange existence, one I can't relate to. But then I remember some mementos in his room.

"You like baseball," I start. "Your dad told me about some of the games he took you to."

"Did he tell you about the time he bought me a Cardinals t-shirt and how we got ten of the guys to autograph it?" He unwraps a taco. "Dad bought this really heavy duty marker and when we got home I seen all this writing on my back. It took four days till it wore off."

He sounds so normal. And for the moment, he's a regular, happy kid. Medora sips her soda, looking relaxed. We've needed this time to just sit and talk about nothing important.

We all chip in and clean the table off. The conversation is light as we throw out the trash, and stack dishes in the sink. But by the time Kathy gets a sponge to wipe away crumbs, the air is heavy again.

"This is your call, Stevie," I say. "We can watch TV or talk about Jimmy."

His face drops. "Might as well get it over with."

"Would you be more comfortable in the living room?" Kathy asks.

"Here's fine." When he sits back down, we follow his lead and position ourselves around him.

"How did you meet Jimmy?" Medora begins.

"Mister brung him home, like he done with the others. I always stayed at whatever house we was livin' at when he done business."

"Business?" Medora asks. "What kind of business?"

That's when Stevie tells us about Jesus Parents and the Jubilation. He recites the craziness as if it were gospel. I'm too stunned to say anything.

"But when we got to Jimmy's new home, no one was there. Mister wanted to just leave him. Just leave a little kid by hisself...in the front yard like an old dog no one wants. But it was night time an' rainin' real hard. I told him Jimmy would get sick—or worse. That's when he talked about Sacrifice."

Kathy gasps. "He didn't..."

"He tried to hurt Jimmy, but I grabbed him an' made a run for it."

"Did you see Benny? He lives in that neighborhood."

Stevie looks up to the ceiling, thinking. "Was that old guy the same dude who was here before?"

Medora nods. "Yes. He said that a man was chasing some boy with a little kid in his arms. That was you?"

"Guess so. We ended up gettin' back in the truck. But at least Jimmy was okay."

"You should be proud that. You saved his life," Kathy says, smiling weakly.

"But he got sick an' Mister got meaner cause he wouldn't be gittin' no money for Jimmy."

"Where's Jimmy now?" I ask, not really wanting to hear what I know he's going to tell us.

"We buried him. He was real weak." Stevie breaks down. His sobbing comes from a deep place that I've visited a few times. There's no voices down there. No light. Just the echo of your own agony. And the deeper you go, the darker it gets.

I kneel down in front of him, grab him tightly and we rock back and forth. The women look frightened. There's nothing they can do now except watch.

It takes twenty minutes for Stevie to calm down. Kathy goes to run a washcloth under cold water. She comes back, timidly, holding it out to me. I press it on the back of his neck. And it's as if I've slapped him.

Jerking up, he's embarrassed but says nothing. Taking the cloth, he wipes his eyes. I stay there, in front of him, my hands on his shoulders. When he looks into my eyes he...smiles. Slightly, so very slightly, but it's there.

He leans close to my ear. "Thanks for bein' here. For me an' my Dad." Then, unexpectedly, he hugs me.

It feels...wonderful.

"Will you take me to see his grave? Please, Mr. Lloyd."

"Of course I will."

CHAPTER SIXTY-FIVE

"A nd this Jimmy," Medora asks. "do you know his last name?" We've all moved into the living room where it's more comfortable. After Stevie calms down, he seems clear-headed. It's like the dam burst and now we're all moving forward on dry ground.

"No. Sorry."

"Did Mister…kill him?" I ask.

"Not with a gun or nuthin' like that. But he hit him a few times. Jimmy got sad after that night in the rain. We had to take him back with us. Mister didn't know what to do with him. Jimmy was scared all the time. He didn't eat nuthin'. He got weak and then just…didn't wake up."

Kathy's trying not to show how stunned she is, but I see. She sands up and walks over to Stevie. "It's been a long day and we're all tired. I think we can talk some more tomorrow." She looks to me for support.

"And if I leave now, I can get to my office before midnight," Medora says. "I need to work through all this with my secretary. We have to prepare our case if we end up in court facing off with Barnes."

"You're not going to stay and watch the news?" I ask. "Laura's report airs tonight. You can go home tomorrow."

"I really should see that. Guess you're right, Vince."

"I wanna see it, too," Stevie says.

"Are you sure?" I ask.

He nods. "More than sure."

Regular programming has been cancelled for the hour preceding the ten o'clock news. A special report: "Journey of a Lost Boy."

Laura's dressed in a tailored suit and opens with five minutes about Kathy and me. Our struggle with personal loss and thankfully, glossing over specific details. She applauds Kathy's organization and my stamina. "If it weren't for these two strangers who came to our state just to offer help, this story might have a very different ending."

Old pictures of Stevie flash in the background, a generic soundtrack plays softly throughout. Shots of the town, the river, details rehashed covering the past three years. When they show his interview at the police station this morning, I figure it's almost over. But there's more.

There's a shot of Carla Reese's home and a statement after she surrendered Troy to the police. A short interview with the Whitehills, smiling, holding their little boy. Franklin Dayton, the boy who witnessed Stevie stab Barnes, talks about his impression of the man.

"He seemed like an ordinary guy. Nothin' special, know what I mean? That's why I was shocked when that kid done him like that. But now I know how close I come to bein' grabbed. An' I wanna thank Stevie Kracher for protectin' me like that."

Sheriff Stoffel comes on next, all smiles, standing there in his shiny shoes and freshly pressed uniform. "Baylor Kracher and his boy were family friends." His eyes are wide with...honesty? "I was heartsick when Stevie went missing but never gave up hope. For years we searched for that boy. Thousands of reports came in daily. Believe me when I tell you, we followed every one of those leads. Drove all over creation when someone called with news of a sighting. And when Roy Willis came after him, well, there was nothing to do but my job. I had to protect the poor boy."

"That idiot didn't do anything!" Stevie says. "You done it, Mr. Lloyd. You protected me."

Laura reports neighbors have conflicting stories—most unsure what they saw during the scuffle. But all agreed that the guard, who had a record since he was a juvenile, would have killed Stevie if someone hadn't stepped in. The pictures she shows are blurred and distorted. She admits she isn't good with a camera.

"I can't believe this," Kathy says turning to me with a big grin on her face.

"No charges will be pressed, no investigation. Looks like you're in the clear, Vince," Medora says.

"And Stoffel's a hero." I have to laugh at the idiot. "But he can't afford one false move or he'll fall off that pedestal of his and the public will nail him."

"Give a man enough rope and he'll hang himself," Medora says. "And people love to sit in the front row with their popcorn and watch the show."

Laura comes back on the screen. "After almost four years of being held captive, Steven Kracher is home. His friends in Kimmswick welcome him back to their community with open arms." Then she pauses a moment and looks directly into the camera. "We all love you, Stevie."

An announcer continues. "Stay tuned for reactions to this exclusive report. You'll only see it here, on Channel Four."

A few commercials drag by and then an anchorman takes over. "Tonight we're live at the Vandalia Correctional Prison with Tammy Kracher, mother of Steven. She has a lot to say about the man who kidnapped her son." He looks to his right. "Are we ready?"

"I'm here, Stan. Can you hear me?"

"Loud and clear."

The interview area appears dark and gloomy. I recognize the woman I spoke to. But this time she has on make-up and her hair is styled differently.

Before the reporter can ask a question, she begins. "Hey, baby. It's Mommy." She waves into the camera. "I'm so sorry all this bad stuff happened to you, darlin'."

"I ain't your baby!" Stevie yells at the TV.

"We understand Mr. Barnes was a guard here. That you met while serving time, right?" the reporter asks.

"Right. An' I believed when he talked all the time about Jesus an' tryin' for a good life. But never, ever, would I think that when I told him how my poor little boy wasn't bein' cared for right, that he'd go an' just steal him away."

"Why didn't you tell anyone when you suspected him?"

"Who's gonna listen to an old druggie like me? Besides, I figured Stevie was better off with a Preacher than his lazy-ass old man."

"You must have known Mr. Barnes was taking children of other inmates?"

"I heard things. But what am I supposed to do? That's for the law to fix, not me."

"You know he's claiming that you're involved in this with him? That you were getting a cut of all his so called, 'donations?'"

She spits. "That's crazy. Just like he is."

"There was a boy found buried off a county road in a small town west of here. Mr. Barnes claims that your son and another boy killed him. An autopsy is being done as we speak. Do you know anything about that?"

"Now how the hell would I know anything that goes on outside here?"

She rants for a few more minutes. Then there's a shot of Barnes being taken into custody.

Stevie flinches.

The man walks slowly, refusing to let police on either side of him dictate his speed. He faces the camera, taunting it. How many times have I seen criminals hide from the camera, covering their face under a coat or shirt? Not Barnes. It's obvious he feels invincible.

I glance over at Stevie. He's staring at the TV now, his jaw tight, back straight and stiff.

"He told us it was a treasure hunt. That's how he made that dumb little kid help dig Jimmy's grave. Thought he was so smart throwin' them coins in the hole. Troy worked so hard for a few lousy nickels an' dimes."

I'm afraid to press him for more information. Kathy and Medora must feel the same because none of us turn to look at Stevie.

When the news is over, Kathy turns the TV off. Then casually, she asks, "Why do you think he'd bury Jimmy out in the open like that? Can he really be that arrogant to think he'd get away with it?"

"We was in a hurry. An Mister thinks he's better an' smarter than anyone…'cept for God. He told me a million times that people are like cattle. All of em' stupid an' lazy. Said how everyone in those parts was used to seein' that pink cross. An' after a while, you don't see it no more cause you don't wanna. It's too sad."

We sit there, digesting his words…until Medora coughs.

"Well, it's been a long day and I'm pooped," she says. "If everyone will clear out, I can make up the couch."

Kathy and I have been sleeping in the guestroom. It hadn't felt right stretching out on Baylor's bed when we first came, and it still doesn't.

As we all stand, stretching our legs, Stevie starts to leave the room. Then he turns. "'Night. See you guys in the morning."

CHAPTER SIXTY-SIX

"Did Stevie see my report last night?" Laura asks when she calls the next morning. "Was he okay with the way his interview was edited?"

"We all saw it," Kathy tells her. "You handled the whole thing great. Thanks."

"I promised you and Vince I'd keep you informed and wouldn't go behind your back."

"And you've been true to your word. A real friend."

I wave at her to let me talk.

Kathy hands me the phone. "What's the word on Jimmy's autopsy?"

"Just got a copy this morning." I can hear papers being shuffled around. "Malnutrion, dehydration, bruises and trauma to the brain."

"Must be from a beating. Stevie says Barnes hit them."

"But there's no proof that it was Barnes who was responsible for any of it. He claims the boy's parents hurt the child, of course."

Stevie walks in the kitchen, wearing a Cardinals t-shirt. He smoothes down the front, petting it.

"We'll talk later," I tell Laura.

He obviously knows who's on the other end when he asks if he can have the phone.

"Go to where they found Jimmy," he tells her. "Near that cross, over by a tree is a medal Mister always carried in his pocket. It's gold, with Jesus on one side an' his initials on the other. He was real proud of that thing. When he tried to trick Troy with the coins, he dropped it by mistake. He didn't see what happened, but I did an' mashed it into the grass with my foot. That should prove he was there, right? That Troy an' me didn't do nothin' on our own."

When he was finished, he handed the phone back to me. "Is there any cereal?" he asked Kathy.

Stevie repeats his story to Medora who wildly takes notes. She's anxious to get back to her office, convincing herself that the long drive will allow time to organize things in her brain. She asks Kathy three times for Laura's number.

"There's nothing more for you to do now," she tells me and Kathy. "Laura can work from here and I'll take care of all the legalities from my end. All the three of you have to do now is relax and let us handle things."

Relax?

"Okay...I guess." I kiss her cheek. "What would we do without you, Medora?"

"Drive safely," Kathy tells her as they hug.

She must be reading my mind as we wave goodbye from the driveway. "Did you hear that? She tells us to relax like it's so easy. But I don't have a clue how to even begin."

"We'll have to work at it."

"Work at relaxing. Doesn't that sound a little weird to you?"

We can hear Stevie slurping his cereal, catch sight of milk dripping from his chin as we enter the kitchen. The way he sits there, looking so...average...he seems like a boy far younger than his eighteen years.

"I like your shirt." Kathy pours me a cup of coffee.

"It's from my dad. He bought it for my birthday a few years ago."

"We saw those gifts on your bed," I say. "You know, your father would have wanted you to be happy and enjoy them."

"I know." He strokes a sleeve.

We sit with him and the three of us talk about nothing important, trying to find things we have in common. Trivial, silly things that hardly seem noteworthy to most people. But I've come to learn that tragedy is like a barbed wire fence surrounding a lush, sunny field. It's there and it hurts. But after acknowledging it you have to jump down, stop jamming those barbs deeper into your skin and live in the light.

"Are you guys going back to Chicago?" he asks out of the blue.

"It is our home," I tell him. "Have you thought about living here? In this house?"

"It don't feel like my home no more. Not without Dad."

"Vince has the paperwork and a letter your father left. Baylor wanted you to have everything. You can sell it all, get yourself an apartment. A new house, maybe? And your father's car's in the garage." Then Kathy laughs. "But you better learn how to drive first."

"I don't know how to do any of that stuff by myself. Sell a house? I'm just a kid. I need…help."

"You got it," I tell him.

"There ain't really apartments here. Not like in Chicago," he says.

I'm anxious when I ask, "Would you consider living up there? Maybe with us until you get used to things."

"Maybe."

"If you could live anywhere in the world," Kathy asks as she touches his hand, "where would it be?"

"Not near no water, that's for sure." When he smiles, he looks like a different person. Eager, excited about his life. "I like cowboy movies, ya know? Me an' Dad would watch John Wayne every Sunday mornin'. He was all the time talkin' about New Mexico. They shot a lot of Westerns there, he said. So…I guess I'd live out west."

"Sounds nice."

"What about you?" he asks her. "Is Chicago this perfect place or would you live somewhere else?"

"That city has a lot of bad memories for us."

"Yeah, Vince told me."

Would Kathy really move? She can run her work from anywhere, just needs a computer. We both have needed a change for such a long time.

"I've always loved the Southwest. So colorful and peaceful. The big city can really get to you. All the noise and crowds."

"Maybe we could go out there sometime," Stevie says. "You know, a trip to see how we like it?"

We. He said "we."

"But I can't stop wonderin' what happened to all them kids Mister took. Maybe I could help you find 'em?"

"It gets real hard. And you know so much we don't. That would be great if you wanted to work with me," she says.

"Do I have to decide anything now, Mr. Lloyd?"

"No, Stevie, there's no deadline or anything like that. Take your time."

He relaxes a little. "An' you guys will stay here...with me... until..."

"We're not going anywhere, don't worry."

ABOUT THE AUTHOR

CHRISTINE MATTHEWS is the author of the "Gil & Claire Hunt" series. She has also written over 60 short stories, many of which have been collected into two single-author collections, *Gentle Insanities and Other States of Mind* (2001) and *Promises Made and Broken* (2014). Her current novel, *Sapphires Aren't Forever* (Dagger Books, 2015), is the first novel in her Jewelry Designer series. She is also a member and officer in long standing of the Private Eye Writers of America. She is a published poet, produced playwright and her work has been optioned for film. Her children's book, *Wilbur, The Bubblegun Dragon*, is scheduled for 2015 publication.

Curious about other Crossroad Press books?
Stop by our site:
http://store.crossroadpress.com
We offer quality writing
in digital, audio, and print formats.

Enter the code FIRSTBOOK
to get 20% off your first order from our store!
Stop by today!

Made in the USA
Columbia, SC
27 June 2019